Zelda's Guilt

Agnes Alexander

A Wings ePress, Inc.
Western Historical Novel

Wings ePress, Inc.

Edited by: Jeanne Smith
Copy Edited by: Joan C. Powell
Executive Editor: Jeanne Smith
Cover Artist: Trisha FitzGerald-Jung

Wings ePress Books
www.wingsepress.com

Copyright © 2018 by Agnes Alexander
ISBN-13: 978-1-61309-661-1
ISBN-10: 1-61309-661-5

Published In the United States Of America

Wings ePress Inc.
3000 N. Rock Road
Newton, KS 67114

Dedication

To Norma Freeman,
a devoted fan of my Western Historical Romances
and a wonderful friend.

* * *

One

As Zelda Jordon trudged from the barn to the house, anyone observing her would have thought she was much older than her twenty-one years. Her battered hat was pushed back on her head and ringlets of black hair had escaped from the bun on the back of her head and hung to her slumping shoulders. The faded brown skirt and once white blouse she wore were covered in dirt, sweat and grime. She knew she smelled as bad as the hog pen, though she'd bathed the night before. Tired wouldn't begin to describe the fatigue she felt. Exhausted would come nearer, but would still not explain the fact that every bone in her body ached and that her work for the day still wasn't finished.

"It's time you got here," her stepbrother Hugh said as she climbed the two steps from the yard to the back porch. "I'm hungry and there's nothing in the house to eat."

Zelda wanted to tell him that at his age, he could have at least started cooking supper, but she only said, "I'll get supper ready as soon as I can. Where's Pansy?"

He shrugged. "She was playing over there near the hen house last time I saw her."

Zelda sighed. "Hugh, you're supposed to watch her when I'm not at the house. She could get hurt out here. Your mother would be furious at you."

"She'd blame you for leaving her. She wouldn't blame me." He gave her his twelve-year- old snide smile.

Zelda wanted to slap the boy, but instead she called, "Pansy, where are you?"

There was no answer so Zelda called again.

Finally, the three-year-old came toddling around the edge of the porch. "I here, Zewie."

Shaking her head when she looked at her little half-sister, Zelda said, "Where in the world have you been?" Pansy was muddy from her shoulders down. Now the child would have to be bathed before supper could be cooked.

"I play in water."

"I see you did." She reached out her hand. "Come with me. I need to get you washed up."

"What about supper?" Hugh asked.

"If you hadn't let your little sister get in this mess, I'd cook supper right away. Now she has to be bathed first."

Hugh stuck out his mouth. "She's nothing but a half-sister to me."

"She's my half-sister, too, but I love her and would never let her get in this mess when I'm watching her."

"You should have been watching her then."

A muddy little hand took hold of Zelda's. "I wove you, too, Zewie."

Zelda couldn't help smiling at the bright-eyed child. "Yes, we love each other, sweetheart. Now, let's get you cleaned up so we can fix supper. I bet you're hungry."

"I eat berries."

"What berries?"

"I pick 'um."

Before Zelda could answer, her stepmother's shaky weak voice came from the bedroom down the short hall. "Is that you, Zelda?"

"Yes, ma'am."

"I'm beginning to get hungry. Whenever you quit lazing around and cook supper, bring my meal to me."

Because of the hassle it created, Glenda had stopped coming to the table to eat shortly after the accident, but Zelda didn't mind. After all, if it hadn't been for her selfishness, Glenda would be able to walk without assistance and Zelda wouldn't be compelled to wait on her stepmother. She glanced at Glenda. "Supper will be ready shortly and I'll bring yours to you."

"Well, hurry up. As I said, I'm hungry."

After giving Pansy a bath and cooking a pot of potatoes and frying what was left of the bacon, supper was ready. Hugh came to the table and began eating without saying a word.

"Do you want to wait to eat your supper while you go with me to take some food to your mama, Pansy?" Zelda hoped she would because when the child tried to feed herself, she got more on her than in her stomach. One bath a day was enough. Zelda didn't want to have to give her another one before they went to bed tonight.

"I go feed Mama, Zewie."

"Good. I have it on the tray. Let's go."

When Zelda entered the room with the tray in her hands, her stepmother said, "You must have been wasting time again. I don't understand why you can't get your work done around here. You're young and strong and healthy. Not like some of us, which is no thanks to you."

Zelda grimaced. Not only because the speech left Glenda gasping for breath, but because what she said was true. Zelda knew it was her fault that she had the full responsibility of her stepbrother and her half-sister. It was her fault that her stepmother was confined to bed and would be for the rest of her life, which according to the doctor wouldn't be that much longer. The saddest thing of all, Zelda knew it was her fault that her father was no longer there to take care of his family and to keep things on their small ranch running as they should. It was all up to Zelda now.

~ * ~

Wiley Hendrix reined his horse to a stop, removed his black Stetson and wiped his forehead with the back of his arm. He looked first one way then the other. He knew if he kept traveling north he'd head in the direction of Oklahoma and if he rode long enough he'd come to Wyoming. But did he want to go that way? He'd shared some happy times with Janet on their small ranch there. On the other hand, some of the time had been horrible. Especially when Janet's health deteriorated and they had to sell their place and move to Chicago for her medical care. Then when he realized he was going to lose his wife, he felt as if his life was over. Going that way again would only bring back the hurt.

Though he never adjusted well to the big city, after his wife's death, he felt lost without the woman he'd loved enough to give up everything for. Though her father offered for him to stay and continue to work in the bank the family owned there, Wiley knew he couldn't. No matter that he'd spent the two years in the city before losing Janet, he was still a cowboy at heart and he knew he always would be.

Therefore, eight months after Janet's funeral, he took what little money he had left and headed back to his home state of Texas. Instinct led him to the Swinging C Ranch owned by his best friend, Blake Cantrell. Before marrying Janet and purchasing their own place in Wyoming, Wiley had been the foreman at the Swinging C for several years. He'd counted on Blake welcoming him back and he wasn't disappointed.

Blake was glad to have him on the ranch once again and so were the hands. Then he met Camilla. She was one of the most fascinating women he'd ever encountered and it wasn't long until he decided he'd make a play for her hand. It wasn't that he'd forgotten Janet. He'd never do that. His wife would always have a place in his heart, but Wiley liked being married and he hoped to do it again someday. After one look at Camilla, he thought she could be the woman he wanted to spend the rest of his life with.

Problem was, Blake Cantrell felt the same way about the woman.

When Wiley learned Camilla was just as much in love with Blake as he was her, he knew he didn't have a chance. He also knew he wouldn't interfere with the feelings they had for each other. After Blake and Camilla were married, Wiley stayed several months and worked on the ranch, but seeing their happiness was almost more than he could stand. When winter slipped into spring, he knew he had to move on. He couldn't be this close to Camilla and keep his feelings hidden from Blake any longer. It was better his friend never know how he coveted the new Mrs. Blake Cantrell.

Now here he sat on his horse watching the sun ride lower in the western sky and wondering in which direction to go to find another ranch that needed a hardworking cowhand. Blake had paid him well and he'd saved most of his money. Maybe, with a few more jobs, he'd have enough to buy a small place of his own. He'd decided before leaving the Swinging C that demanding work on a ranch was the only thing he could do to cope with his loneliness from losing Janet and to get over the heartache of not being able to express his hidden feelings for Camilla.

Replacing his hat, he turned his horse a little to the east. Why not go that way? If he remembered correctly, Waco was somewhere in that direction. He'd never seen the place, but he'd heard it was a right nice town. He also figured there had to be a few ranches in the area where he could pick up work as a cowhand to tide him over until he settled down, if he ever did.

~ * ~

The next day Zelda paused the plow horse and loosened the strap around her shoulder as she looked upward. She could tell by the position of the sun and by the shadows it cast on the ground that it was approaching noon. Maybe she could plow another row or two before she went to the house to fix the mid-day meal.

She shook her head. Why was she wasting her time plowing anyway? Unless she figured a way to find the money to pay the mortgage on this place, they wouldn't live here long enough for the fields to yield any produce. But she knew she had to keep trying. Her stepmother wouldn't survive a day if they had to leave here. Zelda didn't know how much longer Glenda would live, but she knew she had to keep the woman comfortable as long as there was life in her. Besides, Glenda always said she was only happy here on the ranch. Of course, Zelda didn't think her stepmother was happy anywhere.

Things might be different if she could only get Hugh to help her out a little with the things that had to be done. But since her father married Glenda and brought her and her little boy to live at the ranch, Hugh had done little to help anyone, inside or outside the house. Since he'd had the fever as a toddler and survived, Glenda would excuse his laziness by saying, "He's a delicate child and the doctor told me not to let him overexert himself." Hugh played on this excuse from his mother to the hilt. He never let anyone forget he was too weak to work.

John Jordon had believed his wife knew best about the child and had never pushed Hugh to do much of anything around the ranch, though he occasionally gathered the eggs or did some other menial task that didn't consist of arduous work. Now that the head of the family was dead, Hugh did nothing to help his stepsister. He didn't even bother to gather the eggs anymore or slop the hogs or feed the chickens and his mother said he shouldn't have to do anything that tired him. Of course, everything tired Hugh.

Zelda sighed. She often wondered if things wouldn't have been better if her father had never married Glenda, but she realized how lonely he had been after losing her mother to a snake bite. When Glenda and Hugh first come to live at the ranch things weren't too bad. Though she was fifteen at the time, Zelda knew Glenda wasn't too thrilled to have an almost grown stepdaughter. The two had as little to do with each other as they could, but when Pansy came along two years later, things again changed. This time for the better.

Pansy was a happy baby who seldom cried and she was a joy to take care of. Zelda delighted in having her in the house and often, without being asked, offered to help Glenda take care of the little girl. Glenda seemed to mellow toward Zelda and acted grateful for the help with the baby. For the next two years the Jordons were a happy family. Then the tragedy happened and changed everything.

Zelda shook the thoughts away. There was no need to rake up the past. Things were the way they were and there was no changing them. It didn't matter how much Zelda wished they were different. It was time to get to the house and fix the midday meal for what was left of the family, but before she unhitched the horse from the plow she saw a rider approaching.

"Why don't you stay on your side of the creek, Mace Palmer," she muttered through clinched teeth, though she knew he wasn't yet close enough to hear her.

The one thing she found almost as upsetting to think about as her father's death was Mace Palmer, the son of the man who owned the adjoining ranch. Mace Palmer had lusted after Zelda since she was thirteen. She hated him, but as long as her father was alive she didn't have to fear the man. John Jordon once told Mace that if he ever came near his daughter, he wouldn't leave the Jordon ranch alive. Palmer must have believed him because he didn't begin his pursuit of Zelda again until after her father's funeral. Though Glenda had been warned about the man, for some reason he was one of the few people the new widow let visit her.

Zelda often wondered what they talked about, but she could never overhear their conversation. Her stepbrother, Hugh, always had some reason to get her out of the house when Mace was with his mother.

Mace reined up his horse a few feet from Zelda. "Been plowing?"

She wanted to tell him she was only walking the old plow horse around the ranch for the fun of it. Instead she ignored his question and asked, "What are you doing here, Mace Palmer?" She knew her voice was snappy and she didn't care.

"Now, Miss Zelda, don't get your dander up. I just happened to be down at the creek and thought I'd ride up here and see how you were doing."

"Well, now that you see I'm fine, you can turn around and go home."

He laughed. "I will get on after I tell you what I learned in town today."

She lifted her chin and said nothing.

"Pa talked to Caruthers at the bank. He told him your mortgage is coming due." He grinned at her.

"Your pa has no business talking about this ranch to Caruthers or anyone else."

He ignored her statement. "You got the money to pay it?"

"It's none of your business if we have the money."

He gave her a snide smile. "I happen to know you don't have it. Maybe we could talk a little business and I'd be able to help you out of your predicament. Pa says that's what I should do and I agree with him."

"I have no idea what you're talking about."

"If you was my woman I wouldn't let the sheriff come here and run your poor sick mother and her helpless children off this place. Pa says we'll take care of this ranch and he and I both know I can take care of you."

Anger gripped Zelda. "I don't care what your pa says. I'll die before I become your woman, Mace Palmer. Now, get off this ranch or I'm going to get my father's shotgun and run you off."

He laughed again. "Just think about it, sweetheart. You don't want to add the death of your mother and her children to your conscience, do you?"

"How dare you say such a thing!"

"You'll see I'm telling you the truth." He raised his eyebrow. "You might as well accept it. Glenda and I have talked it over and you marrying me is the only answer to all your woes."

"I'll never marry you, Mace Palmer."

"I've wanted you for years and now that your pa is no longer here, I'll get you. Whether you like it or not, you'll eventually be mine, Zelda Jordon."

"Never!"

He laughed. "I'll see you tomorrow after you've calmed down and thought it over."

Before she could retort, he turned his horse and rode away.

Trying her best to shake the conversation out of her head, Zelda turned the plow horse into the run-down corral and headed to the house. Hugh sat on the bench her father had built under the cedar elm tree in the side yard. He glanced at her, but continued reading his book. Something his mother insisted he do often. Zelda liked to read, too, but she never had the time anymore.

Hugh looked up again as she approached the house. "It's about time you got here."

She ignored his sarcasm. "Where's Pansy?"

"Over by the chicken coop. I'm watching her."

Zelda nodded. "Dinner will be ready in a minute. All I have to do is warm it up."

He didn't reply, but went back to his book.

In twenty minutes Zelda stepped out on the back porch. "The food is almost ready, Hugh. Get Pansy and wash your hands. I'll feed your mama if she's awake then I'll make your plate."

He didn't answer, but closed his book, stood and headed toward the chicken coop.

Zelda went inside and went to Glenda's room. "I wanted to see if you were awake and ready to eat."

Though her voice seemed to grow weaker every day, Glenda never passed up a chance to throw barbs at Zelda. "Yes, I'm awake and it's about time you brought me something to eat. A woman could starve to death before you brought her food. Especially a sick woman like me."

Zelda gritted her teeth. "I'll get you positioned and then bring your dinner to you." She placed pillows behind Glenda's back. "I'm sorry the food is a little later than usual. It took a few minutes for the potatoes to get done."

"Wait a minute. I thought I heard a horse outside. Who was it? Are you having company at my ranch when I can't see who you're entertaining around my children?"

"It wasn't company. It was that terrible Mace Palmer."

"Honestly, Zelda. A man like Mace comes to visit and you didn't invite him in to see me?"

Zelda refused to get into an argument with Glenda. "I'll be back in a minute with your dinner."

"It's a shame I can't get to the kitchen and cook food for my children. Of course, you know the reason for that, don't you, Zelda?"

It was as if Glenda's brown eyes were burning a hole in her back as she turned to leave the room, but Zelda didn't respond. She didn't have to. Her stepmother's words were like a knife in her heart and she knew the woman realized that. Otherwise why would she say such things?

Before she was out the door, Hugh came running into the room. "I can't find Pansy."

"What? Where is she?" Glenda cried. "Why weren't you watching my baby, Zelda?"

Zelda glared at Hugh. "I thought you said she was playing by the chicken coop."

"Don't you dare blame him," Glenda would have shouted if she could, but it only came out as a raspy whisper. "You should have been watching my baby like you were supposed to do."

"Hugh was to watch her while I plowed the garden."

"I was watching her."

Glenda lifted a shaky finger and pointed at her stepdaughter. "This is your fault, Zelda. You're irresponsible and you never take your job seriously. What would your sainted father say if he was still alive, like he would be if it weren't for your selfishness?"

"I don't have time to argue with you, Glenda. I've got to find Pansy." As Zelda ran out of the room she could still hear Glenda ranting in the raspy voice. She ignored her. Her one goal, now, was to find her little sister.

Two

Wiley saw an outcropping of thick mesquite and figured there was a good chance there was water nearby. Since it was about time to rest his horse and he was a little hungry, he decided this would be a good place to stop, let the horse graze and fix himself a bite to eat. He'd wanted to get on the trail early this morning so he hadn't taken the time to make coffee when he woke up. He'd settled for hardtack and water from the canteen. A cup of strong coffee sure would taste good and there was no reason why he couldn't make camp near the creek he felt sure he'd find in the trees.

He wondered why he'd been in such a hurry this morning. Nobody was chasing him and he still had plenty of money to buy supplies until he found a place to settle for a while. Maybe it was the fact that he kept dreaming about his late wife, Janet, and Blake Cantrell's wife, Camilla, last night. In his dream the two women were interchangeable. He'd thought about it a lot today. He'd finally decided it was because both women were sweet, kind and understanding. The kind of woman any man would want to settle down with for the rest of his life. Too bad both were out of his reach. But he wasn't giving up hope. There was a woman for him out there somewhere. Maybe even in Waco.

Heading toward the trees, he saw something flit in the bushes before his eyes. He frowned. What kind of animal was that shade of blue? A few birds he'd seen were the color of the sky, but whatever it was that passed in front of him was too large to be a bird, though in his estimation it wasn't big enough to be any familiar animal either. It must have been human. Not taking a chance, he drew his gun and moved his horse forward slowly. He'd wait until whoever it was came into plain sight before making his move.

The blue object became visible and Wiley was shocked. He holstered his gun and dismounted. So he wouldn't frighten her, he walked slowly up to the berry bushes and looked down at the auburn haired little girl. "Hello there."

She looked up at him and smiled, then reached out a red-stained hand full of mashed berries. "You wike berries?"

He was surprised she wasn't afraid of him. He said in a gentle voice, "Yes. I like berries."

"I wike berries."

Wiley glanced around, but didn't see anyone. Looking back at the child he asked, "Where's your mama, little girl?"

"Bed."

Wiley didn't understand, but tried another approach. "Well, where's your daddy?"

The child frowned at him and shook her head.

"Is there anybody to watch you?"

She grinned again. "Not Hugh. Zewie."

Finally understanding the child was trying to say "Zellie," he lifted an eyebrow. "Where's Zellie?"

"Plow."

That made no sense. "What about Hugh? Where's he?"

"Read book."

He decided to change his tactic. "What's your name, sweetheart?"

"Pansy."

"Well, Pansy, what are you doing here by yourself?"

"Eat berries." She held up her berry-stained hand again and asked, "Who you?"

"I'm Wiley."

"Wiwey."

"That's close enough." He grinned at her and remembered she'd said something about somebody named Zellie.

He decided to try to question her again. "Can you tell me where Zellie is?"

"Plow."

He knew he had to try to figure out what she was talking about. "Where does Zellie plow?"

"There." She waved toward the east.

"Why don't you and I go find Zellie?"

She held out her small arms to him. "I wove Zewie."

"Then we'll go find her." Wiley had no choice but to pick her up, berry-stained hands and all. "We're going to ride on my horse. Is that all right with you?"

"Hold me."

"Don't worry. I'll hold you." He mounted his horse with her in his arm and then settled her in his lap. "Now you tell me how to go find Zellie."

She pointed again. This time to the north.

Wiley figured he'd have to rely on his own senses. The place couldn't be too far away if this small child had wandered off and found her way to the creek.

When they cleared the trees, Wiley smiled to himself. He saw smoke in the distance. Not quite a quarter of a mile away. Where there was smoke there was usually a chimney and where there was a chimney, there was usually a stove and where there was a stove there was usually a house. Now he knew which way to go.

He'd only gone a short distance when a cabin came into view. A woman stood in the yard with her hands around her mouth. Even over the horses' hoofbeats he heard her calling Pansy's name. She looked as if she were about to panic, but if she cared so much he wondered why she'd just now missed the child. From what he could see from all the juice on her hands and the front of her dress, Pansy had been at the berry bushes near the creek for quite some time.

He entered the yard and she came running toward his horse, reaching for the little girl. In a frantic voice she demanded, "What are you doing with Pansy?"

He reined the horse in and handed the child to her. "I found this little girl down by the creek. Seems to me somebody here should have been watching after her."

Pansy stuck her berry juice-covered hands toward Zelda. "I eat berries."

Zelda ignored her. "How dare you grab a small child?"

Wiley observed the woman. He couldn't help thinking she'd probably be pretty if she weren't dressed in rags and her beautiful black hair wasn't going in all directions except into the bun where he figured it was supposed to be. Her jade green wide eyes did look concerned, but he still couldn't get over the fact she'd not noticed the child was missing until now. What kind of mother was she not to look after her little girl? Camilla would have never let one of her daughters get out of her sight for any length of time. The fact that they were adopted didn't matter. Camilla was their mother and a good one. That was one reason Wiley had been so attracted to his best friend's wife.

He spoke slowly. "As I said, I found her at the creek. If you're so concerned about the child, why weren't you looking out for her?"

"Her brother was supposed to be watching her."

"Obviously he wasn't."

Pansy spoke before Zelda could answer. This time the child spoke louder. "I eat berries, Zewie."

"Yes, I know you did, honey." Zelda swallowed and looked back at Wiley. "I'm sorry I was so abrupt with you, but I was frightened. Thank you for bringing her home."

"I was shocked to see someone so little at the creek by herself." He couldn't keep the accusatory sound out of his voice.

"I was working in the field and her brother was supposed to take care of her."

"Well, he didn't do a very good job. She could've drowned or been bitten by a snake or gotten lost or a million other things."

"I know. It's just that..."

A boy who looked to be around eleven or twelve, came out onto the porch. "Zelda, Mama wants to know what you're doing to find Pansy.... Oh, I see you found her."

Zelda whirled to face the young man. "Yes, thanks to this gentleman. He found her at the creek. How could you let her wander off so far and not notice she was gone?"

He shrugged. "What difference does it make? She's here now. I'll tell Mama, then I'm ready to eat." He didn't give her time to answer, but turned and went back into the house.

Wiley couldn't believe it. What kind of family was this? For some reason he felt compelled to find out. But how was he to do it? He decided to be direct. "I'm Wiley Hendrix and I'm on my way to Waco. Would you mind if I water my horse and sit under your shade tree and eat what's left in my saddlebag?"

"I wike Wiwey."

Zelda smiled at her, but said to him, "I'm sorry if I accused you of grabbing Pansy, Mr. Hendrix. As I said, I was frightened when I saw you ride up with her in your arms."

"I understand that, ma'am."

"Her Zewie."

Zelda continued to smile at her little sister. "She's right. My name is Zelda Jordon. Pansy has a little trouble pronouncing Zelda."

"I see. She has a little trouble with Wiley, too."

"Well, Mr. Hendrix, as I said, I appreciate you bringing Pansy home. I'm just thankful it was you who found her rather than some unscrupulous character."

"I was happy to bring her home, ma'am. She seems to be a special little girl."

"I is. Zewie tell me that."

Zelda hugged her. "Yes, you are special, sweetheart."

Pansy grinned. "See. Her tell me."

"I do see, Pansy."

Zelda took a deep breath. "Would you like to come in and have a cup of coffee, Mr. Hendrix? At least I can offer you that for your good deed."

"Thank you, Miz. Jordon. I'd very much appreciate it. I haven't had coffee all day and I was getting ready to set up camp and make myself some at the creek."

"Then follow me."

Wiley was surprised when he stepped into the small home. Though the furnishings weren't expensive, everything was clean and seemed to be in its place. He didn't know why he expected it to be as messy and as unkempt as the lady he followed across the parlor to the kitchen table. Though he thought there was probably a lot of pretty woman under all the ragged clothes and messy hair.

The boy she called Hugh was sitting on a bench beside the table with a fork in one hand and a spoon in the other. His voice sounded irritated as he said, "It's about time you got in and fixed me something to eat."

Zelda ignored him. "Pansy, can you wash your hands by yourself? I need to take food to your mama."

Again, Wiley was surprised. The woman with pretty black hair wasn't the child's mother, as he'd assumed. He swallowed. "I need to wash my hands, too. I'll help her."

"Hurry, Zelda. I'm hungry." Hugh ignored everyone else in the room.

Zelda quickly washed her own hands and headed out of the room with a steaming bowl of food.

Wiley went to the sink, dipped water from a bucket into a pan and proceeded to hold Pansy up so she could put her hands in the water. He washed her face then handed her a towel so he could wash his own hands. He then turned and took a seat on the bench on the opposite side of the table from the young man.

"My name's Wiley Hendrix." He introduced himself.

"So?" Hugh sneered at him.

Zelda came back into the room. "Hugh, that's rude. You should introduce yourself to Mr. Hendrix."

"I don't see why. He's got no business knowing who I am. Now give me something to eat."

Wiley couldn't stop himself, he said, "Young man, that's no way to talk to a lady."

Hugh laughed. "She ain't no lady. She's just my stepsister."

"What does that have to do with showing good manners?"

He shrugged and Zelda moved to the stove. "Your mother is feeding herself, but said she wanted to see you after you ate." She poured a cup of coffee and sat it in front of Wiley.

"Hey, why are you giving him something before serving me?"

"I served him first because he's a gentleman who uses good manners." She placed a pone of cornbread on the table, then turned to the stove and filled a bowl. She sat it in front of Hugh. "Now eat."

Hugh turned up his nose. "Potatoes again. We had potatoes last night. Now you've gone and made potato soup. Can't you cook nothing but these stinking potatoes?"

Before she could answer him, Wiley said, "There must be something wrong with your nose, young man. I think it smells wonderful."

"Would you like a bowl, Mr. Hendrix?" Zelda smiled at him.

Wiley wasn't prepared for the way her smile affected him. Although there were smudges of dirt on her face, her clothes were tattered and she looked as if she hadn't had a good night's sleep in a long time, that smile went straight to his heart and made it beat a little faster. He tried to ignore it as he said, "I'd love a bowl, Miss Jordon."

Hugh began eating, but every so often he looked over his bowl at the big cowboy that sat across the table from him.

Each time Wiley looked back at him to let him know he didn't approve of his actions. He knew this made Hugh uncomfortable. He was pleased with the effect because making the boy squirm was his intention.

Zelda shook her head, but didn't say anything. She filled a bowl for Pansy. "Climb up to the table, honey."

"I wanna sit side Wiwey."

Wiley moved over a little. "Come right on, Miss Pansy. I'd like for you to sit beside me."

She scurried up on the bench, turned and grinned at him. "I sits here."

Zelda put a small bowl of soup in front of Pansy then moved beside her and said, "Here, sweetie, let me put this towel around your neck. There's no need of getting your dress any dirtier than it is already."

Pansy grinned at Wiley. "I spills stuff."

Zelda got the last bowl for herself and moved to the table. "Slide over, Hugh."

He didn't move. "Just stand at the cabinet and eat. I don't want you to sit beside me."

"For heaven's sake, Hugh. I'm tired and I've got to go finish the plowing."

"That's not my problem."

"It won't hurt to let me sit down."

"Sit over there like you usually do."

Wiley stood. "Miss Jordon, please take my place. I'll sit by the boy and there's no question but that he'll move over for me."

Hugh stared at Wiley as the cowboy moved to the other side of the table, but he did slide over.

Wiley could tell Zelda was trying to hide a grin.

Pansy looked at them. "Why Wiwey move?"

Zelda patted the little girl's arm. "He knew I wanted to sit beside you, sweetheart."

"All right," she said as a spoonful of soup dribbled down her chin. "I woves you, Zewie."

"I love you, too, Pansy."

"You two are disgusting." Hugh's voice sounded as if he growled.

"Don't be so rude, Hugh."

He glared at her. "You can't tell me what to do."

Wiley couldn't keep quiet any longer. "Seems to me somebody needs to tell you what to do."

"It ain't none of your damn business."

"You've just proved my point, young man. No decent fellow would curse like that in front of his sisters."

"I told you they're not my real sisters."

"Why Hugh mean to Wiwey, Zewie?"

Before Zelda could answer, Hugh jumped up and threw his spoon down. "I need to go see Mama."

"Miss Jordon, I don't mean to butt into your business, but why in the world do you let that boy get away with talking to you like he does?"

"It's a long story, Mr. Hendrix, but his mother has convinced him that he's delicate and must not overwork himself."

"Why?"

"Because he was sick and almost died when he was a little boy."

Pansy butted into the conversation. "I eat it all, Zewie."

Zelda laughed. "Yes, you did. At least you ate what you didn't get on the towel around your neck. Do you want more?"

"Yes, pease."

"How about you, Mr. Hendrix? Would you like more?"

"I don't want to make a pig of myself."

"Eat all you want. We have plenty."

He handed her his bowl. "Thank you."

As she sat the filled bowls on the table, a shrill, but raspy voice called, "Zelda, get in here."

Three

Zelda bit her lip and blushed. She knew she was in for a scolding from Glenda, but that didn't matter. She was more concerned about being embarrassed in front of Wiley Hendrix. "I'll be right back," she muttered and left the kitchen.

As she walked into her stepmother's room she asked, "Yes, Glenda. What do you need?"

"I want to know why you have a stranger in my house who is being rude to my son?"

Zelda took a deep breath and kept her voice as calm as she could. "That stranger saved Pansy's life when Hugh let her wander off."

"How dare you say that? It's not Hugh's responsibility to watch Pansy. It's yours. Where were you?"

"I was trying to plow so we will have something to eat. All I did was ask Hugh to watch her for a little while."

"Don't you dare ever do something like that again. It's your place to keep up with Pansy, not Hugh's." Glenda glared at her. "Now get that man out of my house and fix my boy something decent to eat. He says he's tired of potatoes, and frankly, so am I."

"There's very little else to fix. If you'll give me a little money, I'll buy something different."

"What did you do with the last money I gave you?"

Zelda's shoulders slumped. "I had to buy feed for the animals as well as for us."

"And what did you buy for yourself?"

Biting her lip to keep from screaming at Glenda, she said, "I didn't buy anything."

"Likely story. Now get back in there and fix Hugh something he likes to eat. He needs decent food to grow as a young man should."

Zelda heard Hugh giggle from his seat on the other side of Glenda's bed. She ignored him, but knew if she didn't get out of there she might say something she'd regret. Without another word she turned and left the room.

She was surprised to see Wiley at the sink with his hands in dishwater. Pansy had a clean white towel tied around her waist and was standing on a chair beside him.

She grinned at Zelda. "Me and Wiwey wash dishes, Zewie."

"I see. It was nice of you to help him."

Pansy giggled.

"Mr. Hendrix, you don't have to wash those dishes." She walked up beside him. "I'll take over now."

"I don't mind. Why don't you sit there and rest a bit? Besides, I see you need help around here and this is one way I could thank you for a delicious meal and be of a little help at the same time."

"I appreciate it, but my stepmother thinks you should leave."

"I heard."

"Oh."

When he continued washing dishes and said nothing else, she said, "Maybe you should stop working and leave, Mr. Hendrix."

"I never start a job I don't finish, Miss Jordon."

"But Glenda said ..."

Hugh came into the room and interrupted. "Mama told you to fix me something else to eat. Where is it?"

"There's nothing to fix, Hugh. I have to get back to the plowing."

Hugh whirled around and headed back down the hall. "Mama, Zelda won't fix me anything to eat. She'd rather let me starve."

Zelda looked at Wiley. "I wish Hugh could be more understanding. There's nothing here I can fix him."

"Zelda!" Glenda's angry voice rang down the hall and into the kitchen.

Zelda sighed and started toward her stepmother's room, but a wet soapy hand on her elbow stopped her.

"Come with me."

"Oh, Mr. Hendrix, she'll be upset if I ignore her."

"Let her." He turned to the stool and picked up Pansy with his free arm. "We're going outside."

Pansy giggled and threw her arms around his neck. "We pick berries?"

"Not this time, sweetheart."

Zelda tried to free her elbow, but he wouldn't let go. "Mr. Hendrix, you're making this hard for me."

"We'll see about that."

Glenda's weak voice carried to the back porch and Zelda bit her lip and whispered, "I need…"

Wiley continued walking her down the steps, off the porch and into the side yard where the large cedar elm tree grew.

"I said, I need to …."

"You don't need to do anything except sit down here and listen to me." He stopped in front of the bench her father had built around the tree.

When she only glared at him, he said in a deep voice that left no room for argument, "I said, sit."

She sat and he placed Pansy on her lap.

Hugh came out of the house yelling, "Mama's calling you and she said you'd better get in there right this minute."

Zelda started to get up, but Wiley put his hand on her shoulder and said, "Don't you get off this bench. I'll handle this and be right back."

"But…"

"No buts. Now promise me, you'll stay here."

Zelda closed her eyes and thought a minute. Finally, she said, "I'll stay here for a little while."

"That's all the time it'll take."

~ * ~

Wiley didn't have the foggiest idea what he was going to do or say to the woman called Glenda, but he knew Zelda needed somebody to help her deal with the woman. Pansy certainly couldn't be any help and she seemed to be the only one in the household who cared a whit about Zelda. In long strides he headed to the house.

"Where're you going?" Hugh glared at him.

Knowing he'd give Zelda a hard time if he were left outside, he grabbed Hugh's arm. "I'm going to talk to your mama and you're coming with me."

Hugh jerked his arm, but was unable to dislodge Wiley's grip. "I ain't going nowhere with you."

"Come along peacefully or I'll carry you. It's your decision."

"You wouldn't dare."

"Want to try me?"

Hugh didn't answer, but turned toward the house with Wiley.

Glenda was still screeching Zelda's name when Wiley and Hugh entered her bedroom. She looked startled and she got quiet.

"Zelda won't be coming, ma'am."

Her eyes grew big and she muttered, "Why not?"

"He made her sit on the bench, Mama."

Wiley turned to him and narrowed his eyes and pointed to the chair beside the bed. "Sit down over there and shut up. I don't want to hear another word from you unless you're spoken to."

Glenda grabbed her chest. "How dare you speak to my son in such a manner."

"Ma'am, somebody should've talked to your son like that a long time ago, but he's not my main concern right now."

She began to flail her arms about. "Get out of my bedroom. You have no business talking to me about anything."

"You're upsetting my mama."

"Didn't I tell you not to speak unless I spoke to you?"

"Leave him alone."

"Mrs. Jordon…that is your name, isn't it?"

"Of course, it's my name, but…"

"Then, Mrs. Jordon, I want you to know things are going to change around here. And they're going to change today."

She looked scared as she clutched her chest. "This is my ranch and if anything needs to be changed, I'll see to it. I won't have a stranger coming in here and upsetting my son and the rest of my family."

"Well, the way you're running your ranch, it looks to me like you're not going to have it or a family either for very long."

"We're doing fine," she snapped.

"I can see you are. You lie in this bed and give orders like you're Queen Victoria. Your son is as lazy as any hog I've ever seen wallowing around in the muck in his pen. And your exhausted stepdaughter is working as hard as she can to keep this place going with no help from anyone. Pansy is the only one who seems to be doing fine."

"How dare you compare my son to a hog! He's a sweet boy. He can't help that he's delicate."

Hugh smirked.

"He doesn't look very delicate to me."

"He almost died and the doctor said he needed to be careful because he had delicate lungs. He said they had to build up, but it wasn't a fast process." She was breathing hard, but despite it she threw back her head and gave him a smug smile.

"When did the doctor tell you this? Last week? Last month? Last year? When?"

"After Hugh almost died."

"And when was that?" She didn't answer and he prodded. "How old was he when the doctor said these things?"

"He was four at the time."

Wiley chuckled. "Do you mean to tell me this boy had a lung problem seven or eight years ago and you're still coddling him like a baby?"

"How I raise my children is none of your business."

"Maybe not, but you do want to see them grown, don't you?"

"Of course I do. That's why I have to protect Hugh. I'm a good mother and I love my son."

Wiley figured he wasn't going to get very far with this woman, but he felt he had to try. "Mrs. Jordon, what do you suppose will happen to Hugh if something happens to you?"

"I don't plan to leave this world any time soon, but I know everything here will go to Hugh when I'm gone."

"I don't see that Hugh is equipped to run a ranch or a farm, whichever you call it."

"Zelda will do it."

"What if Zelda is gone?"

"Ah." Glenda smiled. "I'm sure Zelda won't leave the ranch her father started."

"I didn't mean she'd run off. I meant at the rate she's working around here, you're killing her. She may make it to the graveyard before you do."

Hugh's eyes grew big. "Is Zelda gonna die, Mama?"

"Of course not. She's young and strong."

"She's not going to be strong much longer if you keep working her the way you're doing now."

"Mr. whoever you are…"

"Wiley Hendrix."

"Well, Mr. Hendrix, it might interest you to know it's Zelda's fault that we're in this fix in the first place."

"What do you mean?"

"Go ahead and tell him, Mama. Tell him how Zelda killed Pa John."

Taken aback, Wiley stared at her. He wanted to ask her to explain, but he heard the back door open and was sure Zelda was coming inside. He cleared his throat. "I've said my piece. I'll leave now."

"Good." Glenda gave her red hair a flip. "We can now get back to our normal way of doing things."

"I'm afraid you misunderstand. I've leaving your room, not this homestead." Without giving her a chance to answer, he marched out of the room.

He met Zelda in the kitchen. "I thought I asked you to stay outside."

"Actually, you *told* me to stay outside, but I decided I'd better come in and see what was going on."

"I see bee," Pansy said. "Zewie not let it sting me."

Wiley reached and tickled her cheek. "I'm glad she protected you. You're too pretty to get stung by a mean old bee."

Pansy continued giggling and Zelda asked, "Is everything all right?"

He smiled at her. "Everything's fine. Now, I'm going out and walk around this place. I want to see what needs doing."

"I know what needs doing, Mr. Hendrix." She sounded irritated.

He reached over and touched her cheek. "I know you do, but don't turn down help. Maybe I want another bowl of your potato soup."

Before she could say anything, he went out the door.

"Zelda!" Came from her stepmother's bedroom.

Four

Zelda took a deep breath, squared her shoulders and went down the hall to Glenda's room. The woman was propped on a pillow with one hand clutched to her chest and she gripped Hugh's hand with her other one. Her raspy breath seemed to fill the room. *Oh, my lord, is she dying? I should have told Mr. Hendrix how sick she is. She isn't strong enough to stand up to his questioning, no matter how carefully he went about it. And I don't figure he was very careful. If she dies, that'll be another death on my conscience.*

"How could you let that awful man come into my house, Zelda?"

"I'm sorry, Glenda, but he found Pansy at the creek and..."

"Why did you let my baby go to the creek? Why weren't you paying better attention? She's just a little girl."

"I had to plow the garden if we're going to eat. We're almost out of food and I have no money to buy ..."

"So, that's what it's all about. You want my money."

"Why are you talking like that? You know I don't want your money for myself, but you and the children need food. If I don't have money to buy it, I have to grow it."

Glenda coughed and gasped for breath.

Zelda rushed to the bed and held Glenda's head higher. "Please calm down. You know getting upset is not good for you."

"I bet she's trying to kill you, Mama." Hugh looked at Zelda with the snide grin he gave her when his mother was fussing at her.

"She may be, son, but it's not going to happen today." She looked into Zelda's eyes. "I'm going to tell you one time and one time only, don't you let that man come back into my house. He's evil and he wants to hurt my Hugh."

Zelda wanted to defend Wiley Hendrix, but she knew there was no use. Glenda would never believe a word she said. "I'll keep him out, Glenda."

"Good." She dropped back to her pillow. "Now get out of here and start cooking supper. And you need to make something besides potatoes and bacon. Hugh and I are tired of them."

Zelda sighed and spoke before she could stop herself. "I won't fix bacon because there is none. We had the last of it yesterday."

Pansy came toddling into the room "I see you, Mama."

Glenda glanced at her daughter. "My heavens, Pansy. What's that on your dress?"

Pansy giggled. "I eat berries."

"Zelda, how dare you let my baby run around here in a messy dress like that? I only wish I was able to take care of my children myself. You're sure no good at doing it. Go wash Pansy and put her in a clean dress. I don't want her crawling into my bed looking like she does."

"I'll do it right away." Zelda grabbed Pansy up in her arms and hurried out of the room.

Just outside the door, Pansy asked, "Why Mama mad at me?"

Zelda wanted to tell the child that Glenda was an evil person and didn't care about anything except herself and Hugh. But she wouldn't do it. She wanted Pansy to have good memories of her mother. "Your mama isn't mad at you, sweetheart. She's just worried that you'd eaten too many berries and might get a tummy ache."

Pansy laughed. "I not have tummy ache."

"I know, but your mama doesn't know. So, we'll put you in a pretty clean dress then you can go show her you're fine."

"Yes, Zewie." She flung her arms around Zelda's neck. "Wove you."

"I love you, too, sweetheart."

Glenda's voice came into the hall. "Listen to that, Hugh. Zelda's trying to get Pansy to love her instead of me."

"She's always doing that, Mama."

"Well, it won't work. I'll tell my little girl how mean Zelda is."

Zelda gritted her teeth and moved away from the door. She didn't want little innocent Pansy to hear anymore.

~ * ~

Wiley stood beside the chicken coop, pushed his hat back and shook his head. There wasn't a building on the place that didn't need a lot of work. Some more than others. The first thing he thought he'd tackle was the corral. Though there was only the work horse on the place, his horse needed a place to exercise. And the way the fencing had been patched would never do. It would certainly hold the horse in, but he was sure it wouldn't withstand the coming summer storms and it definitely wouldn't hold through the winter. The barn needed a new roof and the chicken coop was almost dilapidated. It was a wonder all the chickens hadn't escaped and probably some had. This would be the second project.

He chuckled. *What am I doing? I need to head on toward Waco and find a job on a ranch where they'll be able to pay me for my work.*

Then, he saw Zelda coming out the back door. She had a floppy straw hat on her head and her shoulders sagged a little as she headed toward the barn. He figured she planned on resuming her plowing. He knew then there was no way he could desert her. Money or no money, this little woman needed help and he intended to give it to her. *You're such a fool, Wiley Hendrix. Never could resist a woman in need, could you?*

He left the chicken coop and intercepted her. "Where you headed?"

"I need to get a few more rows plowed while Pansy is with her mother. I know I'll not be able to finish, but I'll do what I can."

"Zelda, you're exhausted. You're not going to be plowing anymore today."

She frowned at him. "What gives you the right to tell me what to do, Mr. Hendrix?"

"I'm taking the right on myself and for a start, call me Wiley. If Pansy can use my first name, I don't see why you can't."

"Listen here, Mr. Hen …"

"Wiley."

"Wiley. I appreciate you rescuing Pansy, but now I think it's time for you to be on your way."

"Why?"

"Well, I have my work to do and Glenda said she thought it was time you left." When he said nothing, she added, "This is her home and she has the right to say who can come and who must go."

"Then I'll explain to her why I'm not leaving."

"She's a sick woman, Mr. Hen…"

"Wiley."

"Oh, all right, Wiley. The doctor says she doesn't need to get distraught. I think you upset her when you told her Hugh was lazy."

"He's not only lazy, he's rude, too. Somebody needs to straighten him out before it's too late."

"True, but I've already decided it's not going to happen. Glenda will never permit anyone to correct him. She wouldn't even let Daddy when he was alive."

"What's going to happen if and when his mother doesn't get any better? Surely you don't intend to let him continue to treat you the way he does now."

"I don't know what'll happen, Wiley. I'm just trying to get from one day to the next. I don't think about the future at all. And right now, I need to go plow the garden."

"No, Zelda. As I said, no more plowing for you today. I'll finish the plowing. It won't take me long."

She frowned. "Why would you want to do that?"

"I don't know. Maybe it's because I haven't plowed in a while and I want to see if I still remember how." He was almost positive he saw the hint of a smile on her face.

~ * ~

Zelda scrounged around in the root cellar hoping to find something she could add to the potatoes for supper. Glenda would never let her hear the end of it if she didn't come up with something different for Hugh. Behind the last can of pickled-peaches she found a withered apple. Then another one was in the corner of the shelf.

I wonder if I could do something with these. They're not rotten. Just dried up. I remember Mama making pies with dried apples....I wonder....

She snatched the can of peaches and the apples and climbed out of the cellar with enough potatoes to make potato pancakes. At least that was one way she hadn't fixed the tubers that might keep Hugh from complaining.

Glancing toward the cedar elm tree, she saw him relaxed with a book. At least he wouldn't be in the house running his mouth to her as she cooked. She didn't need him telling her what to do. In fact, she didn't need anybody ordering her around, and that included Wiley Hendrix, though that hadn't stopped the man. *What's wrong with me? I'm a big girl and I can take care of myself and this ranch. I've been doing it ever since the accident and so far, we've survived. Why am I letting a stranger come into the picture and start ordering me around as if I can't ... can't what? I can't seem to do anything around here to satisfy anyone except Pansy. She is such a sweet child. Hugh on the other hand...*she paused and thought a minute. *Wiley Hendrix is right. Hugh is rude and lazy and he's been getting away with it for years. It's grown so much worse in the last year.*

I can't believe I let him treat me like he does. But she knew why she did. If she didn't, Glenda would keep reminding her that it was her fault they were in this mess in the first place. Though she hated to admit it, Glenda was right. *I was the one who asked Father to please come home and not stay in town that day. Then the storm came up and...Stop it, Zelda. You can't keep reliving the past. There's no changing what happened.*

She glanced toward the garden. Wiley looked as if he were close to finishing the plowing, a job that would have taken her at least another two or perhaps three days to complete. Though she was thankful he'd insisted on doing the job, she couldn't help but resent the fact he'd ordered her to rest for a while, even if she did think he was one of the handsomest men she'd ever seen.

Rest! Zelda didn't know the meaning of the word. It was only at night that she was able to grab a few hours of sleep and managed a little rest. And those were the nights she was lucky. Most often, her stepmother, who took naps off and on during the day, would yell that she wanted a cup of tea or she'd need help using the thunder pot or need her back rubbed or a multitude of other reasons she came up with to roust Zelda from sleep.

Shaking her head, she went back into the house. At least she would try to give Wiley Hendrix enough to fill his stomach. Even if the main course was another potato dish. After all, it was the least she could do for getting the garden plowed.

"Zelda!" Hugh rose from the tree bench and ambled toward her.

"What, Hugh?"

"When are you going to start cooking supper? I'm hungry."

"For heaven's sake, Hugh. It hasn't been that long since you ate dinner."

"You mean that old potato soup? That couldn't be called a meal. It was awful."

Zelda shook her head, ignored him, and headed to the house. *Hugh's attitude is so hard to put up with. I know his mother says he's sickly, but he should be able to help around here a little. There are things he could do that wouldn't tax his strength. He sure manages to do anything else he wants to.*

In the kitchen, she pulled out the makings of the apple and peach cobbler she planned. She knew it would take longer to cook than the potato cakes.

Pansy came ambling into the room. "Mama sleep."

Zelda smiled at her. "I see. Would you like to help me cook supper?"

"Cook." Pansy pulled the stool close to the work table. She always stood on this when she helped. Or at least thought she was helping, though sometimes it took more effort to clean behind Pansy than the little help she was.

Zelda tied an apron around her waist and a clean towel around Pansy. She then gave the little girl a bowl and a big wooden spoon. "I'll have something for you to stir in a minute."

Pansy giggled.

~ * ~

Wiley's temper was rising when he guided the horse toward the barn. From the garden he'd heard Hugh yell at Zelda about cooking supper. Though he knew he was taking on an almost impossible project, he was going to do something about Hugh's attitude or he would die trying. The boy might be stubborn, but so was Wiley.

"Hugh!" He yelled as he began to unharness the horse.

Hugh ignored him and he yelled again.

This time the boy looked over his book. "What do you want?"

"I want you to come here."

"No!"

Wiley bit his tongue to keep from cursing. "Either come to me or I'll come get you. Your choice."

Hugh glared at him. "You can't make me come there."

Though he was tired, Wiley dropped the horse's rein and stomped toward Hugh as if he were ready to fight.

A frightened look crossed Hugh's face. He put down his book and stood. "All right, damn it. I'm coming."

As soon as he reached him, Wiley grabbed his arm. "When I call you, you answer me immediately and there'll be no cursing."

"Who says I have to do what you say?"

"I say."

"You're not my boss."

"As long as I'm here, I am."

"Mama won't let you stay on her ranch."

"We'll see about that."

"Mama won't let you tell me what to do while you're here."

"She'll have to come out here to stop me."

"She's sick. She can't come outside."

"Then I guess you'll have to do what I say."

Hugh glared at him, but didn't seem able to think of a comeback.

Wiley led him up to the horse. "I'll get him in the barn and you're going to brush him down and cool him off."

"I'm not gonna do that. Call Zelda. She can do it."

"Zelda is busy, so you're going to do it."

"I said I'm not going to do it."

Wiley stared at him a moment, then said, "All right, it's up to you. You can either rub the horse down as I told you to do. Then you can go inside and eat when supper is ready or you can refuse to rub the horse down and sit out here in the barn while the rest of us eat."

"Mama won't let you get away with this." Hugh was almost shouting.

"As I said. If she wants to stop me, she'll have to come out here to do it."

Hugh stomped off toward the barn muttering, "I hate you."

"Do you think I care?" Wiley followed him. He knew he had to make sure Hugh did the job because if he were left alone he'd probably not take correct care of the horse.

They were half through with the brushing job when the sound of a horse's pounding hoofs came into the yard. "I bet that's somebody who'll tell you to get off our ranch."

Wiley shook his head and headed for the door. "Nobody's running me off this ranch until I'm ready to go."

Hugh put down the brush and went out the door behind him. He laughed out loud when he saw the rider. "That's Zelda's boyfriend, Mace Palmer. I bet he'll give you what for."

Wiley said nothing and tried not to show he was surprised at the announcement that Zelda had a boyfriend. He crossed his arms and waited.

"Who the hell are you?" the approaching man bellowed as he reined up his horse in front of Wiley.

Wiley didn't blink, but glared at the rider. "What kind of a man comes riding onto someone's property yelling like a wild man without the courtesy of introducing himself?"

The man glared at Wiley. "I have the right to do anything I want to on my property."

"Tell him, Mace." Hugh grinned at the man.

Both men ignored Hugh. Wiley raised an eyebrow. "I was under the impression this place belonged to Mrs. Jordon."

For a minute the man looked flustered, but finally said, "It'll be mine as soon as I marry Zelda."

"Zelda didn't tell me she was engaged."

"She keeps saying she won't marry him, but Mama says she'll have to, so you better listen to him and get off our ranch." Hugh was practically dancing.

"Until you own this property, I have as much right here as you do. Maybe more. Therefore I suggest you turn your horse around and leave."

"Don't listen to him, Mace. He's just trying to show what a big man he is so Zelda will let him stay. He don't understand how things are."

"I don't intend to listen to a drifter who has come in here and tried to take over. This place is going to belong to the Palmers soon." He pointed his finger at Wiley. "This means it's time you saddled your horse and left."

Wiley didn't show any signs of giving in. "When Miss Jordon tells me she is going to marry you and wants me to leave, then I'll consider leaving. Otherwise, I'm not going anywhere."

"She'll give in. This ranch is close to being foreclosed on. She'll never let her mama and the children lose their home. She'll marry me to save it for them."

"Why don't you just shoot him, Mace?"

"I ought to," Mace said, but he didn't reach for his gun.

"What's going on here?" Zelda's voice interrupted them as she came out into the yard. "I've never heard so much yelling.

They turned to see Zelda approaching them. She had Pansy on her hip.

"Mace was telling this stranger that you're going to marry him and...." Hugh began.

"Heck if I am. Excuse my language, but I've told him over and over that I'll never marry him. He just refuses to get it through that thick head of his."

Wiley didn't say anything, but he did raise an eyebrow as a pleasant feeling filled him.

Palmer gave her a big grin. "Now, Zelda, honey. Don't be that way. You know you're going to have to marry me in the end. I'll make you a good husband and your family will have a place to live when Pa and me own this place and..."

"Mace Palmer, accept the fact that I'll never marry you. I can't stand the thoughts of it. Now get out of here. I have supper ready for Mr. Hendrix."

"Who the hell is Hendrix?"

"I'm the new foreman on this ranch and that gives me the authority to tell you it's time you left."

Mace sneered. "You ain't no foreman. I know for a fact they ain't got the money to hire a foreman."

"Who said I was working for money?"

"If you ain't getting paid, you got no right to tell me to leave."

Hugh interrupted. "That's right, he's got no right."

Wiley ignored Hugh, but said to Mace, "It's none of your business if I'm being paid for the work I'm doing here. Now turn your horse around and leave, Palmer, or I'm going to pull you to the ground and show you who has authority around here."

"I'm not leaving. I came to see Glenda, not any of you."

Zelda took a breath. "Glenda's asleep. I'll not let you disturb her."

"Don't listen to her, Mace. She's probably lying just to keep you from seeing Mama."

"I'm not lying. You'll have to come back later if you want to see Glenda. Now, leave. We're going to eat supper and you're not invited."

Mace didn't say anything else to her, but jerked his horse's head around and glared at Wiley. "You ain't seen the last of me, Hendrix, or whoever you are."

"Don't go, Mace. Zelda will change her mind. Mama will make her."

"You're wrong, Hugh. I'll never change my mind about marrying him."

"Zelda, you ain't got no choice in the matter. I'll be back when you come to your senses." He rode off.

She shook her head at his back and turned to Wiley. "Thank you for standing up to him."

"It's not hard to stand up to a bully and you don't have to thank me for doing so."

She smiled. "As I said, I came out to tell you supper is ready. I know you're tired and hungry after all that plowing."

"I'm hungry." Hugh started toward the house.

Wiley put his hand on the boy's shoulder. "Not so fast. You've not finished brushing the horse."

He whirled around. "But supper is ready."

"And you can eat as soon as you finish the job I told you to do."

Zelda couldn't believe her ears. Wiley was actually ordering Hugh to do some sort of job. She wanted to smile, but didn't dare. She turned back to the house. "Don't worry. I'll put supper on the back of the stove to keep warm until you men finish the job."

Pansy, who hadn't said a word during the interchange, smiled and waved. "Bye, Wiwey."

"Bye, sweetheart and thanks, Zelda. We'll be in shortly." He grinned at them and turned with his hand still on Hugh's shoulder. "Let's go, boy."

Hugh jerked his shoulder from under Wiley's hand, but he did head to the barn.

It didn't take them long to finish what they needed to do. Wiley insisted they wash up at the pump before going in for supper. Hugh was fuming as he went in the back door, but he didn't say anything. Wiley figured he was waiting to go complain to his mama. It didn't matter. Wiley had made up his mind what he was going to say to Glenda Jordon the next time he talked to her.

Five

Zelda watched as Wiley ate the last bite of his pie, then turn to her with a grin. "This was a delicious meal, ma'am."

"I don't see that it was so great. We had potatoes again." Hugh glared at Zelda.

Zelda shook her head. "You managed to eat the potato cakes, Hugh. And I see you ate all your pie, too."

He sneered at her. "A body has to eat enough to stay alive even if the food ain't no good."

Wiley chuckled. "I'm glad you realize that people have to eat to live, Hugh, because we have a long day of hard work before us tomorrow."

Hugh stared at Wiley. "I ain't doing no work with you tomorrow."

"Oh yes, you are. It's time you stopped being a spoiled brat and began taking some responsibility around this ranch."

"Mama says I'm too sickly to do ranch work."

"You don't look very sickly to me."

Zelda watched them in amazement. She appreciated the fact that Wiley wanted Hugh to take on some responsibility, but he had to realize Hugh probably did have some health problems. She thought she ought to butt in and tell him so, but for some reason she kept quiet.

"Zelda!" Glenda's voice came down the hall.

Hugh jumped up. "Mama's awake. I'm going to tell her about you."

He didn't get out of the room before Wiley's hand clamped down on his shoulder. "Not now. I'm sure your mama wants to eat. You'll only upset her."

"I don't care. I..."

"You don't care much about anything but yourself, do you, Hugh?"

"It's none of your damn business."

Wiley shook his head and ushered Hugh toward the door. "I think we need to have a private talk."

"Wiley, maybe ..."

"This is between Hugh and me, Zelda. Why don't you go see about Mrs. Jordon?"

"I go see Mama, Zewie."

"Yes, sweetheart, you can go with me."

"Zelda!"

"I'm coming, Glenda." She hurried down the hall as Wiley and Hugh went out the back door.

Entering Glenda's room, she didn't get a chance to say anything because Glenda blurted, "Were you going to make me starve?"

"Of course not. I just didn't want to wake you because you were resting so well."

"Likely story." She glanced at Pansy. "Come here, baby. Come sit on Mama's bed while Zelda goes and gets Mama something to eat."

Pansy climbed on the bed and Zelda left the room. *At least she didn't say anything too mean about me in front of Pansy. I don't want that innocent little girl to be subjected to the bitterness Glenda often spews.*

When she returned with two potato cakes and a bowl of the pie, she placed them on the table beside the bed and fluffed pillows behind Glenda's head. "I brought you coffee, but I can make some tea if you'd rather have it."

"So, you haven't drunk up all my tea?"

"No, Glenda. I mostly drink coffee or water."

"I see we have potatoes again." When Zelda didn't answer, she went on, "You keep saying we don't have any money, so why did you splurge and make pie?"

"I found a couple of apples and a can of peaches in the root cellar. I thought it would be a treat to have something sweet for a change. I hope you like it."

"I wike it," Pansy giggled.

"I'm glad you do, honey." Glenda patted her arm. "I guess it's all right. Now why don't you jump down and let Mama eat."

"I wash dishes."

"Are you making my little girl do your job, Zelda?"

"Of course not. She likes to stand by me and try to wash dishes."

"I dare say, even though she's a baby, she probably does as good a job as you do." She put a spoon full of the potato cake in her mouth. "Where's Hugh?"

"He went outside."

"Probably reading one of his books. Whenever he comes in, send him to see me. I want to make sure he's all right."

Zelda sighed. "I'll send him." She left the room leading Pansy. She needed to get away before she said something she shouldn't to her stepmother. Though she knew when Hugh told his mother what had happened today, the woman was going to be furious. Zelda wanted to put the confrontation off as long as possible.

~ * ~

The calm didn't last as long as Zelda hoped it would. As soon as Hugh came in, he went directly to his mother's room. Wiley dropped to a chair in the side of the room used as a parlor and Pansy climbed into his lap. Before Zelda could sit, Glenda yelled for her.

She took a deep breath and squared her shoulders. It helped when Wiley winked at her and whispered, "It'll be fine."

Glenda's eyes bored into Zelda's when she said, "Hugh tells me that man is still here. I told you to send him on his way. Why didn't you?"

"He plowed the garden for me and the least I could do was feed him supper."

"It's too late to stop you from feeding him now, but it's not too late to tell him to get on his horse and leave my ranch this very minute."

Zelda didn't know Wiley had followed her into the room and she jumped when he said, "I'll leave your ranch, if you insist, Mrs. Jordon. But let me inform you that when I leave, I'll be taking Zelda with me. Probably Pansy, too."

Glenda gasped. "That's ridiculous. Zelda's not going anywhere."

"Of course I'm not," Zelda muttered.

Wiley ignored her. "As far as I'm concerned, slavery ended with the war. You nor anyone else has the right to treat a human being the way you and your son are treating Zelda. Thank God, little Pansy is too innocent to know what's going on."

"How dare you talk to me in such a way?"

"Oh, I dare, Mrs. Jordon. Somebody should have done it before now. So, either you accept the fact that I'm going to stay around here and try to get this ranch back on its feet or as I said, I'm leaving. But I'm not going alone."

"Mama, can he do that?"

"No, he can't, Hugh. I own this ranch and what I say goes and it's my command that he leave this ranch immediately."

"Fine," Wiley nodded at her and turned to Zelda. "Go pack what you and Pansy will need."

"You'll not take my baby!" Glenda screamed.

"Why? Are you going to make her do the cooking and cleaning and everything else that has to be done around here for you and your lazy son?"

"She's a baby. She can't...."

"That's why we have to take her with us. Unless you plan to get out of that bed and take care of her needs, we have no choice."

"I can't get out of bed and you know it."

"Well then, you must face the fact that with Zelda gone, there'll be nobody around here to look after Pansy. You say you're not able and you know good and well Hugh won't do it. He can't even look after himself, much less a little girl."

"But...but..."

"There are no buts, Mrs. Jordon. Either you accept the fact than I'm going to stay around here for a while or you get out of that bed and run the ranch yourself."

Glenda grabbed her heart and burst out crying.

Pansy's eyes got big as she reached for Wiley. "Is Mama sad?"

"Oh, yes, Pansy, my darling. I'm very sad. This stranger has pushed his way into our lives and made us all sad." Glenda wiped her nose and started to reach for her daughter, but Hugh walked up to the bed.

"I thought you were going to run him off, Mama." Hugh glared down at his mother. "I don't like him and I want him gone."

She held her arms out to him. "Come here, baby." Hugging him close, she said, "We'll be fine. I'll see that he doesn't make you do anything you're not able to do."

Hugh looked out from under his mother's arm and stuck his tongue out at Wiley. He then began to smile and nod at something his mother whispered in his ear.

~ * ~

Zelda followed Wiley out the back door. He was still carrying Pansy.

"Where we go?" The little girl asked.

"I thought we'd go sit on the bench under the tree. Is that all right with you?"

"Can Zewie come?"

"I think she's right behind us."

Pansy giggled, looked over his shoulder and waved at Zelda. "Hey, Zewie."

"Hello, sweetheart."

They reached the bench and Wiley took a seat and sat Pansy down beside him. "Have a seat here with us, Zelda. I think it's time you and I had a talk."

"I think you're right about that, Mr. Hendrix."

He lifted an eyebrow. "So, we're back to last names?"

"What difference does the name make? You'll be leaving."

"Didn't you hear what I said to Glenda?"

"Of course, but …"

"No buts, Zelda. You need help around here and I've decided I'm going to help you since there's nobody else to do it. Or at least, there isn't until Hugh learns to pull his weight around here."

"But…"

"There you go again with that word *but*."

"All right, let me put it this way. I appreciate you plowing the field for me, but I have no money to pay a ranch hand."

"I know you don't have any money; therefore, you don't have to pay me. I'll work for a place to sleep and food."

"That can be a problem, too. We have very little food and there's no room in the house for you to sleep. The big bedroom is used for storage."

"Why?"

"Not that it matters, but when Glenda married Father, she refused to sleep in the bedroom he shared with my mother. She insisted they use her bedroom suit and sleep in the room where she is now. Since I was sleeping in the room with Pansy, she decided to use the big bedroom as a place to store the rest of her furniture and what belonged to my mother she didn't want. It's still there."

He winked at her. "Don't worry about a place for me to sleep. The barn will do. As for food, don't worry about that either. I like potatoes."

"But, Wiley, as much as I'd like the help, I don't own this ranch. Glenda does and there's no way she'll allow you to stay here."

"She has no choice. I'm pretty sure she believed me when I told her if I left, you'd be going with me."

"You know that's not going to happen. I can't leave with nobody here to look after her."

"You realize that, and I realize that, but she's not sure of it, so relax. We need to decide what should be done first to get this place back on its feet or has it always been just hanging on like it is now?"

"When my father was living we had a nice profitable ranch. We had cows, horses and other livestock."

"What went with them?"

Zelda shrugged. "Glenda let Mace Palmer and his father buy all the cows that hadn't wandered off. We did keep our old milk cow. I'm sure the Palmers cheated her when they took the herd, but she wouldn't listen to me when I told her not to let them go so cheap. As I said, my father left the ranch to her so there was nothing I could do about it."

"What about the other animals?"

"We have a few chickens, but they aren't laying many eggs and I've been afraid Glenda will decide we should kill and eat them."

"You said some cows wandered off. Do you think they could be rounded up?"

"I don't know. I guess they could be, that is if somebody hasn't already claimed them."

Pansy began to wiggle. "Get down."

"Sure, honey." Wiley helped her to the ground.

"I make play house." She began to move around and collect pebbles to add to a small pile off to the side of the bench.

"That'll be a petty play house, Pansy." Zelda smiled at her. Looking back at Wiley, she said, "Pansy loves her rocks and keeps a collection here to make shapes with when we sit here."

Wiley nodded. "At least her mother's attitude hasn't rubbed off on her."

"Not yet it hasn't."

"And with your influence, it never will."

"Thank you, Wiley. I hope you're right."

The back door slammed and Hugh came out of the house. He paused and looked at them, but instead of heading their way, he walked around the side of the house.

Wiley chuckled. "I don't guess he wants to join us."

"Probably going to sit on the front porch. He often does that when Pansy and I are in the backyard." Zelda stood. "I better get back inside. Glenda might want something."

"You sure do take looking after her seriously, don't you?"

"I have to, Wiley. There's nobody else to do it."

He looked as if he wanted to make a comment, but instead he said, "I think I'll check out the barn loft and see where I want to lay out my bedroll."

"Are you sure you want to stay here?"

"I'm positive." He grinned at her and headed toward the barn.

Zelda reached down and extended her hand to Pansy. "Come on, sweetheart. Let's go check on your mama."

~ * ~

Wiley climbed the ladder to the loft of the barn and tested the floor boards as he walked across them. There were a couple of loose ones he knew should be nailed down. He hoped there was a hammer among the tools here. He'd have to ask Zelda where she kept them.

He walked to the window at the front of the structure. It was over the main door and looked toward the side of the house. Of course, from here he could see the entire yard, even that in the front of the house.

He frowned when he saw Hugh sneaking around the corner of the house and looking in the direction of the bench Zelda and he had vacated. The boy must have decided it was safe to come to the backyard because he hurried to the tree bench. But instead of sitting, he looked toward the house then turned toward the barn. Wiley figured the boy must have thought he had gone inside with Zelda and Pansy.

Wiley wondered what Hugh was up to, but he decided he wouldn't ask. He'd wait and see because he was sure the boy would give himself away.

It didn't take long. Hugh came into the barn and in minutes he was leading the plow horse out with a bridle on him. There was no saddle, but the boy threw a blanket across the animal's back and led him from the barn, across the yard and toward the woods. When he was in the trees, he stopped and climbed on the horse.

Wiley knew the boy had something on his mind and he knew he was going to find out what it was, but there was no big rush. It would be easy to follow his trail. Climbing down from the loft, Wiley walked to the corral and got his horse. He saddled him and mounted.

He decided he'd keep out of sight until he saw where the boy went. Knowing Hugh wouldn't notice him following, he still stayed back a safe distance.

In a little while Hugh turned the plow horse into the road leading to a neighboring ranch. Stopping his horse on top of a knoll where he could see the cabin and the surrounding buildings, Wiley pulled out his spy glass and trained it on the front yard.

It was only minutes until the man called Mace Palmer came out the front door, walked down the steps and put his hand on Hugh's shoulder. He guided the boy onto the porch and through the door into the house.

Wiley had seen all he needed to see. He replaced the spy glass in his saddle bag, turned his horse around and headed back to the Jordon place. He'd find out later what went on at the Palmer ranch though he almost knew Hugh had gone there because that's what his mama told him to do. That must have been what they were whispering earlier.

It didn't make a difference. Wiley knew he would keep his eyes and ears open and be prepared for whatever scheme Glenda tried to pull off through her son.

~ * ~

Zelda tucked Pansy into bed, kissed her cheek and smiled as the little girl turned on her side hugging her worn rag doll. She grinned up at Zelda. "You kiss BeBe to sleep, too."

"Of course I will." Zelda leaned over and kissed the doll. "Good night, BeBe. You sleep tight with Pansy."

Pansy giggled. "Wove you, Zewie."

"I love you, too, sweetheart. Now you go to sleep and I'll be in to sleep soon."

"All right."

Zelda blew out the lamp and slipped out of the room she shared with Pansy. She would have liked to climb into the small cot in the corner where she slept, but there was still work to do in the house. She knew she had to wash the dirty clothes the next day and they had to be checked to see if there were places that had to be mended. Especially on Pansy's clothes. The child tended to accumulate rips, tears and other damage to the clothes she wore daily. Hugh's weren't as bad because he seldom did anything except sit around. If he were willing to do a little work, his clothes might have shown more damage, too.

She sighed and wished she had the money to buy some things for Pansy. The little girl was growing fast and would soon have to have a few things. But Zelda kept putting off asking Glenda for the money to add to the child's wardrobe. She knew there would be a fight when she did ask. The woman didn't have a lot of cash, but she guarded every penny because she seemed to think Zelda was trying to take what little there was away from her.

Nothing could be further from the truth. Zelda didn't want Glenda's money, but she knew it took money for the family to survive.

<h1 style="text-align:center">Six</h1>

Zelda was pinning the wet clothes to the backyard clothes line when she paused to watch Wiley pull the rickety ranch wagon into the yard. He had hitched up the wagon after breakfast and headed to town. He didn't tell her why he was going and she didn't ask. She was intent on getting her wash started because she knew it would take most of the day.

Wiley stopped the wagon next to the back porch and jumped down. "I'm back."

She smiled, looked down at Pansy where the little girl had been building something with rocks. "Let's go see were Wiley has been, Sugar."

She dropped the pebbles and reached for Zelda's hand. A big grin spread across her face. "I wike Wiwey."

"I know you do, sweetheart." She wanted to add that she did, too, but she didn't dare.

"Where's Hugh?" Wiley asked when she walked up to the wagon.

"He read," Pansy said and reached for Wiley.

He took her in his arms and tickled her belly. "Do you know where he's reading?"

She giggled and pointed toward the tree with the bench. "There."

"Let's go get him."

"Wait, Wiley..." Zelda started.

He raised his eyebrow at her. "Why?"

She sighed. "I just don't want an argument today."

"Don't worry about it." He walked off toward the bench with Pansy in his arms.

She didn't know what he said to Hugh, but in a matter of minutes the boy returned to the wagon with Wiley and Pansy. He didn't speak to Zelda, but glared at Wiley. "What do I have to do?"

"Start taking these supplies in the house and put them in the kitchen."

"Why should I? Zelda can do it."

"No, Zelda can't do it. You're going to."

"I don't want to."

"All right, Hugh. I changed my mind. You don't have to do it."

Hugh grinned.

It faded when Wiley said, "It's your choice. You can return to your seat under the tree and start reading again or you can carry these supplies into the house."

"I'll go read."

"That's your choice, but I want you to understand that unless you carry these boxes into the house, you will not eat a bite of what comes out of them. You'll only be allowed to eat the potatoes that are already on this ranch."

"You're lying."

"I'm not, but if you want to wait and see, it's up to you. Of course, you'll be only eating potatoes by then."

Hugh grabbed a box and muttered, "You damn bastard!"

"Watch the language or I'm going to wash your mouth out with the soapy water Zelda has used to wash the clothes."

Hugh didn't say anything else, but clomped into the house, a box in his hands.

Zelda looked into the wagon. "Wiley, what have you done?"

"I thought you might like something different to cook, so I went into town and picked up a few things at the general store."

She shook her head. "Why? You know I can't afford to buy anything."

"Well, I can afford it, so forget it."

"No, I won't forget it. I don't want you coming in here and ...."

"Listen, Zelda. I'm here because I want to be. I also want to have enough food to eat while I'm doing the work that has to be done. It's not that you don't do what you can with what little you're allowed to have, but you deserve more. As long as I'm here, there will be plenty of food on the table."

"But..."

"Don't argue. Now, go finish hanging your clothes on the line and then sit down and rest." He looked at Pansy and sat her on the ground. "You go with Zelda, sweetheart. You and I will play later."

"All right." She looked up at Zelda. "Go hang, Zewie?"

Zelda felt she had no choice and she didn't understand why she felt that way. She was under no obligation to obey when Wiley Hendrix told her what to do. But for some reason, she always did. She reached for Pansy's hand. "Yes, baby. Let's go hang."

~ * ~

Wiley checked his smile when a furious Hugh came back to the wagon and picked up another box. Without saying a word, he turned back to the house with it.

"You do know that if there's anything ends up broken in these boxes, you will have to be punished, don't you, Hugh?"

"I haven't broke anything."

"Good." Wiley picked up a box and followed the boy into the house.

Hugh sat his box on the table and started out the door, then paused when he saw Wiley began to take things out of the boxes. "Ain't you coming to help me carry the rest of it?"

"You can handle it. I'm going to start putting things away."

Hugh went out mumbling under his breath. Wiley knew the boy was cursing him, but he ignored it. It was going to take a while, but he felt sure he could help Hugh face his laziness and overcome it. He also felt he could eventually clean up the young man's language. He was certainly going to try, because the young man would probably be worth it in the end.

The back door opened as Zelda and Pansy entered. She looked at the groceries on the table. "Why in the world did you buy all of this?"

"I think I explained that."

"Yes, but..."

Hugh came in. "This is the last box."

"Then get the other bags."

Hugh looked at Zelda. "You go get them. You're not doing anything."

She started to speak, but Wiley spoke first. "I think I told you to get them, Hugh. In case not, I'm telling you now. Go get the bags."

Hugh didn't argue. He turned and went out the door.

"He's furious," Zelda said.

"Being mad never hurt anybody."

Hugh came back in and slammed a bag of flour, one of sugar and one of apples on the side board. "That's all. Are you satisfied now?"

"I am, Hugh. You did a good job. Now, you can go back and read your book until I want you to do something else."

"I'm not doing anything else." He stomped to the door.

"We'll see about that."

Hugh ignored Wiley and went out the door.

"You shouldn't antagonize him so much, Wiley."

"I know you think I'm being rough on him, Zelda, but somebody has to take that boy in hand and teach him how to be a man. If not, it's no telling where he'll end up."

"But his health. His mother says..."

"Forget what his mother says. I stopped in and had a talk with the doctor today while I was in town. He says Hugh got over the disease he had as a baby years ago. It was bad at the time and probably made his mother worry it would happen again, but his chances of getting it again are no greater than yours or mine. There's no reason the boy can't become a working cowboy on this ranch and I'm going to do my best to see that he does just that."

"I guess you checked up on Glenda's health, too."

"I did." He glanced at Pansy who had climbed up on the stool by the table and was looking at the supplies in the box. "What are you looking at, little darling?"

"Don't know."

Wiley laughed. "Well, I bet I can find something in there that you will like."

She looked at him with her big brown eyes. "What?"

Wiley opened one of the small bags and pulled out a cookie. "What about this?"

Her eyes got big. "Cookie."

"Yes, it's a cookie. Would you like it?"

She nodded and Wiley handed it to her.

She climbed down and looked up at Zelda. "Eat now?"

"Yes, precious. You can eat it now. Why don't you sit there by the fireplace and eat it?"

"I will." She moved to the side of the room beside the fireplace and sat on the hearth. In a matter of seconds, she was showing her doll the cookie. "Look, Be-Be. Cookie."

Zelda turned to Wiley. "Now, tell me. What did the doctor say about Glenda?"

Before he could answer, the sound of a horse came clomping into the yard. Hurrying to the door she looked out and sighed. "It's Mace Palmer."

"You stay inside and I'll take care of this."

"No, Wiley. It's not your problem."

"I'm making it mine." He winked at her. "You put up the rest of these groceries and let me handle it."

It felt good to have someone else deal with Mace, but she felt a little guilty about it. "Are you sure you want to face him?"

"I'm sure. Might better keep Pansy in here with you. She doesn't need to see it if I have to knock the man's teeth out."

"Teeth?" Pansy said.

"Yes, honey. Do you have cookie in your teeth?"

She looked puzzled, but shook her head.

Wiley grinned and stepped outside. He noticed Hugh put his book down and walk up to Palmer, who was dismounting.

They were saying something, but Wiley couldn't hear at the distance. He stepped off the porch and headed in their direction. "How can I help you today, Palmer?"

"I'm not here to see you. I have business with Mrs. Jordon."

"Mrs. Jordon is asleep, so you're wasting your time coming here this time of day."

"I'll wake her up. This is important."

"Yeah, Mace is right. Mama would want us to wake her up for this."

"For what, Hugh?"

"To sign the papers."

Mace swatted at him. "Shut up, Hugh."

"All right, fellows. What's going on?"

"Tell him, Mace."

"I told you to shut up, Hugh. He's got no right to know anything." He turned to Wiley. "Now get out of my way. I'm going to see Mrs. Jordon, just like I said in the first place."

"I told you, she's asleep."

Mace stepped close to Wiley. "I said I'd wake her up."

"And I said you weren't going to do that."

"Hit him, Mace. He's not so brave since he's not wearing his gun."

Mace smiled and put his hand on his gun butt. "Hugh's right. Looks like I hold all the cards here. Now get out of my way."

Wiley stood his ground. "You're going to have to shoot me to get into that house, Mace Palmer."

"Shoot him, Mace."

Mace reached for his gun, but Wiley was faster. He struck out with his right hand and hit Mace on the left side of his face.

Mace staggered backward and managed to get his pistol out of his holster. As he raised it to shoot, a bullet whizzed by his head. He whirled around.

Zelda stood on the porch with the rifle raised to her shoulder, ready to shoot again.

Mace holstered his gun and held up his hands as she walked toward them. "I weren't gonna shoot him, honey. I just wanted to scare him a little," Mace said.

She didn't answer. She only kept coming toward him with the gun trained on his head.

Hugh looked scared. "Mama wanted to see him, Zelda," he muttered.

Zelda didn't say a word. She just kept coming.

"Don't shoot, Zelda. I've put my gun up."

She paused a few feet away. "Get on your horse and get out of here, Mace Palmer. If I ever see you on this ranch again, I'll kill you."

"Now, darling. You don't understand. Glenda sent for me. She wanted to ... well she wanted to see me about some business."

"You and your father have cheated Glenda enough. You have no more business with her today or ever."

"Don't you understand, Zelda? Mama told me to get Mace to come see her so she could straighten things out and old Wiley would leave and you could marry Mace and ..."

"Hugh, get this through your thick head. I'm never going to marry Mace Palmer. I'd rather die."

Hugh frowned. "But Mama said you had to."

She ignored him and glared at Mace. "Are you leaving or am I going to have to shoot you?"

Wiley hadn't said a word, but he walked to Zelda's side and took the rifle from her. "I'm not going to let this sweet innocent woman shoot you, Palmer. It would make her feel more guilt than what has already been laid on her by Glenda Jordan. But I don't have the conscience Zelda does. I'll shoot you in a heartbeat if you don't do like she says and get out of here."

"You'd hang."

"I don't think so. A man has a right to protect his woman."

"She's not your wo..."

"Can you prove that?"

Mace looked confused, but shook his head. He turned to Hugh, took a folded paper from his pocket and handed it to the boy. "Give this to your mother and get her to sign it."

"I will, Mace. I'll do it right now." He started for the house.

Wiley had a feeling he knew what the paper was. He grabbed his arm. "Not so fast, boy. You don't go back in that house until we all go inside."

Mace climbed on his horse. Whirling around, he yelled as he left, "You think you've seen the last of me, but you're dead wrong. I'll be back and when I get here you'll be sorry you caused me so much trouble."

Before anyone could say anything, Pansy came out of the porch and said, "Mama yell."

"I'd better see what she wants."

"I want to see Mama, too. I'm going with Zelda."

Wiley turned him loose. "Go ahead."

Following everyone to the house, he knew he had to get the paper Mace had given Hugh. It would be prudent to do so and this he intended to do. In the meantime, he was going to tell Zelda how impressed he was by her interference in the argument. The woman might be riddled with guilt, but she was sure full of spunk. He admired that about her.

~ * ~

Zelda hurried into Glenda's room. "I'm here now. What did you need?"

"Need? I could've died it took you so long to get here. Why didn't you come when I first called? Where were you?"

"I was outside." She didn't see any need to inform Glenda of what had really happened.

"You should have been in the house."

"It's wash day, Glenda."

"That's no excuse."

Hugh came running into the room. "Mama, Mace came like you asked him to, but Zelda tried to shoot him and he left."

"Zelda did what?"

"She tried to shoot Mace."

"That's not true, Hugh. I only kept Mace Palmer from shooting Wiley."

"Stop arguing with him, Zelda. Hugh wouldn't lie to me. Why don't you get out of here and let me talk to my son? He's the only person on this ranch I trust."

"But…"

"I said get out of here."

Zelda turned and walked out of the room. Oh, how she wished she could tell this woman what she really thought of her. She had never cared much for Glenda, but since she'd been bedridden, she was impossible to please. *I'm so tired of trying.* She smiled to herself. *I can't believe I'm thinking this way, but I almost wish Wiley had been serious about taking Pansy and me away. It would be good to get away from Glenda and Hugh, but I know I shouldn't think that way. Lord, please forgive me for letting it enter my mind. I know this is my lot in life and I'll handle it as long as I must. There is no other choice for me.*

She found Wiley and Pansy in the kitchen putting up the supplies. "I can do that."

"Sure you can, but I don't mind."

"I help, Wiwey."

"I see you are." She glanced at Wiley. "I hope you didn't let her eat anything else."

"Nope. We talked about it and decided we'd wait for supper."

"Some clothes should be dry in this heat. Why don't I go get them off the line and then start supper?"

"I'm sure Pansy would like to help you."

"I help."

She looked at him. "Should…"

"There's something I need to do."

"Then, come with me, Pansy. We'll get the clothes and I'll let you hold some of the clothes pins."

She scrambled down from the stool. "I like hold pins."

Hugh came into the room. "Mama wants a pen so she can sign something."

Zelda stopped and looked at him. "What?"

"I don't know. She just told me to get a pen."

"Go on, Zelda. I'll get one for her."

She looked at Wiley. "Do you have one?"

He nodded.

"Then, let's go, Pansy." They went out the door holding hands.

"All right, Mr. Bossy. Give me the pen to take to Mama."

"I'll take it to her, Hugh. You need to go outside and put the wagon in the barn and rub down the horse."

"I'll not do it."

Wiley didn't argue. He walked over to Hugh, took him by the arm and led him to the door. "Now, do like I said."

"Why are you trying to ...?"

"It doesn't matter why, Hugh. You're a kid. I'm a man and I'm the one in charge. Now, get out there and do what I said if you want to eat any supper tonight."

"But Mama wants a pen."

"I said, I'd take care of your mama. Now, go."

Hugh gave up and went out the door.

Wiley watched to make sure he was going to stay outside, he then turned and headed to Glenda's bedroom.

Seven

Wiley walked into Glenda's room and closed the door behind him. "I think it's time we talked."

She hurriedly folded the papers in her hands and stuck them under the sheet. "Where's Hugh?"

"Hugh's busy right now."

"I sent him to get me a pen. I want it right now."

"He's not coming with the pen. I said you and I need to talk and we're going to do it now."

She turned her head. "Well, say what you have to say and then get out of here and send Hugh to me."

"I had a nice long talk with your doctor today."

She snapped her head toward him. "You had no right to do that."

"Oh, I think I did, but that's beside the point. You realize what I found out, don't you?"

"He wouldn't have told a stranger anything about me."

"He didn't think I was a stranger."

She frowned. "Who did he think you were?"

"Does it matter?"

"To me, it does."

Wiley gave her a sly smile. "All right, if you must know, I told him I was the man who would be taking on the responsibility of Hugh and Pansy when you die."

"He wouldn't have believed that?"

"When I told him I was marrying Zelda, he believed it."

Glenda's shoulders slumped. He knew she understood he was telling her the truth. She shook her head. "So, you know."

"I know."

"What are you going to do about it?"

"I think it's more important to ask yourself, what are you going to do about it?"

Glenda was silent for a moment. "But she had to be punished."

"Why?"

"Because it's her fault that I no longer have a husband."

"Are you sure about that?"

"I'm sure."

"What about the fact that you're the one who insisted you and your husband leave town that day instead of staying at the hotel. You couldn't stand the thought that Zelda was here alone with your son. You were afraid she'd make him do some work for a change." He glared at her. "Don't you think she deserves to know the truth?"

Glenda was quiet for a minute. Then, "She had already asked her father to come home, so I'm not going to tell her a thing."

"I figured you'd say that, but I decided I'm going to give you time to think about it. You don't have to tell her anything now."

"I won't change my mind."

"That's up to you. Just know that if you don't tell her eventually, I will."

"It'll be too late then."

"I doubt that." He stared at her a minute, took a deep breath and said, "Give me the papers."

"What papers?"

"Give them to me, Glenda. I don't want to take them away from you, but I will."

"You would, wouldn't you?"

He nodded. "You know I will."

"What gives you the right to come to my ranch, then into my house and now into my bedroom and tell me what to do?"

"Mrs. Jordon, I had no intention of even staying on this ranch longer than it took to eat a bowl of potato soup and rest a bit. Then little by little, I discovered what was going on around here and I felt somebody should put stop to it."

"Nothing that's happened here is any of your business. It's my ranch and..."

He interrupted. "I know that. It's your ranch and if you die you intend to leave it to Hugh. That is, if you still own it."

She stuck her chin in the air. "Who says I won't own it until the day I die?"

He grinned. "You can fool a lot of people, Glenda Jordon, but you can't fool me. You have made plans for your stepdaughter to marry that fool, Mace Palmer, if it cost you the ranch and your children."

"Again, that's none of your business."

"I like Zelda, so I'm making it my business. There's no way I'm going to stand by and see you destroy her and your children." When she only glared at him, he added, "Now, give me those papers. Or, as I asked before, would you prefer I take them away from you? You'll not be signing them either way."

She had hate in her eyes as she eased the papers out from under the sheet and handed them to him. "I suppose you're going to look at them."

"Of course." He unfolded the papers and read them. Shaking his head at her, he said, "It's just what I thought it was. I knew you were vindictive, Mrs. Jordon, but I never dreamed you were stupid."

"How dare you call me stupid!"

"There is no other word for what you were about to do except *stupid*. Yes, you would have been hurting her, but she would still not marry Palmer. In the end you'd only be hurting your children. In fact, you would have ruined their lives because what you expected to happen, never would, and they would have to pay for their mother's hate and greed with their lives."

"That's not true."

"Oh, yes, it is."

"How can you be sure of that?"

"Don't worry about it. I'm just sure." He ripped the papers in two sections, then into four. "I'll burn this and nobody will have to know it ever existed."

"I can get another set."

"Don't bother. I'll never allow it."

She glared at him. "Get out of my room."

"Gladly." He walked out of the room and directly to the kitchen. He opened the stove lid and dropped the papers inside.

He heard Glenda sobbing, but he didn't return to check on her. Instead he plastered on a smile and walked outside to check on Zelda and the children.

~ * ~

Glenda looked at the tray of food Zelda brought her. "I knew you were lying when you said we didn't have anything except potatoes to eat."

"We didn't have anything except the potatoes until Mr. Hendrix decided to go into town and buy supplies for the family. He thought we needed something better to eat."

"How much of my money did he spend?"

"He spent his own money, but I think you should pay him back for the supplies."

"I will not. He had no business buying them, but since he did, he can just pay for them himself." She picked up her fork and stabbed a piece of ham that Zelda had cut up into small chunks for her. "If he's stupid enough to buy food for us, I'll let him do it."

"It's not his place to buy for us."

She shrugged. "So."

"Honestly, Glenda, don't you care about anything?"

"I had a husband I cared about. I had good health that I enjoyed. I had a wonderful life until somebody took it all away from me."

Zelda's shoulders slumped. "I know and I'm so sorry. I'd change it all if I could. You should know I'd do anything to change what happened, but I can't."

"And you won't even try."

"What do you mean?"

"You know if you would marry Mace Palmer, he and his father would combine these two ranches and make a home for all of us."

"I'll never marry that awful man. I know you hate me, but I can't believe even you'd want me to do that."

"I knew you were too selfish to think of us instead of yourself."

"Marrying Mace Palmer would only complicate things, Glenda. Now that the Palmers have the cattle and most everything else of value here, they don't care about anyone or anything else here except getting their hands on this ranch. They would never take care of you and your children."

Glenda shook her head. "You're wrong. Mace would make a good home for my children and you, too, even though you don't deserve it. I'm sure his father would agree to that."

"I can't stand the man. The thoughts of him touching me gives me the shivers."

Glenda laughed. "Then if you marry him I won't have to worry that you're not still being punished for what you did to me and my family. Every time he touched you, you'd be sorry for what you did."

"I'm already sorry for what happened, but marrying Mace Palmer won't help matters."

"Oh, yes it would. I would know my children would be cared for."

"He would never take care of your children, so give it up. I won't marry the man, Glenda, and I'd appreciate it if you didn't mention it to me again."

"Why? Are you going to run to your friend Wiley Hendrix about it?"

"This is none of Wiley's business."

"That's the only thing you've said that I agree with. Now get out of here and let me eat my supper in peace. Then send my children to me. I want to spend some time with them before I go to sleep."

~ * ~

Wiley came out of the barn and walked up to the tree bench where Zelda sat. He dropped down beside her. "I'm surprised to find you out there under this tree alone."

"Glenda wanted to visit with the children and I got the feeling she wanted me out of the house."

"Do you trust her with them alone?"

"Why shouldn't I? They're her children."

"I know that, but she's sure done a poor job of mothering them."

"You shouldn't say that, Wiley."

"Why not? It's the truth."

Zelda shook her head. "Honestly, Wiley. You sure say what you think, don't you?"

"Most of the time."

She looked across the open land. "I think tomorrow will be a good day to start planting the garden. I appreciate the seed you bought. I told Glenda she should pay you for them, but I'm not sure she'll do it. If she doesn't, I'll repay you whenever I can."

Before he could answer, a shot rang out and a bullet embedded itself in the tree just above Wiley's head. He grabbed Zelda and pulled her to the side and behind the tree where he sheltered her with his body.

She was shaking. "What happened?"

"Somebody shot at us." He looked around. "I sure wish I had my gun on."

"Oh, no," Zelda cried and pulled out of his arms. "Pansy is coming out the door."

Wiley had no choice. He ran to the porch behind Zelda. Another shot hit the ground behind their backs, but they made it to the house. Zelda scooped Pansy up, pushed Hugh backward and hurried inside.

"Why you run, Zewie?"

"What's going on?" Hugh demanded.

Zelda didn't answer. She just held Pansy close to her and whispered, "Thanks to the good Lord we made it inside."

"Yes, we did. Now, I want you and the kids to stay inside."

"I asked, what's happening?" Hugh's voice was sarcastic.

Again, she ignored him and glanced at Wiley. He was buckling on his gun belt. "What are you doing?"

"I'm hoping I can catch whoever it was shooting at us. Like I said, keep the children inside."

"Do you think you should go outside?"

"I can't hide in here with somebody shooting at the people on this ranch, Zelda. Now, don't worry. I'll be back soon. Hopefully, I'll have the shooter all tied up across his horse Just keep the children and yourself where you'll be safe."

"Somebody tell me what happened." This time Hugh almost yelled.

Glenda's raspy voice came down the hall. "What's going on?"

"I hate to leave you to explain this, but I need to go."

"Don't worry. We'll be fine."

Wiley turned. "Hugh, lock the door behind me when I go out. I'll knock when I get back."

"Why?"

"Just do it, Hugh." Wiley's voice left no room for argument.

"Somebody come in here and tell me what's going on," Glenda demanded.

After Wiley went out the door, Zelda turned toward Glenda's room. Pansy was still in her arms. In a minute Hugh followed. "She won't tell me what happened, Mama."

"Why won't you tell him, Zelda?"

"I was too busy trying to get him and Patsy in the house to answer his questions."

"Well, you're in here now. What happened?"

"Someone was shooting at us while we were in the backyard. When Pansy started out, all I could think of was getting her back inside out of danger."

"You're being ridiculous. Nobody would be shooting at anyone at our place."

"Well, they were. One bullet hit the tree where the bench is. Another hit the ground."

Glenda put her hand to her throat. "Were you sitting under the tree, my precious son?"

"No, Mama. I was in here with you. They must have shot at Zelda."

"I don't think anybody would shoot at her." It was as if something dawned on Glenda. Her face broke into a smile. "I'm sure they were shooting at that Wiley person you're hiding here. He's probably an escaped outlaw or something."

Zelda stared at her. "Wiley is no outlaw."

"How do you know? You bring a stranger into my home and all these terrible things begin to happen. This proves he has to go and I demand that you run him off today."

Zelda didn't know where the courage came from, but she looked directly into Glenda's eyes and said, "Wiley Hendrix is the best thing that's happened here since my father died. I will not run him off. If you want him gone, you'll have to do it yourself."

Fury crossed Glenda's face. "You ungrateful bitch! How dare you talk to me like that after all I've done for you! I'm glad your father isn't here to hear how you treat the women he loved and would still be with if it wasn't for your selfishness."

"Tell her, Mama. She's sorry and no good. I hate her."

"So do I, Hugh, darling, but it's too late to get rid of her now."

"Why?"

"Why, indeed?" Zelda turned and went out of the room.

"Get back here, Zelda."

"Mama call."

"I know, Pansy. We'll see her later." Zelda went into the small parlor and sat in the rocking chair by the fireplace.

Pansy laid her head on Zelda's chest. "Rock me."

Zelda smiled down at the little girl and hugged her against her chest. "Yes, my darling, Pansy. I'll rock you."

Hugh came into the room. "Mama said for you to go back in there. She wasn't finished talking to you."

Zelda shook her head. "I'm not going back in there now. I'm too angry. I might say something I'd regret for a long time. You go talk to your mother. I'm sure you two have a lot to say about me."

"But Mama said..."

"Right now, I don't care what your mama said. I'm not coming." She began moving the chair back and forth in smooth slow motion and ignored him.

Shortly, Pansy dozed off. In spite of the fact that Glenda was still ranting and raving in her bedroom and without realizing how tired she was, it wasn't long until Zelda slipped into dreamland, too.

~ * ~

Wiley tracked the gunman to the edge of the ranch, then lost his tracks when they came to an end at the small stream that separated the Jordon ranch form the one owed by the Palmers. Though he checked on the other side of the branch, Wiley couldn't pick up the tracks again. He figured the man had traveled by water for some distance before leaving the stream. Maybe all the way back to the Palmer homestead.

Turning his horse, Wiley headed back to the ranch. He was sure the gunman had wanted to kill him. Therefore, he didn't think the man would return to shoot at anyone else at the Jordon place, but there was the slightest chance he could be wrong. In case he was, he felt he had to make sure they were all safe.

He wished he could have caught the man, because it was next to impossible to prove the shooter had been Mace Palmer. Yet it had to be him. Nobody else on any of the other ranches knew or cared that Wiley Hendrix was helping Zelda Jordon. And he did consider that he was helping Zelda, not the rest of the family. After all, she was the one who needed the most help, though Hugh came in a close second.

On the way back, Wiley noticed a couple of cows, one with a calf, grazing near the line. He rode over to them and looked for a brand, but they didn't have one. He raised an eyebrow. This could be the beginning of the Jordons' new herd.

He decided to drive them closer to the ranch house and check to see if there happened to be some fences up where he could pasture them. If not, he could probably find a small canyon and head them in there until fences could be built.

Driving the cows and the calf was easy, but he wondered if he could handle all the work alone that needed doing around there. He knew Zelda would do what she could, but she had the responsibility of Glenda and little Pansy. She couldn't be away from the house for very long. Then there was Hugh. With the right training, he could learn to be a good ranch hand. Of course, he'd not be able to handle some things because of his age, but he could do a lot more than he thought he could. Only thing, it wasn't going to be easy to train him, though Wiley thought it would be worth it in the end. The boy didn't know it, but he was in for a rude awakening. *And unless I change my mind, that awakening is going to begin tomorrow.*

Eight

"Want me to go yell at Zelda and make her come in here like you said?"

"Not right now. I'm too tired to deal with her, darling. I will make sure she realizes that refusing to come when I called her was a big mistake."

Hugh looked at his mother and frowned. "Mama, why didn't Zelda come when I told her you wanted her to come in here?"

"I'm not sure, son. It seems she hasn't acted the way she should ever since that Hendrix man showed up here."

"I hate him."

"I know you do, dear." She reached over and patted Hugh's hand. "I hate him, too."

"Then why can't you run him off?"

"I'm trying, sweetheart, but he's a stubborn man. It's not as easy to get rid of him as I thought it would be."

"I bet he'd go if Zelda told him to leave. He listens to her."

"I know, but she wants him to stay here. I think she likes to torment me because she knows I can't get out of this bed and run this household as it should be run."

"I wish you could get out of bed, Mama. If Zelda hadn't done what she did, you wouldn't be here, would you?"

"That's right, honey. It's all her fault."

Hugh was quiet for a minute, then he grinned. "Want me to go get Mace while that Wiley man is gone?"

Glenda lifted an eyebrow. "It would be a good time to conduct my business with Mace."

"I can get him here and Wiley will never know it."

Glenda seemed to be thinking out loud. "I could sign the papers then all our worries would be over. Mace and his father would own this ranch and Zelda would have no option but to marry him and you would have a home forever here with them."

Hugh frowned again.

"What's the matter, son?"

"I don't want to live with old mean Zelda forever."

Glenda chuckled. "You wouldn't have to worry about that. I'm sure Mace would make her be nice to you."

"Would Pansy have to live here, too?"

"Of course she would. Pansy's your sister."

"She's only my half-sister, Mama."

"True, but she's still a sister to you."

"Do you love Pansy more than you love me?"

She reached for him and pulled him close to her. "I don't love anybody more than I do you, Hugh. You're my baby boy and you always will be. I'll always love you more than anyone else in the world."

"I'm glad. I don't want you to love Pansy."

"Well, I do love her. She's my daughter, after all. You need to love her a little, too, especially since she's your half-sister."

"Does that mean that since Zelda's my stepsister, I have to love her, too?"

"No, darling. You don't even have to like Zelda because she's in no way related to you. She just happens to be the daughter of the man I married so you and I could have a good home."

"Why does she live with us?"

"I was hoping John would make her leave after we married, but he insisted she was his daughter and she had to live here, too."

"I didn't like John much, but I sure liked him better than I do Wiley."

"Why's that, son?"

"Even if John did make me do some work around here, he wasn't as bad as Wiley."

"I knew John wanted to make you do things you shouldn't be doing, but I stopped him from forcing you to work, didn't I?"

"Yeah. Do you think you can make Wiley stop making me work?"

She frowned. "What has that man made you do, Hugh?"

"He makes me unbridle and rub down the horse every time he uses him, and when he got back here with supplies, he made me unload the wagon all by myself. I think he's trying to kill me, Mama."

"That's terrible." She shook her head. "I'll put a stop to that. Find him and tell him to get in here right now."

"He's not here now. He went after that man who shot at him and Zelda."

"Well, when he gets back, tell him to come see me immediately."

"I will, Mama."

Glenda laid back against the pillows. "Hugh, my darling, I'm getting tired. Would you mind if I took a little nap?"

"Why do you get tired, Mama?"

"It's my illness."

"I don't see why. You can't walk, but that shouldn't make you tired all the time."

She reached for him. "Don't you worry about it, my sweet boy. Mama will be all right."

"Do you want me to go get Mace while you rest?"

She patted his hand. "Yes, dear. That's a clever idea. Tell him to bring another set of papers because that Wiley tore the others up."

"See how mean he is, Mama?"

"Yes, dear. I see. Now give Mama a kiss and hurry over to Mace's ranch before that awful Wiley gets back."

He obediently kissed her forehead and hurried out the door.

~ * ~

Wiley had the cows in a small make-do corral in a canyon and headed back to the ranch. He paused on the knoll looking down on the property when he saw Hugh hurrying from the house to the barn. In a matter of minutes, the boy came out leading the plow horse. He climbed on the horse's back and headed in the direction he'd gone the night before.

Turning his horse across the meadow below, Wiley hurried to head him off. When he was sure he was ahead of Hugh, he pulled his horse to a stop behind some trees and waited.

When Hugh rounded the curve, Wiley urged his horse forward and stepped out in front of a surprised Hugh. "Where you headed, boy?"

Hugh glared at him. "It's none of your business."

"I think differently, so turn your horse around and head back to the barn with him."

"I won't do it."

"Hugh, you're going to do like I said. There's no way I'm going let you go running to Mace Palmer for your mama."

Hugh frowned. "How do you know I'm going to see Mace?"

"I just know. Now, turn around."

Hugh must have realized he wasn't going to win the argument with Wiley because he made a face, then turned his horse around and headed back to the ranch with his head hanging down.

Wiley knew Hugh was pouting, but he had no intention of giving up on the boy. The young man had to begin growing up and taking some responsibility, not only on the ranch, but in his own life. If he didn't, there would be no future for him. When his mother was gone, nobody else was going to coddle him the way she had done and he would be left to flounder. Zelda, as forgiving as that sweet woman was, would probably give up on him when he became a man.

Pulling his horse up even with Hugh's, he glanced at the boy and asked, "Hugh, what do you plan to do when you're a grown man?"

Hugh gave him a puzzled look. "What do you mean?"

"Just what I said. You do plan to grow up, don't you?"

"Of course, you fool. Everybody grows up."

"You're right. Most people do, but that doesn't answer my question. What are your plans for the future?"

"I'm going to live on the ranch with Mace and Zelda."

Wiley shook his head. "That'll never happen, Hugh. Zelda will never marry Mace. I think she's told you that more than once."

"Mama says she'll have to when he has the ranch."

"It doesn't matter what your mother says. Zelda won't marry that man."

"But she'll have to."

"No, Hugh. She won't have to and when she doesn't, what do you think Mace will do?"

Hugh frowned. "I don't know."

"Well, I have a good idea of what he'll do. He'll throw you and your mama off the ranch and he won't care what happens to you or her."

Still frowning, Hugh asked, "What about Zelda and Pansy? Will he keep them?"

"No. They'll already be gone."

"What do you mean?"

"If your mama signs your ranch over to the Palmers, I'm leaving here with Zelda and Pansy before the ink is dry."

"You can't do that."

"Oh, yes I can and I will. Now, I want you to think about that. Then decide if you really want the Palmers to get their hands on this ranch."

Before Hugh could answer, Wiley kneed his horse and it galloped forward.

~ * ~

"So, you missed him when you saw him under that tree with your woman?" Elias Palmer started eating from the plate the middle aged Indian woman sat before him. "Warm up my coffee, Two Feathers."

"Yes, sir." She poured coffee into his cup and then into Mace's when he held it out to her and muttered, "Give me some, too."

"You didn't answer my question, Mace."

"I didn't have a clear shot, Pa. If I could've got closer I wouldn't have missed."

"Why didn't you kill him when you saw him out on the range today?"

Two Feathers turned back to the stove as if she weren't paying any attention to what they were saying, but she was hearing every word.

When Mace said nothing, Elias said, "I'm still waiting for your answer. Why didn't you kill him earlier today."

"I thought about shooting him when I saw him earlier, but then I changed my mind."

"Why did you do that?"

Mace took a bite of the stew in front of him. "I'm not sure we have to kill him, Pa. I got a feeling he'll get tired and leave the Jordon place soon."

"You're a damn fool, Mace. He'll get that woman to looking at him and then she won't have nothing to do with you."

"She don't have nothing to do with me now, Pa. She says she won't never marry me no matter what happens with the ranch. Sometimes I think she means it."

"And you're going to let her get away with that?"

"What can I do? I've tried talking sweet to her and telling her how good it'd be when we got married, but she won't listen to me. There ain't nothing more I can do about it. No matter what I say, she says she don't like me and ain't never gonna marry me."

"Hell, son, do I have to do all your thinking for you?"

"What are you talking about?"

"Don't take no for an answer. Go get her and bring her back here. No matter what she says, the damn woman will marry you when you show her you're the boss. She won't have no choice in the matter."

"I don't think you're right, Pa. She has to take care of Glenda and those brats of hers."

"To hell with Glenda Jordon and those damn brats. As soon as I get that ranch I don't care what happens to them. I been thinking about letting her lay there in her bed and die."

"But it might take a long time for her to die."

"Not if we don't feed her."

"You mean you'd starve her to death?"

Elias shrugged. "Why not?"

"What about the young'uns?"

"We'd put that youngest one in an orphanage so your woman wouldn't have to fool with her. I'd whip that boy into being a man. He could make a good working hand and the best part is we wouldn't have to pay him. When I get him in shape we could get rid of Dub and save the twenty dollars a month I pay him." Elias thought a minute. "I guess we would have to feed the brat, though."

"Glenda says he's sickly and has to be looked after."

"He don't look sick to me. I think he's just lazy."

"That all sounds good, Pa, but if I take Zelda away, Glenda Jordon will never sign that paper giving us the ranch. She thinks we'll always look after her and them young'uns of hers and that's the only reason she'll sign it."

"I guess you're right. We have to keep her thinking that." He sighed. "Then you better not go dragging that Zelda over here until after the paper is signed."

"That's right, Pa." Mace turned to look toward the stove. "Two Feathers, dip me some more of this stew. It's better than usual this evening."

"When that Zelda woman gets here, we're gonna get rid of Two Feathers and let your woman take over the cooking and the other chores in the house. I never liked the idee of a Injun being in our house in the first place. With her and that half-breed, Dub, gone, it'll be a lot nicer around here."

"I think so, too, and I'm sure Zelda can handle the work Two Feathers does. She's been doing it for Glenda Jordon and her young'uns for over a year."

Elias shook his head. "It beats me why you want Zelda Jordon in the first place. You know I hated her father. When he was alive, the old cuss was hard to get along with."

"I know. He was mean to me, too. When Zelda was a young girl he never let me come around her. Always said I was no good." Mace chuckled. "He'd probably turn over in his grave if he knowed I planned to get her in spite of all the things he said and did to keep her away from me."

"He was always selfish with his women. His first wife was quite a looker, but he didn't want me coming around her. She didn't seem to like me either, but she was always nice to me. Of course, from what folks say, she was nice to everybody."

"Too bad she died. If she was still his wife, you could go sparking her."

"Well, she ain't alive and I don't care much for this Glenda he married and I ain't interested in sparking her. By the time John Jordon moved her in, I was only looking for a way to get his ranch."

"And now we have the perfect chance. That Glenda he married is all ready to sign the place over to us just to get that Hendrix man to move on."

Elias laughed out loud. "You're right, son. We're going to get what we both want. I'll have Jordon's ranch and you'll have his daughter. We'll get rid of the Injuns and Glenda and her offspring and everything will be just the way we want it. Couldn't ask for more than that."

~ * ~

Two Feathers frowned. She was glad the fools thought she was too ignorant to know and understand what they were talking about, but they were so wrong. They'd been wrong ever since they'd taken her in to do their cooking and cleaning over a year ago. She knew they would have never done that if Elias's wife hadn't died six months earlier and they had let the place become as nasty as a pig's sty. They needed somebody to do the work around there and no woman in Laster would take the job as their housekeeper. Two Feathers knew that when they learned she was wandering around town looking for a job, they decided she'd have to work for them for almost no pay.

She knew they also thought she was content to work for room and board and a dollar a month, but again they were wrong. She let them think they used her as almost free labor, but all the while she was planning her escape. It had taken almost a year, but she'd managed to get her hands on some of their money in the time she'd worked there. They were careless with their coins and would often drop some in their rooms or in the barn. It was usually a penny or two, but it was beginning to amount up. After she'd been on the ranch six months or so, she almost had a dollar to add to the four she'd saved from her salary. She'd set her goal to get twenty dollars and she thought eventually she'd be able to do it.

Then things changed. Six months ago, Dub showed up. She knew the Palmers had been in town trying to hire a ranch hand and at breakfast the next morning they told her they'd hired one and she'd have to carry his meals out to him in the almost-falling-down bunkhouse. She wondered why until Elias said, "We can't have no half-breed coming in here to eat at our table."

She understood this because she knew being an Indian was hard, but being a half-breed was even harder. That evening when she knocked on the bunkhouse door and stepped inside without waiting for him to answer, her whole life changed. Putting the food down on the rickety table, she turned to leave, but he turned around and their eyes met.

Dub said, "I heard you were working here; that's why I agreed to hire on as their hand."

In that moment, she knew she'd only leave the Palmer place whenever Dub was ready to move on, too.

But from hearing the conversation today, she knew if they intended to get rid of her, she might have to change her plans. Even if she left with almost nothing, she would see that things didn't work out the way the Palmers wanted them to. They might think they were going to bring the woman called Zelda in, but she had a suspicion that Zelda would never go for the plan. They might also think it would be easy to work out their scheme, but again they were wrong. If she were still around, she'd never stand by and let them starve a woman to death, or send an innocent child to an orphanage, or make a slave of a young boy. If they tried, she knew Indian ways to take somebody out of the world. Ways that nobody in the white world would ever know about. Though she didn't want to do it, she would if she had to. She was sure Dub would help her, too.

Nine

Wiley was surprised when they reached the barn and Hugh climbed down from his horse and removed the blanket. He then removed the bridle and gave the nag a few strokes of the brush before putting him in the corral. Though he didn't say a word, Wiley was pleased. He'd been correct. With the right direction, Hugh would become a working cowboy whether that had ever been part of the boy's plan or not.

After taking care of his own horse, Wiley headed to the house behind Hugh. They didn't talk, but Hugh seemed to be thinking. Wiley hoped it was about the conversation they'd had concerning the Palmers. Though he was sure he could keep Hugh from bringing Mace back to sign the papers giving the Palmers the ranch, he wanted Hugh to reach his own decision about the almost surety that the men would not only break their word about taking care of the Jordons, but the absolute fact that Zelda would never marry the man, no matter what happened. Wiley was never going to let that evil man get his hands on Zelda.

Following Hugh into the kitchen, he smiled to see Pansy on the kitchen stool making wads of biscuit dough with a handful of the bread makings Zelda had left in the bowl for her to play with. Zelda worked bedside her. Wiley nodded to Zelda and said to Pansy, "Hello there, little darling. What are you doing?"

She grinned at him. "I make bread." She held a wad of dough toward him.

"I see you are. Will you make a biscuit for me, sweetheart?"

"I will, Wiwey."

Hugh asked, "Is Mama awake?"

"I'm not sure, Hugh." Zelda glanced at him. "You can peep into her room and see."

Hugh headed down the hall.

Wiley turned to Zelda. "Something sure smells good."

"I'm cooking a roast. I hope you approve."

"I sure do. Nothing like beef for a cowboy to fill up on when he's hungry."

"Did you happen to catch the man who was … uh…?"

"Nope, but I'm pretty sure who he was because there's only one man in the area who wants me off this ranch, dead or alive."

She frowned. "Do you really think he'd kill you?"

"I have no doubt. Now, let me tell you what I did do."

"What was that?"

"I found a few cows with no brand. Since they're up for grabs, I ran them into a canyon and plan to bring them to pasture on your ranch as soon as I can get some fences in the ground."

"We used to have fenced pastures, but I guess they've fallen into disrepair."

He lifted an eyebrow. "Maybe I can repair them. We do need some place to put the cattle I intend to round up."

She laughed. "When did this get to be a 'we need' thing?"

"The minute I decided I was going to get this ranch up and running again."

Zelda shook her head. "I don't know if it's worth it or not, Wiley. Glenda seems bent on giving this place to Mace Palmer and his father. If that happens…"

"I'm not going to let that happen, Zelda. If Glenda Jordon doesn't understand that by now, she will soon."

"What can you do to stop her?"

"Don't worry. I'll think of something." He turned to Pansy. "When you get through making your bread, I'll take you in the other room to play, or maybe read a book while Zelda finishes up supper."

Pansy threw the wad of dough she'd been rolling around in her hands to the pan. "I through."

"Let me get her cleaned up before you take her in there."

"Wiwey can wash me."

"I sure can." He picked her up and moved to the pan of water sitting on the drain board.

Zelda laughed. "You've certainly become her knight in shining armor, Wiley Hendrix."

"It's nice to be somebody's knight." He winked at Zelda, dried Pansy's hands and headed for the rocking chair in the connecting room. As he went out the door he said, "Maybe I can work up to be her sister's knight one of these days."

~ * ~

Zelda shook her head and tried to concentrate on getting the bread into the oven. It was all she could do not to tell Wiley he was already her shining knight. It had made things harder for her interacting with Glenda since he'd been here, but for the first time in a long time, she was able take a break from all the arduous work. When she thought about it, it was worth having the fights with Glenda just to have him here... and not just because he made her work easier. She simply liked it when he was around.

She glanced into the parlor section of the room and saw him take a seat in the rocking chair by the fireplace. Pansy climbed into his lap and said, "Read me."

"I'd be pleased to read to you, Pansy. Where's your book?"

"Don't know."

"Well, let's look around here and see if we can find it."

"There on table."

Wiley leaned over and picked up a worn picture book. "Is this the one you want me to read?"

"Yes, pease."

Wiley opened the worn book and his soft voice carried to the kitchen as he read the children's story, putting in expressions and actions. Pansy giggled at the appropriate times and Zelda knew she was enjoying the story she'd heard hundreds of times.

Turning back to the stove, she wondered if Wiley was married and if he had children of his own. It stood to reason that he did because he was wonderful with Pansy. He knew just the right things to say to her and how to entertain the precious little girl. It was almost certain he was a father. If not, he certainly must have had lots of younger brothers and sisters.

Oh, my goodness. The man may be married. If so, why is he on his way to Waco as he said he was? Is that where his family is? Were a wife and children waiting for him to return from some sort of business trip or something pressing? If that were the case, why has he decided he's going to stay here and get Glenda's ranch on its feet again? Shouldn't he be on his way?

Or could he be on the run from something or someone? Maybe he was an outlaw. The area seemed to be full of them lately. If he was, she needed to know. She didn't want him around the family if he was a wanted man. Since Glenda couldn't protect the children, Zelda felt she had to do it. And if Wiley were a threat, she needed to know. But she had to be wrong. He was too kind to be an outlaw. At least she hoped that wasn't his profession. She also hoped he wasn't married and had a family.

With these thoughts tumbling in her mind, Zelda decided she needed to ask the man more about himself. After all, he was a stranger and no matter how nice he'd been, she didn't want to subject the children to someone who wasn't who they claimed to be. Of course, Wiley hadn't claimed to be anybody or anything. Something else she had to ask him about.

Hugh came back into the room, glanced at Wiley and Pansy, then walked to the kitchen area. "Supper about ready?"

"It won't be long. Is your mother awake?"

"No, but I'm hungry."

"It will be finished in ten or fifteen minutes."

Again, he glanced at Wiley and Pansy. Turning back, he said, "I'll wait on the porch. Call me when you have it on the table." He didn't wait for her to answer, but went out the back door.

Zelda couldn't help noticing it was the first time he'd spoken halfway decently to her, even if he was giving her orders. She glanced at Wiley and wondered if the tall cowboy had anything to do with that.

~ * ~

Hugh sat on the steps of the back porch and tried to disregard everything Wiley had said to him, but it wasn't easy. His mother had told him many times that Zelda would marry Mace and that would assure that he and Pansy had a home with them forever. He had no reason to doubt this, but still...what if Wiley was right? What if all Mace and his daddy wanted was the Jordon ranch? What if Zelda didn't marry him, as Wiley said, and his mother still signed the ranch over to the Palmers? What would they do? He couldn't take care of his mother and he sure wasn't going to take care of Pansy. He could hardly stand the little girl at times. He wished she'd never been born. Why did his mother and John Jordon want to have a kid anyway, especially a girl? He might could have tolerated a boy, but a girl was different. He doubted he'd ever like her.

Hugh didn't know what he was supposed to do. He'd always been told to listen to his mother, but he was smart enough to know his mother hadn't been the same since the accident. Oh, she still loved him and she tried to make Zelda take care of him, but it was hard for her to know everything that was going on while confined to bed as she had been.

He knew he took advantage of that fact at times. Yes, he liked to hear his mother yell at Zelda. He'd never much liked his stepsister, though he liked her better at times than he did at others. He even liked her better than he did Pansy most of the time. He guessed that was because his mother loved Pansy and didn't like Zelda at all. He didn't have to compete with his grown half-sister for his mother's attention like he did Pansy.

But that didn't help his dilemma today. He wasn't sure if he should slip off after supper and get Mace to come again as his mother had asked him to do. Maybe it would be better to wait until morning, if he could get his mother to agree. Tomorrow, Wiley would be busy doing some kind of work around the place and it would be easier to slip off. He just had to convince his mother of this.

But what was he going to do if Wiley was right? Should he convince his mother to wait to sign those papers? Should he encourage her to sign them now?

Lord, he wished making this kind of decision wasn't something he had to do. He didn't like thinking about things like this. He'd rather read his books or even brush down the horse than decide what he should do.

Laughing a little, Hugh couldn't believe he'd told himself he liked brushing down the horse. But he had to admit, it hadn't been that bad and the horse seemed to enjoy it. Only thing, he sure wasn't going to let that mean old Wiley Hendrix know he felt that way about the job. He figured this was one fact he was going to keep to himself forever.

Zelda stuck her head out the door. "Supper's ready, Hugh. Come on in and wash up."

He entered the door and the good smells hit him. He almost told her something smelled good, but he caught himself. He had no intention of ever complimenting Zelda's cooking.

Wiley and Pansy came to the table and Wiley said what he was thinking, without knowing he was expressing Hugh's thoughts. "Smells wonderful, Zelda."

She smiled. "Thank you."

"I washed outside," Hugh said and sat at his usual place. He saw Wiley's eyebrow shoot up, but the man said nothing. *Now, he'll think I got the idea to wash up outside because of him. But it was really because I didn't want to have to wash in here with Zelda in the room.*

"Since Glenda is still asleep, we'll go ahead and eat." Zelda slid into her chair and added, "Want to come sit beside me so I can put a towel around your neck, Pansy? I have made gravy with the roast and I know what you do with gravy."

"Wanna sit with Wiwey."

"Hand me a towel. I'll fix her up." Wiley winked at Zelda.

They were about halfway through the meal when Glenda's raspy voice called, "Zelda, come in here."

Zelda immediately stood. "I'll make her a plate."

Wiley reached out and put his hand on her arm. "Why don't you finish your supper? I'll see what she wants."

"No, Wiley. It's my job." Zelda made the plate and hurried out of the kitchen.

Wiley looked at Hugh. "Why don't you help your sister look after your mother?"

To hide his anger at hearing Wiley call Zelda his sister, Hugh said with a smirk, "She ain't my sister. Besides, it's her job to look after Mama, not mine."

"Why is it her job?"

"What do you mean why? She's a woman and she's supposed to do things like that."

"But Glenda is *your* mother, not Zelda's."

"Don't matter. She was married to Zelda's dad. That makes it Zelda's job."

"I wike Zewie."

"Of course, you do, stupid. It's because she pets you," Hugh said in a snapping voice.

Wiley shook his head. "That was uncalled for, Hugh. You shouldn't ever call your sister stupid."

"Why not? She is stupid."

"She's only a child, Hugh."

"That's no excuse for you to act like an even smaller child yourself."

"Is I stupid, Wiwey?"

"No, Pansy. You're a very smart little girl. You shouldn't listen when your brother says things like that. He's wrong."

Zelda came back into the room. "Your mother wants you to go in there, Hugh."

"I'm not through eating."

"It's up to you if you go, but I've delivered the message." Zelda sat and picked up her fork.

Hugh frowned, pushed back his plate and stood. He mumbled as he stomped out of the room, but he knew nobody could understand what he was saying.

Entering his mother's bedroom, he asked, "What do you want, Mama?"

"I wanted to know if you got those papers from Mace."

"No."

"Why not?"

"Wiley caught me on the road to Mace's ranch and I had to come back here."

Glenda shook her head and he could tell she was gritting her teeth. "That man has come in here and taken over. I don't like it one little bit."

Hugh leaned close to his mother. "I want to ask you something."

"Sure, honey. What is it?"

"What if Mace isn't telling the truth about looking after us when he gets the ranch? What if he throws us all off the place? We won't have anywhere to go."

"Oh, Hugh. That would never happen."

"How do you know, Mama?"

"Mace gave me his word and I believe him."

"Are you sure you can?"

Glenda frowned and looked as if she were getting agitated. "What in the world gave you the idea that Mace wouldn't keep his word, Hugh? He's always been honest with me and I'm sure he's being honest now."

"Don't get upset, Mama. Forget I asked."

"Somebody put the notion in your head that Mace has been less than honest with me. I bet it was Zelda. She's always saying I let him have the cattle too cheaply. Now she thinks I'm going to give away the ranch and leave her homeless."

"It wasn't Zelda, Mama."

"Then who was it....oh, I see. It was that awful Wiley person, wasn't it?" When Hugh nodded, she went on. "How dare him say such a thing? He doesn't know Mace Palmer. How could he say something about the man's character?"

"You're right, Mama. I shouldn't have listened to him."

"No, you shouldn't, Hugh. Promise Mama that you'll not do such a thing again. Wiley Hendrix is the one who can't be trusted. I don't know what he wants, but we have to keep a sharp eye on him."

"I promise, Mama. I won't listen to anything he says ever again."

"That's my boy." She looked down at her tray. "Would you like to sit with me while I eat my supper?"

"I need to go back and finish my supper before Zelda throws it out."

"Yes, you should. You can't trust her not to dispose of it." He started out the door and she reached for his arm. "One more thing, Hugh."

"What's that, Mama?"

Her voice dropped to a whisper. "Go get that paper from Mace as soon as you can. I need to get it signed before it's too late."

"I'll go first thing in the morning." He smiled as he left the room. It was easier to change her mind about him going this evening than he thought it would be.

Ten

The next morning Zelda finished washing the breakfast dishes and hung up the dishtowel she used. She then sat Pansy down from the stool where she stood and said. "I think you and I will go plant some of the seed in the garden Wiley plowed for us. I'm sure I saw some pumpkin seed in the batch he handed me when he got back from town." She tweaked Pansy's nose. "We might get some pumpkins from the garden this fall if we plant them now."

"I wike pumpkins."

"So do I, sweetheart."

"Zelda!" Glenda called.

"Mama want you."

"Yes, Pansy." Zelda sighed. "Let's go see what she wants."

In the room, she asked, "Yes, Glenda?"

"Tell my Hugh to come in here. I need to see him this morning."

"He's not here, Glenda."

"Where is he? Did he go see the Palmers?"

Before Zelda could ask her why he would go see them, Pansy blurted, "He with Wiwey."

"What?" Glenda's brown eyes darted to Zelda. "Why is my boy with that man?"

86

"They rode out on the range after breakfast. Wiley said they were going to check fences."

"How dare that man drag my boy out there on the range? I have something I wanted him to do. Besides, he could get hurt out there."

Zelda took a deep breath. "All I know is Wiley said he was going to check fences and needed Hugh to go with him to make sure he was on the Jordon ranch and not the Palmers'."

"That doesn't make any sense. Hugh doesn't know the boundaries of this ranch."

Zelda didn't say anything and Glenda went on, "Well, get him back. I want him to do something for me."

"I can't get him back, Glenda."

"Why not?"

"Because they're out there on the range somewhere. I have no idea where and besides, I don't have a horse to go looking for them."

"Ride the plow horse."

"What do you think Hugh is riding?"

"Why isn't he riding one of the other horses?"

"There are no other horses, Glenda. You sold them all to the Palmers. Remember?"

She stared at Zelda for a few seconds. "Then, use the rifle to shoot twice in the air. That will bring them in."

"That signal is only used for emergencies. I'm not going to use it to get Hugh to come back here just because you want to see him."

"I don't see why not."

"Be reasonable, Glenda. You can talk to Hugh when they come back."

"Honestly, Zelda. If your father only knew how you treat me, he'd..."

Before she could control herself, Zelda almost yelled, "Stop it, Glenda. He doesn't know what's going on here, but if he did, he'd be very proud of the way I've cared for you and your children and put up with all the complaining you do and the way Hugh treats me. Since my father died, the only one who cares a thing about me is sweet little Pansy and that'll probably end as soon as you manage to poison her mind against me the way you've done Hugh's." She took Patsy's hand. "Let's get out of here, honey. We need to go plant those pumpkin seeds."

"Don't you dare walk out on me you ... you..."

But it was too late to answer. Zelda and Pansy were already across the parlor and going out the back door.

~ * ~

"Why are you making me do this, Wiley Hendrix? I had things I wanted to do today." Hugh held the fence post in place while Wiley beat it back into the ground with the axe he'd found in the barn.

"You need to do this so you will know how to help take care of this ranch when you finally decide you're going to grow up and accept some responsibility around here."

"But Mama says I'm too weak to do such hard jobs."

Wiley shook his head. "Did you know I talked to your doctor when I was in town the other day?"

"No. Why would you?"

"Because I realized your mother had to be wrong. You looked too healthy to be so weak you couldn't do some work around here."

"Did he tell you that I needed to be careful about what I do?"

"On the contrary. He told me you were as healthy as any twelve-year-old boy should be. He said, yes, you were sick at one time and had to take it easy when you were a little boy, but that was years ago. He told me that anyone else, including Zelda or Pansy, would stand as much chance of getting sick from overwork as you would."

"But Mama said..."

"I know what your mama said, but the doctor's told her the truth. He said she makes him examine you every time he comes to see her. He said it was a waste of time because you've been in perfect health for several years. He's even told your mother that."

"Why didn't she tell me?"

"I don't know, Hugh. Maybe she can't accept the fact that you're growing up and will soon become a man and she wants to keep you her little boy. Or maybe she wants to keep you from helping Zelda because she hates her step-daughter so much that she doesn't want you to help do things around the ranch so it will be more for Zelda to do."

"Mama wouldn't lie to me."

"Maybe she doesn't even realize she's lying."

Hugh frowned. "How can somebody not know they're lying?"

"Believe me. It happens. A person can tell themselves a lie so many times they eventually believe it's the truth."

"I don't know."

"Tell you what. The doctor told me he was coming to see your mother later this week. I'm sure she'll want him to check you over. When he does, ask him yourself about your physical condition. Doctor's aren't allowed to lie to patients."

"Are you sure?"

"I'm positive." Wiley laid the axe on the ground. "Now let's tighten this wire on the post and then we'll have this section of the fence in pretty good shape."

Hugh looked as if he were thinking over what Wiley had said and began helping tighten the wire without complaint.

Wiley said nothing, though he noticed the cooperation Hugh was showing, and it pleased him. Maybe he was beginning to get through to the boy.

~ * ~

Zelda stretched her back and looked down at Pansy. "Well, sweetheart. We got the pumpkins planted."

Pansy looked at the ground. "I don't see pumpkin."

She smiled. "I know you don't. We must water them and wait. It will take a few weeks for them to begin to grow."

"Oh." Pansy looked disappointed. "I want pumpkin now."

"It doesn't work that way, honey. It takes a while for the ground to make the seed grow. But don't worry, we will have pumpkins before the first snow."

Pansy made a face. "Well...all right."

"Come on. Let's go wash up and start supper. Wiley and Hugh will be coming in soon and we need to have something to eat."

"I make biscuit?"

"Yes, you can make biscuit." She tasseled Pansy's hair. "Now, let's go."

The house was silent when they got inside. Whispering to Pansy to be quiet, they eased down the hall and peeped in Glenda's room. Zelda let out a sigh of relief when she saw the woman sleeping.

Back in the kitchen, Pansy looked at her. "Can I talk now?"

"Yes, my love, you can talk now."

The little girl giggled. "I hungry."

"You know what? I'm hungry, too. What do you think we should cook for supper?"

"Biscuit."

"That sounds good to me. How about I put on some vegetables, fry some ham and then we'll make biscuits. You can help me wash the vegetables if you want to."

"I want to."

They had supper almost ready when the sound of a horse and buggy came through the window. "Wonder who that can be."

"Don't know."

"We better go see." Zelda dried her hands, then lifted Pansy from her stool.

Pansy held Zelda's hand and as they stepped out on the porch. The little girl muttered, "Doctor."

"Yes, it is." Zelda smiled at the middle-aged man as he climbed from his buggy. "Hello, Doctor Abernathy."

"Hello, Zelda. I was over at your neighbor's house and thought since I was out this way, I'd stop by and check on Glenda. Hope you don't mind."

"Of course I don't mind. Please come in."

"I didn't think you would, but the Palmers said I shouldn't come because you didn't want anybody coming around bothering you."

Zelda's eyes narrowed and her voice was angry when she said, "I hope you don't take anything the Palmers say seriously. Those people will say anything that pleases them."

He frowned. "I'm surprised you seem to be hostile about them. Mace said you and he were going to get married. In fact, he's told that all over town."

"That fool." She shook her head. "I'll never marry that awful man and I've told him that more times than I can count, but for some reason the stupid man seems to think I'll change my mind."

"Glad to hear that. I know your father never wanted you to have anything to do with Mace." He smiled. "He knew you could do better and I see you did."

"What do you mean?"

"I liked the man who came in to see me about Glenda and Hugh. I think he's a much better choice for you."

"Do you mean Wiley Hendrix?"

"Of course."

"Well..." Zelda didn't know what to say because she wasn't sure what Wiley had told the doctor.

"I'm sure John would have liked him, too. He seems to be a good man and your father would've approved of him for you."

"Maybe so." She pointed to a chair. "Have a seat and I'll see if Glenda is awake."

"Don't wake her if she's asleep. I need to rest a bit anyway." He sat where she pointed. "Those Palmers wore me out. Elias is one of the crabbiest men I've ever had to deal with."

Zelda grinned, but didn't answer him as she headed down the hall. In a matter of seconds, she was back. "She's still asleep. Are you sure you don't want me to wake her?"

"Not yet. Little Pansy here is showing me her doll. I think it has a tummy ache."

"Be-Be do." Pansy hugged the doll. "Her cry."

"Let me see if I can make her feel better." The doctor took the doll and put her to his ear. "I think I hear her tummy rumbling." He held it to Pansy's ear. "Can you hear it?"

She looked serious. "I do."

"I bet it would make her feel better if you hugged her close to you, Miss Pansy."

She giggled and hugged her doll.

The doctor turned to Zelda. "By the way, is Hendrix around?"

"He and Hugh went out on the range. I expect them back soon."

"I'm surprised Hugh's mother let him go."

"She wouldn't have if asked, but nobody asked her permission. Wiley simple told Hugh he was going and the boy went." Zelda smiled. "Wiley Hendrix has a way of convincing people to do what he wants them to do."

"Good for him."

"What do you mean?"

"You and I both know that since your father died, you've needed a man around here that knows how a ranch should be run."

"How do you know Wiley Hendrix is that man?"

He chuckled. "When he came to see me, and told me he was working here to see that things got straightened out on this ranch, I took an immediate liking to him. I had a feeling he liked you a lot, too."

She blushed. "But..."

"Let him do what he needs to do, Zelda. I know you're an independent woman, but we all need help at times. And if anybody needs help around here, you do. Everybody knows that."

She didn't want to argue with the doctor. Standing, she said, "If you'll excuse me, I need to finish up supper."

"Of course, I'll excuse you. Whatever you're cooking sure smells good."

She laughed, despite herself. "Are you hinting you'd like to join us for supper, Uley Abernathy?"

"If I remember correctly, the times I came here to tend your parents, what you served was always tasty."

"Then feel free to eat with us this evening. Then you can see if my cooking has gotten better or worse."

"Thank you, Zelda. It'll be like it was when I was coming here as your father's friend, not because somebody was sick."

"I remember, too." She sighed. "As tough as things are now, I still have the good times to remember."

"Zelda!"

"It sounds like Glenda woke up." Zelda headed down the hall. "I'll tell her you're here."

"Where have you been? I've called you for hours."

"You've been asleep, Glenda."

"I have not. I've been lying here in pain for hours and as usual, you ignored me."

"That's not true, Glenda."

"It most certainly is true. I know you want me to die and you're doing everything you can to hurry it along."

"Now, Glenda, that's not so." Uley came into the room behind Zelda. He smiled at the woman on the bed. "I came in to see you when I arrived and you were sound asleep."

She looked surprised to see him, but said, "I must have fallen asleep and not realized it."

"Be-Be sick," Patsy said and held her rag doll up for her mother to see. "Her tummy hurt."

Glenda ignored her. "Go tell Hugh to come inside, Zelda. I want the doctor to check him while he's here."

"I want to check you first." The doctor walked to the bed and took her hand. "How have you been feeling?"

"Awful. It's so hard to lie here in bed and wait for somebody to see to your needs. Zelda either ignores me or she's often outside or so she says. Sometimes I lie here so long I think my kidneys will explode."

"Shall I go out and let Zelda help you so you can relieve yourself?"

"No. I'll be fine for the time being."

"Be-Be belly hurt." Pansy held up her doll again.

"Why don't you go rock your dolly while I check out your mother, Pansy? I'm sure Zelda will help you make her feel better." He pulled the chair up beside the bed.

"Zewie rock. She love Be-Be." She reached for Zelda's hand and they left the room.

~ * ~

"Zelda sure takes loving care of Pansy, doesn't she, Glenda?"

"Too good, if you ask me."

He lifted an eyebrow. "What do you mean?"

"I think she's trying to take my baby away from me. She wants her to love her better than she does me. It upsets me to watch how sneaky she is about it."

He shook his head. "It seems to me like you'd be thankful she cares so much for Pansy."

"Why should I?"

"You know the reason as well as I do. I'll go get my bag. I left it in the main room. You try to calm down and I'll be right back." Uley stood and headed to the parlor. He couldn't help wondering why Glenda had become such a disagreeable person since John's death. The woman knew full well she was dying and she should be happy that her daughter would be well taken care of when she was gone. Instead, she resented Zelda more and more. It seemed worse each time he came to check the woman.

He picked up his bag and went back into Glenda's room. Pulling the chair up close to the bed, he looked at her. "Shall we get started?"

"I suppose so. Did you see Hugh in there?"

"Nope. I guess he's outside somewhere."

"I told Zelda to call him. That woman knows I want you to look at him before you leave and she's probably deliberately trying to keep him away from you."

"I'll make sure he's checked over before I go, Glenda."

"Good. He's been a little sick lately. I'm afraid he's getting the disease back or Zelda is not feeding him well enough."

"No, Glenda. Hugh is well fed and he's not getting the disease. I've told you before, your son is as healthy as he can be. He's a typical twelve-year-old."

"What do you mean, *as well as he can be*? Have you found something wrong with him?"

"Not at all. You're not listening to what I'm saying. Hugh just needs to be more active than he is. He should do some chores around here and concentrate on other things twelve-year-old boys do. Things like fishing, and playing ball and riding his horse. He doesn't need to spend all his free time reading. He needs exercise."

"But he's not well. I can't let him overdo. He might…"

"If you don't let him do something except sit around and read books, he'll end up unhealthy and probably die at a young age. A boy's body needs to stay active."

"I'm his mother. I should know what's good for him."

"I'm not going to argue with you, Glenda. Now quit talking and let me listen to your heart." He put the stethoscope on her chest.

Just as he expected. Her heart was growing weaker. Should he tell her? Would it do any good if he did?

He decided to approach it from another angle. "Glenda, have you made any arrangements for your children when the time comes that they'll need someone to look after them?"

"Of course, I've tried to." She huffed a little then added, "But that blasted Wiley showed up here and managed to stop me."

"How could he do that?"

"You don't know the man, Doctor. He's evil."

"Oh?"

"Ever since he arrived here, he's pushed everyone around and told them what to do. Now he thinks he's going to keep me from doing what's best for my children."

"What do you want to do that he won't let you do for them?"

She eyed him. "Why do you want to know?"

He shrugged. "I just thought that as your doctor, I might be able to help you accomplish your plans. I like your children and I have a responsibility to my patients, you know."

She smiled. "I hadn't thought about it that way, but you're right. If you really want to help, I think I could trust you to do so."

"I'll do whatever I can to assure your children will be all right without you, Glenda."

She was quiet for a minute, then she asked, "Do you know the Palmers? They have the ranch that joins mine."

"I know them. As a matter of fact, I was over there today before I came to check on you."

"Oh, no. I hope Mace isn't sick or hurt."

"He's fine. It was his father I went to see."

"Is the old man all right?"

"He will be. He had a little too much happy juice and fell off the front porch. He has a pretty nasty sprain, but he'll survive."

"I'm glad it wasn't Mace."

"Why? Is Mace special to you?"

"Only because he's the answer to my children's future."

"How is that possible?"

"I head the backdoor open. That's probably that Wiley person. I don't want him to hear what I'm saying. I'll have to tell you later."

"I'm staying for supper. Maybe we can talk after I eat."

Hugh appeared at his mother's bedroom door. "Zelda told me to tell the doctor that supper is ready."

"Oh, Hugh, I'm glad you came inside, dear. I want the doctor to check you over."

"I want to eat first. I'm hungry."

"I agree with Hugh. I think we should eat first." The doctor put his stethoscope back in his bag and stood. "There'll be time for me to examine him later."

Glenda's face turned cold and she straightened her covers. "Tell Zelda I'm hungry, too. I want my food while the rest of you are eating."

Eleven

After everyone finished their supper, Zelda went into Glenda's room to get her dirty dishes. She noticed the women had cleaned her plate.

Without thanking Zelda for the meal, Glenda snapped at her, "Where's Hugh?"

"The doctor is examining him."

"He usually examines him in here with me. Why didn't you let him do it today?"

"I didn't have anything to do with it. Hugh said since he was getting older; he wanted privacy for the examination. I told him he could use either his room or mine."

"Don't you mean Pansy's room?"

Zelda sighed. "Whatever you say, Glenda."

"I just want you to remember this is my home and the bedrooms belong to my children and me. You stay here because it was the way your father wanted it to be."

"If by chance I ever forget that, I'm sure you'll remind me."

"Do you have to be so snide, Zelda?"

Zelda sighed. "I'm sorry."

"You should be. Now get out of here and be sure to tell the doctor to come in here and tell me about Hugh when the examination is over."

"I'm sure he'd do that without me telling him, Glenda." Zelda hurried out of the room.

But she wasn't far enough away from the door to miss hearing Glenda say, "You ungrateful bitch."

Shaking her head, Zelda went to the sink and washed the dishes Glenda had used. She rinsed them and placed them on the towel with the others she'd already washed. She then dried her hands and went out the back door. She needed to get out of the house because she was afraid Glenda would demand she come back and she didn't want to endure any more of her stepmother's insults.

Stepping out on the back porch, she saw Wiley sitting on the bench under the tree. Pansy was intent on telling him something and he was giving her babbling all his attention. Zelda couldn't help smiling as the thought crossed her mind that Wiley would make a wonderful father. If he wasn't one already. If he wasn't, she felt the woman who gave him children would be one lucky lady.

Shaking the thought away, she plastered a smile on her face and crossed the yard. "May I join you two?"

He returned her smile. "We'd be delighted to have you, ma'am."

"Hey, Zewie. I tell Wiwey about horse. I tell you, too." She then launched into an explanation with some understandable words, but very few.

Wiley looked over her head, winked at Zelda and moved over for her to sit beside him.

She nodded and sat. Neither talked. They sat in silence and listened to the little girl tell her story, though it was more rambling than talking. It didn't matter. It felt peaceful and comfortable to be here with Wiley and Pansy. It was almost as if there were nothing else going on in her life. But that was a long way from the truth. Her life was in shambles and she knew it. She lived with a stepmother who hated her. She was responsible for the woman's care and had the burden of taking care of her stepbrother and half-sister. Her brother hated her as much as his mother did, and she had only a passing relationship with him. Her sister was a precious little girl who didn't realize what was going on. To top it all, the ranch was dying and it wouldn't be long until her stepmother sold it or gave it away, leaving them all homeless. But there was nothing she could do about it, except hang on as long as she could and let the darkness continue to surround her.

The only light in the situation was the chance visit of a stranger who came into her life and was trying to help. Though she appreciated his efforts, it wouldn't make any difference in the end. The chances of her ever solving her problems in a permanent way or of her being happy again in this life were slim to none.

She glanced over at him and smiled. She wondered if he could tell what she was thinking, that even if the ranch did die, she'd always cherish the time she'd been blessed with Wiley Hendrix's presence there.

~ * ~

Hugh rushed into his mother's room in front of Uley. "The doctor says I'm a healthy twelve-year-old, Mama. Why did you say I was sickly?"

Glenda's eyes blazed. "You are weak, baby. You almost died."

"But that was years ago, Mama. Doc says I should do some chores around here and get some exercise."

"No, Hugh. You can't overwork yourself. I don't want you getting sick. I couldn't stand it if anything happened to my little boy."

"I worked today and it didn't hurt me."

She frowned. "What do you mean, you worked?"

"Wiley made me help him fix a fence."

"How dare that man make you do something so strenuous! I'll have to have a talk with him."

"For Heaven's sake, Glenda," the doctor spoke for the first time. "The boy helped the man mend a fence. He didn't dig a ditch. It was a simple job and if she was a little older, Pansy could have done it."

"I did a good job. Wiley said I did."

She reached for his hand. "I'm sure you did, honey, but that man had no right to make you do anything. I'm sure you'll pay for it tonight. You'll be so tired you probably won't be able to sleep."

Hugh frowned and looked at Uley. "Is that right, Doctor?"

"No, Hugh. Your mother is wrong. You'll probably sleep the best you've slept in a long time. I told you that if you only sit around and read books, you're going to end up unhealthy."

"Don't listen to him, Hugh. I'm your mother. I know what's best for you." She looked at the doctor. "I can't believe you'd fill his head with such foolishness. I thought I could trust you."

"You can, Glenda. I told you I'd help you and I meant it. But Hugh is a healthy young man and I'm only trying to get you to understand that."

She squeezed Hugh's hand. "Honey, give me a kiss and then go outside and rest from your work. You can read your book for a little while. I need to talk to the doctor alone."

"Ah, Mama. Why do I have to kiss you all the time?"

"Don't shy, baby, and give me a kiss."

A red-faced Hugh kissed her forehead quickly and hurried out of the room without saying anything else.

"You do know you embarrassed him, don't you, Glenda?"

"Don't be silly, Uley. He loves his mother and doesn't mind who knows it."

"I love my mother, too, but I don't want her demanding kisses from me in front of other people."

"Of course you'd feel that way. You're a man."

"I am. I'm also male and I know how it feels when your mother treats you like a small child in front of other people."

"Hugh is a child."

"A child that is on the cusp of becoming a teenager. He told me he had a birthday coming up this fall." He pulled the chair up beside the bed. "I see we will never agree about your son, so let's talk about what this help is that you need from me to ensure your children a good future."

"The first thing I want you to do is help me get rid of Wiley Hendrix."

"Why, Glenda? He's getting things done around here. Things that have needed doing for a long time."

"That's not important. I had everything planned and it was working just as it should, then he showed up."

"What did you have worked out?"

"A plan where my children would be taken care of."

"And how did you accomplish that?"

"After John died and it became known that I'd never walk again, Mace and Elias Palmer were the first to come to me and offer help. I knew right away that I could count on them and I knew there was no way I could handle taking care of the stock. I sold most of it to them at what I figured was a fair price." She shook her head. "Zelda kept telling me that they'd cheated me, but she couldn't know anything about the price of cattle and I knew she was wrong. Later they offered to buy the ranch, but I knew John wouldn't want me to sell it right out. It was a good home for the children and me. Of course, John wanted me to let Zelda live here, too."

"I'm glad you decided to keep the place because you're right. It's a good house and with some work, the ranch can become productive again. If it were run correctly, it could easily support Zelda and both your children."

"That's right, but the problem is, I knew Zelda didn't know a thing about running a ranch." She took a deep breath. "When I learned I wasn't going to get well, I knew I had to make arrangements for the children because I was afraid they would end up with nowhere to go."

"Didn't you think Zelda would take care of them?"

"Not unless she was forced to. She hates me and to get back at me, I'm sure she'd put then in an orphanage or something."

"I can't believe that. She loves Pansy and it shows. I'm sure she cares for Hugh, too."

"Well, she might keep Pansy for a while, but she hates Hugh." When he shook his head, but said nothing, she went on, "Knowing that Mace Palmer wanted the ranch, I struck a deal with him. I told him I'd sign the ranch over to him with the stipulation that my children would be allowed to live here as long as they live. He said he'd do it if I'd convince Zelda to marry him."

Uley lifted an eyebrow. "Zelda can't stand Mace Palmer."

"Once they're married, she'll get over that."

"I think you're wrong, Glenda. Zelda will walk away from here before she marries that Palmer man. It wouldn't surprise me if she didn't take the children with her. Do you think Mace or his pa would take care of you like she does?"

"She'll never run away. She knows it's her fault that John died."

"John's death was a horrible accident. How in the world would it be Zelda's fault?"

"If she hadn't insisted we come home from town that night, we would've stayed in the hotel. John would still be alive and I'd be out of this bed taking care of my children."

"Nobody knew there was going to be a storm. It came suddenly and devastated everything in its path. The hotel was damaged, too. If you'd been in one of those torn up rooms, you both could have been killed."

"Well, we didn't stay there and John was killed and now here we are. I'm dying and I have to make sure my children are taken care of. If you want to help me, as you said you would, you'll encourage Zelda to send Wiley Hendrix on his way. Then I'm sure she'll take Mace's proposal more seriously."

"I will promise you this, Glenda. I'll talk to Zelda."

She laid back and smiled. "I knew you'd understand, Uley." She breathed hard. "I'm tired, so if you don't mind, I'm going to take a nap."

He stood. "That's good. Rest is what you need."

"You will come back?"

"Of course."

"I want you to keep a close eye on Hugh and I also want you to have that talk with Zelda."

"I promise to do both, Glenda."

"Thank you."

He nodded, but she'd already closed her eyes.

Twelve

"Give me some more of that stew, Two Feathers," Elias Palmer demanded.

Mace finished his last bite and held out his bowl, too. "I want some more, too."

Two Feathers ladled the bowls full and turned back to the stove where she busied herself wiping off the dipper. Trying not to be obvious, when she finished this job, she went to the sink and began washing the dishes she'd used cooking supper. She'd been thinking about what she should do with the information she'd learned from these two men. She knew she could use it in several diverse ways, but she hadn't reached a final decision. She wanted to hear a little more of what they talked about before doing anything. She also wanted to pick the right time to discuss it with Dub.

"I been thinking, Pa."

"Bout what?"

"Bout getting the Jordon ranch."

"We know as soon as you marry that gal, the ranch will be ours."

"I know that, but I have an idea about what we can do to get her to marry me sooner."

"What's that."

"I'm going to snatch one of her young'uns."

"What good's that gonna do? They belong to the widow, not your gal."

"I know. That's the point. Zelda feels responsible for them since their mama can't get out of bed and take care of them herself."

"I still don't see what good grabbing one of them will do."

"Don't you see, Pa? She's going to think we'll kill the kid if she don't marry me. She ain't never going to let nothing happen to one of them young'uns if she can help it."

"Maybe she don't like them as much as you think she does, Mace."

"I don't know about that, but Glenda told me she feels responsible for them, and I don't think Glenda would ever lie to me. She wants me to marry Zelda because she thinks when I do, her brats will have a free and happy home forever." He laughed.

"We know better than that, don't we?"

"You're right we do. I don't intend for Zelda to spend her time looking after somebody else's snot nose monsters."

"Are they that bad?"

"The girl might not be, but the boy is a lazy little bastard. We can train him, though. You still got that whip you used on me a few times, don't you?"

"I shore do. I still know how to use it, too."

"So do I, Pa. So do I." He stood and shoved back his chair. "I think I'll go take a ride over toward the Jordon ranch. Might get a chance at one of the young'uns before it gets dark. Want to go?"

"No. My ankle hurts like hell. I'm going to get a drink and lay down." He followed Mace out of the kitchen.

It was no surprise to Two Feathers that neither of them spoke to her. She was used to them treating her as a piece of furniture and she didn't mind. It was something she could always use to her advantage. She knew the information she'd learned tonight was something she had to discuss with Dub as soon as possible. She felt she'd made up her mind how she was going to use all this evidence, but she wanted his approval.

~ * ~

The next morning Hugh walked into the barn and saw Wiley milking the cow. He laughed and glared at him. "Why you doing woman's work, Wiley Hendrix? Are you a sissy?"

"Work is work, Hugh. It doesn't mean a chore can only be done by either a man or a woman. It's just work and whoever sees it needs doing, does it."

"But I thought a man should do things like we did yesterday. Mend fences and such as that. Not milk cows."

"Traditionally, that's the way it happens. Women normally take care of the things in the house and yard and the garden. They also usually do the milking and gather the eggs. Men take care of the things that need doing out on the range such as mending fences and rounding up cows. They do the work around the barn and feed the stock. But there are times when women will have to do some of the things that are thought of as man's work and men have to do women's."

"Zelda did everything in the house until you came along. Now, I've even seen you wash dishes."

"I've noticed that Zelda has way too much work to do around here and that is one reason why I've tried to help her. From what I've seen, nobody except Pansy is interested in giving her a hand, and what little Pansy does is often more hindrance than help."

"Mama said I was too sickly to do strenuous work."

"I don't see that putting your dirty dishes in the sink, taking your mama her meals or keeping an eye on Pansy is strenuous work. It takes almost as much energy to find a place outside to sit and read your books."

"But Mama said..."

Wiley interrupted. "Did you discuss your health with the doctor yesterday?"

"Yes, but Mama said not to pay any attention to him. She said she knew what was best for me and I should listen to her and nobody else."

"Who are you going to listen to when your mother is no longer around to tell you what to do? Are you smart enough to know everything yourself?"

"I'll be smart enough to know what to do. Mama will tell me before she dies and I'll listen to what she says. I promised her I would only listen her and to people she has trust in."

Wiley shook his head and went back to milking.

Hugh didn't like being ignored. "Ain't you going to say anything else?"

"Why should I? You're going to listen to your mother regardless of what everyone else says. I guess you think nobody else in the world knows anything except her, so I'm not going to waste my breath."

Hugh frowned. "She trusts Mace Palmer. I guess I'll listen to him when Zelda marries him and he moves in here."

"That just goes to show you that you and your mother are thinking about something that will never happen. Zelda is not going to marry Mace Palmer. She's told you that and she's told your mama that." Wiley stood and picked up the milk pail. "I've told your mama that and now, I'm telling you. I'll take Zelda away from here before I'll ever let Mace Palmer get his hands on her. As for you and your mother, I don't know what you'll do then. I guess you'll be the one to have to learn to cook and take care of your mama yourself so you won't starve to death. I'm sure Palmer won't bother to do it when he gets hold of this ranch. He'll probably run you off and then the two of you will be on your own with nowhere to go and nobody to help you."

"What about Pansy?"

"She's a little girl and can't be blamed for any of this. She'll go with Zelda and me because Zelda is the only friend she has in this family."

"Mama loves her."

"But your mama can't take care of herself, much less Pansy, and you sure wouldn't look after your little sister. Now, move aside. I'll get this milk inside and then start mucking the barn. It doesn't look it's been done in a while."

"Zelda did it a while back."

"As I said, sometimes a woman must do a man's work if there's no man or a strong boy around to help do the things around a ranch that a male would usually do."

Hugh watched Wiley take long strides toward the house and wondered if the man could possibly be telling the truth. Would he really take Zelda and Pansy away to keep her from marrying Mace? If he did, what would he and his mama do?

What if Wiley is right and Mama is wrong? What if Mace wouldn't help us if he don't get to marry Zelda? What would we do if Mama gives the ranch to Mace and Zelda runs away with Wiley? Would Mace let us live here? Even if he did, how would we have food if there is nobody to cook it? Mama can't get up and I don't know how. After I eat breakfast, I think I need to have another talk with Mama.

~ * ~

Zelda set a stack of pancakes in front of Hugh and Wiley. She gave Pansy one on her plate and a couple for herself. She knew she would give the little girl more if she wanted it, but it was easier for her to eat one at a time.

"These look great, Zelda."

"Thanks, Wiley. My father always liked them. I thought it would be a change from eggs."

"Especially since the few hens you have aren't laying like they should."

Hugh looked up. "Why aren't they laying?"

"They will probably lay more now that Wiley bought feed for them. I think I wasn't feeding them the right thing."

"I wike eggs."

Zelda smiled at Pansy. "I know you do, sweetheart. Here, let me spread the butter on your pancake and you can pour some syrup on it."

"I wike pancake."

"I like pancake, too." Wiley winked at her and she giggled.

Zelda shook her head at him. "You and Pansy seem to have your own language."

"We do, don't we, Pansy?"

"Uh-uh."

"Well in the meantime, I need to be serious. I'm running low on flour. Do you think you could hitch up the buckboard for me so Pansy and I could run into town and get some after Glenda wakes up and I feed her?"

"Tell you what. Why don't I go get it for you and anything else you want? There are couple of tools I couldn't find in the barn that I need." He glanced at Hugh and his question sounded more like a command than a question. "Want to go with me, boy?"

"If I have to."

Zelda smiled. "Thank you, Wiley. I'll make a little list. I don't need much."

"Good. We'll leave as soon as we finish eating. We need to get back and go out and check on the fence we mended before it gets too late. I want to make sure we got it all finished."

Hugh shrugged.

After the meal was over, Wiley stood and carried his plate to the sideboard where the dishpan sat. Zelda was surprised when Hugh did the same thing. Then the two of them went out the back door together.

"Well, Miss Pansy, I think I just witnessed a miracle. I never dreamed Hugh would ever take his plate to the sink."

"What's a miracle?"

"It's something you don't see happen often." She stood and reached for Pansy. "I guess it's up to us to do the dishes and do whatever else that needs doing this morning."

"Need to wash first."

Zelda looked at her and laughed. "Oh, my goodness. You sure do. You have syrup all over your chin."

"Sticky."

"Yes, it is." She stood, picked up a wet a cloth, and said, "Come on and let's get it all off before your mother wakes up and wants to eat."

She had just laid down the cloth when Glenda yelled for her.

"Coming." Zelda picked up a plate, filled it and carried it with her to Glenda's bedroom.

"I see you've made pancakes this morning."

"Yes. I thought it would be a change for all of us."

"I prefer eggs and bacon, but I guess this will have to do."

Zelda sat the coffee on the side table, propped Glenda up with pillows and put the plate on her knees. "Everyone else seemed to enjoy them this morning."

"I guess they didn't have a choice in the matter." Glenda unfolded her napkin and glanced at Pansy. "I bet you wish you'd had an egg, didn't you, Pansy?"

She shook her head. "I wike pancake."

"Humph." Glenda took a bite of the food. "Where's Hugh? Send him in to me. I'm sure he wanted to eat something besides this."

"Hugh isn't here. He went to town with Wiley."

Glenda dropped her fork. "Who gave him permission to go with that man?"

"Nobody gave him permission. He just went."

"I bet that Wiley person made him go. Well, I don't like it. Not one little bit." Her voice was furious. "As soon as my son gets back, send him in here. I'm going to tell him not to ever listen to that Wiley. He's a bad influence on my sweet son."

"I'll tell him, Glenda." She reached for Pansy's hand. "Let's go and let your mother eat her breakfast, honey."

As soon as they were back in the kitchen, Pansy whispered, "Why Mama mad, Zewie?"

Zelda reached down and put her arms around the child. "Don't worry, Pansy. She's not mad at you. She's just upset about something someone else did."

"All right." Pansy hugged her back. "Help wash dish?"

"Yes, darling. You can help me wash the dishes."

Thirteen

Wiley glanced over at Hugh as the wagon bounced along the rutted road. He could tell the boy had something on his mind. "What you thinking about?"

"Nothing."

"I guess that's all right if you think *nothing* is something interesting to have on your mind. Personally, I prefer thinking about other things."

Hugh didn't say anything for a minute, then he broke the silence. "The doctor said I wasn't sick. You say I'm not sick. Even Zelda says I'm not sick, but Mama says I am."

"What do you say, Hugh?"

"I don't know. I always thought Mama was right. I did things like she told me to do so I wouldn't get sick again. Then you came along and made me rub down the horses and help you with the fence and I didn't get sick or nothing. Then the doctor examined me and said I wasn't sick no more and I needed to do some things around the ranch." He paused and looked at Wiley. "I'm confused."

"I guess it is enough to confuse a guy, but there comes a time when we have to decide for ourselves what we're going to believe. You said you'd soon be thirteen years old. Don't you think it's about time you began making some decisions on your own?"

After another pause, Hugh said, "You'd really take Zelda and Pansy away from here before you'd let her marry Mace Palmer, wouldn't you?"

"Yes, Hugh. I would. I knew the first time I saw Mace Palmer that he was an evil man. I'll never let him get his hands on Zelda."

"I don't see why not? She's no good."

"Why do you say that?"

"It's Zelda's fault that Mama can't get out of bed and that Papa John died."

"I don't believe that, Hugh."

"It's the truth."

"How do you know?"

"Mama told me."

Wiley knew he could give Hugh several reasons why Glenda's thinking was wrong, but he wanted the boy to draw his own conclusions about what was going on between Glenda and Zelda. He simply shook his head and said nothing.

Hugh looked around at Wiley. "Ain't you going to say nothing?"

"Why should I? You and your mama have it all worked out the way she wants it. Telling you the truth seems to me a waste of my time."

Hugh frowned. "What does that mean?"

"It means that it doesn't matter what the truth is, you're going to believe whatever your mama tells you about the situation, even if she's dead wrong."

"Are you saying I shouldn't believe my mama?"

"Like I said before, you're getting old enough to start using your own mind, Hugh. I just wonder why your mama is so sure Zelda is the reason her husband is dead and she's in bed."

"I guess because Zelda don't care about nobody but herself."

"I don't understand why you would say that."

"Why not?"

"The way I see it, if Zelda didn't care she wouldn't work herself so hard to look after the three of you. Especially since Pansy's the only one who ever gives her a kind word."

"Pansy's a baby. She don't know no better."

"So, you think it's all right to treat a lady the way you treat Zelda."

He frowned again. "I don't...I mean...Well, she ain't no lady."

"That remark shows me you still have a lot of growing up to do, Hugh. A man never says a woman is no lady whether she is or not."

"That don't make no sense."

"Think about it. It will become clear to you later."

They spent the rest of the ride into town in silence.

~ * ~

When Zelda heard a horse in the front of the house, she looked out the window and saw Elias Palmer rein up at the hitching post near the front porch.

She wondered what he was up to. He never visited without a reason. She took Pansy's hand. "Let's go see why he's coming here this time of day, Pansy."

"Hello in the house!" he yelled before she got the door open.

Zelda stepped out on the porch and stared at him. "What can I do for you?"

"I heard that Miz Jordon was ailing. Thought since I'm not able to do much work with this sore ankle, I'd come by and visit with her for a little while."

"She's asleep."

"Ain't it time you got her up for the day?"

"She isn't a well woman, and she takes several naps a day."

"Well, maybe I'll just come in and have a cup of coffee and wait until she wakes up." He started limping toward the steps.

Zelda felt Pansy move closer to her side. She squeezed the little girl's hand. She didn't bother to ask him what happened to his foot. "I'm sorry, Mr. Palmer. I haven't the time to entertain company this morning."

"Well now, that ain't a very friendly thing to say to your future father-in-law."

"I don't know what your crazy son is saying, but I'm telling you right here and now that you'll never be my father-in-law, Elias Palmer."

"Now, you know that's not so, little lady. Mace is looking forward to taking care of you and your family. I'm even looking forward to being that pretty little girl's grandpa." He pointed at Pansy and gave her a toothy grin. "Come here, little one, and give your grandpa a big kiss."

Pansy shook her head and moved closer to Zelda.

"Leave her alone, Elias. She doesn't know you and she's sure not going to come to you."

"Then I'll come up there and get my hug and kiss from her." He stepped up on the first step.

Through the open door, a cry came from inside. "Zelda, where are you?"

"That's Glenda. I need to see to her. You'll have to visit with her later." She turned and went into the house. "I'm coming, Glenda."

She didn't realize Elias had followed her until he said, "She's awake now, so I don't see no reason why I can't visit with her."

"Get out of here, Elias. She doesn't need company this morning."

"I don't think I'm going anywhere until the lady in there in that bed tells me to go."

"Zelda, what's going on?"

Elias pushed Zelda aside and she fell to her knees. He grabbed Pansy and headed to Glenda's room with Pansy screaming, "Zewie! I want Zewie!"

"What are you doing with my baby?" Glenda yelled when Elias entered her room with the still screaming and kicking Pansy in his arm.

Zelda ran into the room and snatched Pansy from him. "How dare you scare this child like this?"

"I was just trying to let her get to know me a little. We need to be acquainted with each other before we're all one big happy family."

Glenda nodded. "I agree with you, Elias, but we have to be a little more careful about it. You should take it slow with children. Pansy will come around when she gets to know you better."

Pansy was cuddled against Zelda's neck and was settling down. "Since Elias came to visit you, I'll take Pansy out so you can talk."

Glenda reached her arms to her daughter. "Do you want to come to me, baby?"

Pansy shook her head and continued to cling to Zelda.

Zelda didn't say anything. She turned around and walked out of the room. She hadn't gone far when she heard Glenda say, "It upsets me the way Zelda is always trying to make my daughter love her more than she does me."

"Maybe you should look at that as a good thing."

"What do you mean?"

Zelda couldn't help it. She paused so she could hear Elias's answer.

"It means, when the time comes, she and Mace will make good parents to the little one."

"Humph." Glenda grunted. "I guess I hadn't thought of it that way, but it still upsets me."

Zelda moved on. She didn't want to hear any more. She decided to go outside and let Pansy play with her pebbles and see if she could convince the child the bad man wasn't going to hurt her. Though she wasn't sure herself he wouldn't harm the little girl if given the chance.

~ * ~

"Well hello there, Mr. Wiley Hendrix," Emma Wilson said as Wiley and Hugh entered Wilson's General Store. "How can I help you today?"

"Hello, Miz Wilson."

"Who's that young man you have with you? It can't be John Jordon's boy."

"It is John's son. I guess he's grown since you've seen him."

"He sure has." She grinned at Hugh. "How's your mother doing now days, son?"

"She's all right, but she can't get out of bed."

"I know that. It was sure a tragic accident that took Mr. John away from here and left your mama in her pitiful condition. It's too bad your mama insisted they go home instead of staying in town that evening."

Hugh frowned. "What do you mean? Mama said Zelda wanted him to come home."

"Well, she did, but Mr. John said she'd understand if they stayed here, but your mama wouldn't hear of it. She said she wanted to get home to you and your little sister."

When Hugh said nothing else, she went on, "I haven't seen Zelda lately. How's she doing?"

"Fine." Hugh turned away and tried to comprehend what Mrs. Wilson had said as he began looking in a barrel filled with small hand tools.

"Zelda is working too hard, but other than that, Hugh's right, she's doing fine." Wiley walked up to the counter. "Here's a list of what we need in the line of food supplies, but Hugh and I are going to look around for a couple of tools I need out on the ranch."

"Just help yourself, Mr. Hendrix. Delmar and Garth can help you out in the back if you don't see what you need in here."

"Come on, Hugh. Let's see what they have out there."

For a minute, Hugh looked as if he were going to argue, but instead, he shrugged and followed Wiley out the side door and around to the back. They found a tall skinny man working on a wagon in the back yard. A younger boy was holding the wheel.

"You must be Wilson?"

"That's me." He finished fastening the wheel, then turned and looked at Wiley. "What can I do for you?"

"I'm Wiley Hendrix and this is Hugh Jordon. I'm helping out on the Jordon ranch and I need a couple of things I couldn't find out there."

"Well, good for you, Hendrix. Call me Delmar. This here is my son Garth." He wiped his hand on a dirty cloth, then reached to shake hands with Wiley. "The wife said you came in the other day and bought a goodly amount of supplies for the Jordons. Sorry I missed you that day. I was out making deliveries."

Wiley nodded to Garth and shook the man's hand. "Good to meet you both."

"Is there anything I can help you find?"

"I need some lumber to repair the chicken coop and the corral fence. Of course, that means I need nails. The ones at the ranch were bent and rusted. I found an old hammer, but I'll take a new one."

"Garth, why don't you take Hugh there into the store and find a sack of nails and a hammer for these folks? I'll help Hendrix pick out the lumber."

"Sure, Pa." The blond-headed boy looked at Hugh. "Come on. Maybe we can talk Ma out of a treat. She'll usually give me one when I've been helping out around here."

Hugh glanced at Wiley.

Wiley was surprised that the boy was asking permission, but he simply nodded at him and Hugh followed Garth into the store.

"First time that boy's been in here since the accident. Zelda comes in now and then, but she told us his mama always wants him to stay with her and the baby."

"Zelda's with them today, so he came with me."

"Are you a relative of Zelda?"

"I'm a friend."

"A friend, huh?"

"That's right."

He grinned. "I bet Mace Palmer don't like you helping her."

"Mace Palmer has nothing to say about it."

"Glad to hear it. I know the fool thinks Zelda will change her mind and marry him, but I got a feeling you're gonna put a stop to that."

Wiley nodded, but he knew he didn't want to keep talking about Zelda and Mace Palmer. He changed the subject. "Do I need to pull the wagon around here to put the lumber in?"

"Wouldn't hurt."

"I'll be right back with it."

"Fine. I'll start pulling the lumber I think you'll want."

Fourteen

Garth pulled a hammer from the shelf and held it toward Hugh. "Will this one be all right?"

Hugh shrugged. How was he supposed to know about hammers? "I guess so."

"Then we'll go over here where the nails are. What size do you want?"

Why was he getting all these questions? It wasn't his place to choose these things. Wiley was the one who wanted them. He should come inside and pick them out himself. "I don't know."

Garth looked puzzled, but didn't ask anything else. "Pa uses this size to repair the fence in back and since Mr. Hendrix said he was going to repair the corral fence, this is probably what he'll want. If not, he can change to something else when he comes inside." He carried the stuff to the counter. "Pa told me to get this for Mr. Hendrix and for you to put it with his other stuff, Ma."

"I sure will." She reached for the candy jar closest to her and took out two peppermint sticks. "Since you boys haven't seen each other in a long time, why don't you go outside and catch up with what's going on with each other? I can handle things in here and I'm sure your pa is busy with Mr. Hendrix."

"They're getting some lumber. Thanks, Ma." He turned to Hugh. "Come out this way. We can go out back as long as we don't get in the way of the men loading lumber."

"We don't have to help, do we?"

Garth raised his eyebrow at the question, but said, "Probably not. Usually it only takes two men to handle it. Pa says it goes faster that way."

Hugh followed Garth outside. The men were busy loading the lumber and didn't seem to see them. Hugh was glad because he didn't put it past Wiley to make him go help them.

Garth went to the left and they came to a corral beside a small barn. A big red horse pranced around in the fenced area. "I didn't know people in town had a horse."

"Lots of people in town have them. Some folks keep them in the livery stable, but we keep ours here with the wagon. Makes it easier when we have to make deliveries."

"Where do you live?"

"We live upstairs over the store."

Hugh frowned. "You're kidding."

"No, I'm not. Where did you think I lived?"

Hugh shrugged. "I live on a ranch."

"I know you do. Do you have to work hard on your ranch?"

"I didn't till Wiley Hendrix showed up. He makes me do chores."

Garth frowned. "Didn't you do chores before he came?"

"No. Mama says I'm too sickly to work on the ranch."

"Then who does all the work?"

"Zelda does it, but maybe she won't have to when she marries Mace Palmer."

Garth laughed.

"Why'd you laugh? Mama says it's going to happen."

"I can't imagine any woman who'd want to marry that crook."

"He ain't no crook."

"Yes, he is. He owes the store a lot of money and he won't pay it. Ma and Pa won't let him buy nothing else on credit until he pays up what he owes. They call him a deadbeat."

"What's that got to do with him marrying Zelda?"

"I'm surprised you'd want him to marry her. I heard him tell his pa that when he marries Zelda he's going to get rid of the rest of the Jordons."

"When did you hear that?"

"A couple of weeks ago." When Hugh said nothing, Garth went on. "I'd be afraid of him, if I was you."

"Mama says he promised her he'd look after all of us as soon as Zelda marries him. My Mama wouldn't lie to me."

"Probably not, but she might not know how mean Mace Palmer is. I don't trust him."

"I don't think he'd be mean to us if he married Zelda."

"I bet he would, too. He'd probably be mean to Zelda, too. She's a nice lady and I don't think she should marry Mace Palmer. She ought to marry Mr. Hendrix. He's a nice man."

"I don't like him."

"I don't see why not."

"He makes me do things."

Garth shrugged. "So what? Ma and Pa make me do things, but I still like them."

"I don't want to work all the time."

"I don't work all the time. I go to school when it's going on. I go fishing and I play ball with my friends. I do lots of things. What do you do for fun?"

"I read books."

"What else?"

"Nothing."

"Don't you have any friends?"

Hugh shook his head.

"Everybody should have friends."

"Well, I don't."

Garth gave him a strange look. "Want me to be your friend?"

"I guess so. I'd like to have a friend."

"Then count me in." He laughed. "You got any brothers and sisters?"

"Pansy is a half-sister, but she's a baby and I don't like her much."

"Why not?"

Before Hugh could answer, a boy came running across the yard. "Hey, Garth. Me and Sam are going down to the creek to swim. Want to go?"

"I'll have to ask Ma."

"Your Pa is helping that man. Why don't you ask him?"

"I can't bother him because he's busy. I'll ask Ma first. If she says no, that'll be the end of it because Pa will tell me to do what she says, but if she says yes, then Pa will say to go ahead and do it."

Hugh couldn't believe the conversation between these two boys. Something inside him made him want to go to the creek and swim with these fellows, but he knew his mama would never let him do it. Of course, she'd never know if he went for a little while. It then dawned on him that Wiley would never permit him to go. He might as well forget the idea.

"If my folks will let me go, do you want to go with us, Hugh?" Garth asked.

"I'd like to."

"Hugh don't have any friends, Kyle. I bet you'd be his friend, too, wouldn't you?"

"Sure, I will. We'll ask Sam to be one, too."

"Then I'd have three friends."

"Yes you would, and now that we're friends, do you want to go with us?" Garth looked at him.

"As I said, I'd like to, but I guess I'll have to go back to the ranch."

"Maybe you can go with us next time."

"Maybe I will."

"I'll ask Dad if I can go with you in a minute, Kyle," Garth said. "He's almost through loading that wagon.

Wiley and Delmar walked up and Garth explained about what was happening. "We asked Hugh to go with us, but he said he'd have to go back home with you."

Wiley nodded. "Hugh does have to go back to the ranch today, but if he wants to go swimming with you boys, I'll bring him back to town one day soon so he can go."

Hugh was surprised. "Really?"

"Yes, Hugh. Really."

"That'll be great, Mr. Hendrix. When will you bring him back?"

"Like I said, soon."

"Son," Delmar said, "Let's go in and get Mr. Hendrix's supplies out front while he pulls his wagon around. After that, if your mama doesn't object, you can go swimming with your friends."

"Thanks, Pa." Garth turned to his friend. "Go get Sam and come to the store. I'll ask Ma and if she says yes, we'll head out."

Wiley looked down at Hugh. "Come on, Hugh. You can ride in the wagon with me."

Hugh nodded.

"See you later, Hugh," Garth and Kyle both said.

Hugh nodded. He was still trying to absorb the fact that Wiley had said he would bring him back to go swimming with these guys and was too stunned to speak.

~ * ~

Elias Palmer rode his horse into the barn and began to curse as he fumbled with his walking stick trying to help himself down. Mace walked up and took his arm to keep him from falling. "Well, Pa. I see you didn't listen to me and stay home with your bum leg. Two Feathers said you made her harness the horse for you, then you headed out as soon as I went out on the range."

"I wanted things checked out and I knew the only way to do it was to do it myself."

"What things?"

"Things at the Jordon ranch. I picked a good time, too."

"How's that?"

"That damn man who has showed up and seems to be running things there had gone to town and I didn't have to worry about him running me off." They paused at the corral fence and Elias leaned on it. He let out a snide chuckle as he leaned over and spit a stream of tobacco on the ground.

"I'm surprised Zelda didn't run you off. She's been awful ornery lately."

"She didn't want me to come in, but Glenda hollered at her and when she went back in off the porch, I followed her. There was nothing she could do, but let me talk to Glenda. It helped when the little brat began to cry. Zelda grabbed her and hurried out of the room."

"Why did she cry?"

"I think she was afraid of me. I guess she ain't around many men."

"She don't cry when she sees me."

Elias frowned. "It don't matter. Whenever we snatch her, she'll get use to me, too."

"Why didn't you snatch her today?"

"I swear, Mace. Sometimes I think you're crazy. How could I snatch the little gal in the shape I'm in? I wouldn't have been able to get out of that house before Zelda would've hit me in the head with a frying pan or something."

Mace laughed. "You're right. I bet she'd do it, too."

"That's what I figured. But I know for sure how getting that girl will be the best thing we ever done."

"How do you know that?"

"I could tell Zelda was crazy about her and would do anything to protect her. We get that young'un and Zelda will be yours for the taking."

Mace smiled. "That's the thing I want."

"Course we wouldn't have had to worry about gettin' her if I'd had a copy of the papers in my pocket. The old gal would have signed it right then and there and we'd have the ranch."

"I told you not to ever go over there without them."

"I ain't no fool, Mace. It come to me that it weren't the time to get her to sign today, even if I'd had them with me."

Mace frowned. "Why the hell not?"

"Think about it. If we had the paper signed, we'd get the ranch, and frankly that's all I want. But you want that Zelda and after seeing her today, I can understand why. She weren't dirty and nasty like she is when she's been working so hard. She had her hair pinned up and she was clean and I realized she's plum pretty."

Mace frowned. "You ain't thinking you'd want her for yourself, are you, Pa?"

"I would certainly consider it if some other man besides you was wanting her. Since it's you, I'll bide my time."

"What do you mean by that?"

He shrugged. "It's just that if'en she don't come around and marry you, I might see if I couldn't talk her into marrying me."

"I'll be damned if you do that. I've wanted her for years and I ain't giving her up to you or nobody else."

"I'm not sure you're going to have that choice. Glenda told me today that her stepdaughter is dead set against marrying you. She even asked me to help her change the woman's mind."

"How could you help?"

"That's what I asked, but she said she'd figure it out and tell me when she had a clear plan." He chuckled and spit again. "I figured it was a good idee to let the old girl come up with something. If she can do it afore she dies."

"Is she really dying?"

"Said she was, but she doesn't think it'll happen for a while yet. She plans for us to take her in and look after her like a baby."

"Well, we can't just up and kill her."

"I don't know about that. Things happen on a ranch all the time that kill people. Look at my ankle. It could have been worse when I fell off the porch. I could have even been killed."

"But the woman can't get out of bed. She ain't going to have no accident."

"She can't get out unless she decides she wants to get up and there's nobody in the house to help her. She might just try it herself and fall to her death."

"I don't see how we could make that happen, Pa."

"That's your trouble, Mace. You don't plan ahead like I do. Why don't you leave the thinking to me and things will work out just the way we want them to? We've got the stock. That is, what of it that ain't run off. We've got Glenda on our side, and I've got a good plan working to get you or me that woman. Now, all you got to do is what I tell you to do."

"You ain't gettin' Zelda, Pa."

"Maybe not." He laughed. "Let's quit jawing and go on in the house. I want to see what that crazy Injun has cooked up for us to eat. Hope it's somethin' besides stew. Her stew is good, but I'm tired of it."

Mace frowned, but didn't say anything as he followed his hobbling father toward the back door. He knew he was never going to let his Pa have Zelda, if he had to kill the old man to keep him away from her.

Fifteen

Zelda tuned from the sink where she'd stashed the dirty supper dishes and stared at Wiley. "Why do you want me to keep the children out of the house while you have a talk with Glenda?"

"Because I don't want them to hear what I'm going to say to her."

"I figured that, but what are you going to say."

He gave her a crooked smile. Lord, this woman was inquisitive! "Zelda, I'll tell you all about it later. Just please do as I ask for now."

"All right, but you have to tell me later."

"I promise, I will."

She shook her head and frowned at him at the same time. "You better keep that promise."

"Have I ever broken a promise to you?"

"As far as I know, you've never made a promise to me."

"Then, it's for sure that I haven't broken one."

She shook her head and turned back to the kitchen. "Come on, Pansy. Let's go outside and see if we can find Hugh."

Pansy looked puzzled. "Why?"

"Honey, I don't know why, but for some reason Wiley wants us to do it."

"Oh." Pansy laughed. "Bye, Wiwey."

"Bye, sweetheart. I'll see you in a little bit."

Pansy giggled and waved at Wiley as she and Zelda went out the backdoor.

Wiley turned and went down the hall to Glenda's room. "What are you doing here?" she snapped at him as he entered?

"I need to have a talk with you."

"I have nothing to say to you."

"Maybe you do and maybe you don't, but you can decide that after you hear what I've got to say."

"Well, say it and get out of here."

He pulled up a chair beside her bed.

"I didn't ask you to sit down."

"That doesn't matter. I'm sitting anyway."

She scowled at him. "You are the most exasperating man I've ever met."

"You're not the only woman who has ever told me that, Glenda Jordon."

"Well, now you're seated, tell me what you want."

"I heard you had company today while I was gone."

"Not that it's any of your business, but yes I did. I enjoyed it, too."

He ignored that statement. "I had an enjoyable trip into town this morning."

"So, what do I care?"

"Your son enjoyed it, too."

Her eyes blazed. "You took Hugh to town with you?"

"I did."

"How dare you do such a thing! You didn't have my permission to take him."

"No, I didn't. Furthermore, I won't ask your permission the next time we go."

"What do you mean *the next time*?"

"Hugh met a friend and he wants to go back to visit with him."

"I'll not have my son being influenced by those rough-neck boys who live in town. They're not the kind of friends he needs."

"Glenda, the boy is twelve-years-old and he needs to have friends. There's nobody around here he can pal around with. So, if you don't want him making friends in town, I suppose you don't want him to have any friends at all."

"He has me."

Wiley couldn't believe this woman. "For heaven's sake, woman. You're Hugh's mother, not his friend. When are you going to start acting like a mother and let the young man grow up?"

"Damn you, Wiley Hendrix. I know what's good for my son. Get out of here and send him to me. I'll straighten out the damage you've done to his thinking with your secret trips to town."

"You may try to straighten out his thinking, as you say, but you're going to end up losing your son if you keep pushing him. He's beginning to do some thinking for himself and will eventually think he doesn't need you anymore."

"You're crazy. My baby will always need me. He always comes in and tells me what's going on in his life."

"Let me ask you this. We've been back from town since the middle of the afternoon. Has he come in and told you about his trip?"

"I must have been asleep."

"No, you weren't. Zelda came in and brought your supper. Hugh was at the table with us and he didn't bother to come in here."

A tear slipped down Glenda's cheek. "You're trying to take my little boy away from me."

"I don't want your little boy. The way you've coddle him, he's a spoiled brat. Unless you loosen the reins and let him become the young man he could be, nobody will ever want to be around him."

She stuck her nose in the air. "You're just as wrong as you can be. Mace Palmer can't wait to move in with him. His father told me that very thing today."

Wiley shook his head. "All right, Glenda. I see there is no way you'll ever see the logical side of things, so I think it's time I got real with you."

"What do you mean?"

"I had a talk in town with some folks today. They were very informative about the Palmer family."

"Whatever you heard is just gossip. They told me that the folks in town don't like them."

"They have good reason not to like them. Do you realize that for months they came to the general store to get supplies and told the Wilsons the supplies were for you? They had no reason not to believe them, so they put all their supplies on your bill."

"That's a lie."

"Do you remember a few months ago when Zelda came to you and told you that you'd have to pay for your supplies in cash?"

"So what? I guess they needed money."

Wiley went on. "It was because the bill the Palmers ran up in your name was over sixty dollars and not a penny had been paid. When the Wilsons realized what the Palmers were doing, they put a stop to it and now demand they pay from everything they buy in cash. They also demand they pay off the bill they claimed was yours at a few dollars each time they shop."

"I still don't believe you."

"I can't help what you believe, but it's the truth. They also said Mace Palmer is not only paying a dollar a week on the bill in your name now, but he told Mrs. Wilson that as soon as he gets your ranch and your money, he'll let you pay it off." Wiley took a breath. "But none of that is the part that you need to think about."

"Then why are you telling me these lies?"

"On the way home today, Hugh told me something I think you need to know."

"What was that?"

"He said the Wilson boy told him he overheard Mace Palmer tell his father that as soon as he was married to Zelda he was going to get rid of the rest of the Jordons. It scared the boy and he asked me if I thought it was true. I told him I wouldn't bet against it."

"See why I don't want Hugh associating with those evil boys in town? They'll fill his head with lies like that and then you back them up."

"I thought it my duty to tell you what happened, but if you choose not to believe it, I feel sorry for you." Wiley stood and pushed back his chair. "But to be honest, I feel sorrier for your children than I do you. They have a mama who cares more about the hate she feels for her stepdaughter than she does about what will happen to her children if the Palmers ever get their hands on this ranch."

"You stupid man. I love my children more than anything."

"Your actions tell me how much you care for them. It doesn't matter what they'll have to go through just as long as you manage to bring hurt to Zelda."

"You're a fool, Wiley Hendrix. I know if you don't get off the ranch, you'll end up messing up all my plans."

Wiley didn't say anything. He simply turned and walked out of the room, wondering why she didn't tell him to send Hugh in to see her.

~ * ~

Wiley wasn't surprised to see Zelda and Pansy sitting on the tree bench. What did surprise him was Hugh sitting on a patch of grass a few feet away from them. The boy usually headed for the front of the house when others were outside. Wiley tried not to show that he was glad to see the three of them together. He nodded and said, "There's a couple of hours of daylight left. Since I didn't get to go out on the range to look for stray cattle today, I think I'll go check a couple of places now."

Zelda looked at him. "How many have you found."

"I penned twelve head up in a canyon on the left of the creek. As soon as I finish the fences, I'll turn them back into the pasture."

"Can I go with you to look for cows?" Hugh blurted.

Wiley knew that the boy on the plow horse would slow him down, but he didn't want to rebuff the kid when it was the first time he'd asked to do something with him. "Sure," Wiley grinned at him. "Let's go saddle our horses."

Hugh jumped up and ran toward the barn.

Zelda lifted an eyebrow. "I'm surprised he wanted to go with you."

"Me, too, but I think he might be seeing that sitting around and reading books is not the only thing in this world for a boy his age to do."

"Oh, Wiley, I hope you're right. He's been so...." Her voice trailed off and he figured it was because she didn't want to say anything negative in front of Pansy.

"I go get cows, too."

Wiley chucked her under her chin. "I'm afraid not, pretty girl. You have to stay here and take care of Zelda."

She giggled. "I wove Zewie."

Wiley almost said, *so do I*, but he caught himself and instead said, "I'm sure Zewie loves you right back."

"She sure does," Zelda said and hugged the little girl to her.

"Well, you ladies be sweet and Hugh and I will be back before dark."

"We'll be just as sweet as sugar as soon as we go inside and finish the supper dishes."

Wiley winked at her and walked off before he could tell her they both were already as sweet as sugar. What was wrong with him, anyway. Yes, Zelda was a nice lady and right pretty, too, but he wasn't going to be there long. So why was he having these thoughts about her? He knew he'd make certain that Mace Palmer never got his hands on the lady, but other than that, he needed to stay out of her life. He wasn't sure he liked the idea of that last thought. It was almost like since he'd entered her life, he wanted to make the arrangement permanent.

~ * ~

Zelda heard Glenda calling her name as soon as she stepped inside the back door. She hurried to her room with Pansy trailing behind her. "Yes, Glenda. What do you need?"

"Where in the world were you? I've been calling and calling."

"We outside, Mama."

Glenda ignored Pansy. "Tell Hugh to come in here. I need to talk to him."

Before Zelda could answer, Pansy blurted, "Hugh go get cows."

"What?"

"Get cows."

Glenda looked at Zelda. "What is she talking about?'

"Hugh rode out on the range with Wiley to look for stray cows."

"He what?"

"You heard me."

"I know I did. I just couldn't believe what you said. How could you let my baby boy go off with that ruffian? He's a bad influence on Hugh."

"If you ask me, he's the best influence on Hugh anyone has been since Papa died."

"Hugh doesn't need to be doing demanding work like that. Go get him. I want him in this house this minute."

Zelda laughed. "Glenda, that's a crazy thing to ask me to do. Hugh and Wiley left riding horses and I have no idea where they headed. Besides, there's no way I could find them on foot."

"You could at least try."

"Don't be silly. I'm not going out there trying to find two men who could be a mile away from here."

"It's not two men. It's an irresponsible good-for-nothing man and a helpless little boy. How could you let him go?"

"I had nothing to do with it. It was Hugh who asked to go."

"That's a lie."

Glenda shook her head. "Believe what you want to, Glenda. I'm not going to argue with you about it. Now, if there's nothing else, Pansy and I are going to wash dishes."

It wasn't the first time Zelda heard the woman call her a bitch as she left the room. She chose to ignore it, just as she always did.

Sixteen

Wiley stopped at the entrance to the canyon and waited for Hugh to catch up. He had to grin when Hugh said, "Old Hector is slow, isn't he?"

"Yeah, he is. If you want to keep coming out on the range with me, we need to see about getting you a decent horse."

His eyes got big. "A real horse for me?"

"Of course. Don't you think you're about old enough for one?"

"Sure, but I don't know if Mama will let me have one." When Wiley only lifted an eyebrow, Hugh added, "But I'll tell her I need it and maybe she won't get too angry."

"Maybe not." He urged his horse forward into the mouth of the canyon, then paused, dismounted and began moving the brush he'd used to fence them in. He noticed that a lot of it had been disturbed.

Hugh got down and began helping him. "What's wrong?"

"Why do you ask?"

"Cause you're frowning."

"I guess I was. It looks like to me that somebody has messed with the brush here. I just hope the cows have wandered further back than I thought they would."

"Reckon they've got away?"

"I don't see how they could. The brush was still here, but it does look like it's been disturbed."

"Maybe somebody let them out."

"I was thinking the same thing. Somebody who had no business messing with them." He turned toward his horse. "Let's ride into the canyon a way and see what we can find."

When they didn't find any cows, Wiley was certain they had been stolen. "Well, Hugh. It looks like there's a thief around here. Wonder who would just help himself to your cattle?"

Hugh shook his head. "I don't know. Do you think it was rustlers?"

"Anybody who steals a man's cattle is sure a rustler, whether it's a few head of cattle or a large herd."

"That's mean of them, isn't it?"

"It sure is." He turned his horse and Hugh followed. "If it was anybody around here, I might be able to recognize the cows."

"How? Don't all cows look alike?"

"Not really. But the mother to a calf had a torn place on her right shoulder. She probably got it from limb or something. It was pretty bad, but I knew she needed to stay with the baby, so I patched it up."

"Are you saying we should look for a cow with a torn place on her right shoulder?"

"It wouldn't hurt to keep an eye out for her."

"Can we ride around and look for her now?"

"Since the sun is going down, we better wait until tomorrow." When he saw the disappointed look on Hugh's face, he added, "Of course, we can head back by the creek instead of across the field. As we go that way, we need to keep a sharp eye out."

Hugh perked up. "I'll do that. I've got good eyes."

Wiley grinned. *Yep. I was correct. With the right leadership, Hugh can be taught how to be a cowboy. A good one at that. I'm surprised how much he's come around today. Oh, I'm not saying he won't backslide, because I know he will. Glenda will put her ideas in his head and he'll have to learn all over again, but at least today has been a good start. Whether or not I want to admit it, I'm beginning to like the boy. I'd like him even better if he'd be more civil to Zelda, but I know it'll take some time to change the way he demands things of her. It may be harder than making a cowboy out of him, but it can be done. And after today's progress, I'm the man to do it. I just can't expect him to change all his bad habits in one day or one week, for that matter.*

~ * ~

As Wiley went in to breakfast the next morning, he passed Hugh headed for the barn. "Going somewhere, Hugh?"

"Yeah. I'm going to pick Mama some berries. She likes them."

"Watch out for snakes."

"I will."

Wiley stepped into the kitchen. "Good morning, ladies."

"Good morning, Wiley." Zelda sat a filled plate at his place at the table.

He reached over and tweaked Pansy's cheek. "Hey, pretty girl."

As she always did when he showed her attention, she giggled.

"Hugh seemed to be in a hurry this morning."

"He was determined to get out of here before his mother woke up." Zelda put down plates for Pansy and herself.

"Why the rush?"

"I'm not sure. He said there was something he had to ask her and that maybe the berries would put her in the mood to let him have what he wanted."

"Did he tell you what that was?"

"You should know better than to think he'd tell me anything."

"You're right. I should." He grinned. "This is good."

"Thank you."

"Good," Pansy said as she stuffed a slice of bacon in her mouth.

"Let me cut that up in bites for you, honey." Zelda smiled at Pansy. "It'll be easier for you to eat."

"I have something I need to tell you, Zelda."

She looked up at Wiley. "What's that?"

"I had rounded up about a dozen wild cows and penned them in a canyon. When Hugh and I got there yesterday, they were gone."

"What happened to them?"

"All I can figure is that somebody took them."

"Who would do such a thing?"

"I'm not sure, but whoever it was knew where they were. They probably watched me rounding them up and knew where I penned them."

"So it was deliberate?"

"I'm sure it was."

Zelda laid her fork down and whispered, "Mace Palmer."

"I thought the same thing."

"How can we prove it?"

"I don't know, but I'll think of something."

"You might better think fast. It wouldn't surprise me if Glenda doesn't give the ranch to him before we can stop her."

"I'm going to see if I can't do something about that, too."

"What can you do?"

"I don't know if there is anything I can do, but I'm going to talk to your father's lawyer. He did have one, didn't he?"

"If he did, I'm sure it would be Avril Crowder or his son. They're the only lawyers in Laster."

"I'm going into town again today and I'll make it a point to see him."

Before Zelda could answer, Glenda yelled for her to come into her room. She shrugged, stood and filled a plate. "Pansy, honey, you stay here with Wiley. I'll be back in a minute."

Pansy grinned. "I wike Wiwey."

"I'm glad you like me, sweetheart. I like you, too. Now let's see how quickly we can eat our eggs."

~ * ~

Zelda entered the bedroom. "Good morning, Glenda."

"What's good about it?"

"There's a lot good about it, Glenda. I'm sorry you can't see that."

"If you were the one lying in this bed, and knew you were dying, you wouldn't be so cheerful either."

"I'd try to be."

135

"Where's my son? You were supposed to send him to see me before he went to bed last night."

"He came in to see you, but you had gone to sleep."

"He could have awakened me."

"He didn't want to."

"I bet you didn't even let him come to see me."

"It was his choice to go to bed without waking you."

"I'm sure you're lying, but it really doesn't matter. I'll ask him, so send him in to see me right now."

Zelda bit her lip. "He's not here, Glenda."

Glenda glared at her. "Where has that devil, Wiley Hendrix taken him now?"

"Wiley hasn't taken him anywhere. Wiley is in the kitchen eating his breakfast. Hugh ate earlier and went down to the creek."

"Why in the world did you send him to the creek?"

"I didn't send him. He said he was going to pick berries for you."

Glenda's mood changed. "Oh, how sweet of him. He's such a thoughtful son. He knows how much I like berries and he wants me to have some."

Zelda headed out of the room. "I'll send him in here as soon as he gets back."

"I'm sure he'll come directly to me, so you don't need to bother."

~ * ~

Zelda turned from hanging the last sheet on the line and watched Hugh ride Hector into the yard. He went directly to the barn and in a few minutes, came outside. He had a worried look on his face. "Is something wrong, Hugh?"

"Where's Wiley?"

"He left about an hour ago for town. He said he'd be back this afternoon."

Hugh frowned. "I would've went with him."

"He said to tell you he'd check on a horse for you and if he found a good one, he'd go ahead and buy it. He did add that if you didn't like it, he'd take it back."

Hugh's face lit up. "I bet I'd like it."

"I help pin clothes," Pansy said and held up one of the wooden pegs Zelda used to fasten the clothes to the line.

"I'm through hanging things up, honey. You can put that one back in the basket."

"When will Wiley be back?"

"I told you, he said he'd be back this afternoon. Is there something I can help you with?"

"Why would you want to help me?"

Zelda bit her lip. "I know you don't believe me, but I don't mind helping you when you need it, Hugh."

"I guess I'll have to go talk to Mama."

"She wanted you to come to see her when you got back. She even said to wake her up if she was asleep."

Hugh turned and headed into the house.

"Come on, Pansy. We may as well go inside, too. It's time I started cooking." She picked up the laundry basket and reached for Pansy's hand.

Hugh stood in the kitchen drinking water when she stepped inside. "I thought you were going to talk to your mother."

"She'd asleep."

"She said…"

"I know. You told me she said to wake her, but I wanted to get something to drink first."

"I see."

"Zelda!" Came the cry from Glenda's room.

"Sounds like she's awake." Zelda put the basket down. "Pansy, you go over there and play with your dolly and I'll go see what you mama wants."

Pansy toddled off to the side of the fireplace where she kept her few toys.

Zelda looked at Hugh. "Do you want to come with me?"

"I'll be there in a minute."

She nodded and went to the bedroom. It then dawned on her that Hugh didn't have the berries he'd gone to the creek to pick. He hadn't even brought the basket back. What was up with him today?

"There you are. Where were you lazing around now? You're never here when I need you."

Zelda couldn't help the sharpness in her voice. "I was hanging the wash on the line. As you know, I have more to do than to stay in here and wait for you to call me to wait on you."

"Where is Hugh? Don't tell me he hasn't come back from his berry picking."

"He just got back a minute ago. He's in the kitchen."

"Well, tell him I want to see him."

"I'm here, Mama." Hugh came through the door.

"Hello, darling. I've been waiting all morning for you to come see me." She smiled at him. "I'm so pleased that you wanted to go pick berries for me this morning. I'm looking forward to eating them with you."

For a minute Hugh looked flustered. Then he said, "I couldn't find any berries, Mama. I guess the birds have eaten them all up."

"Oh, my. I would have loved to have had some, but the fact that you wanted to get them for me is what is important. Now, have a seat and let's have a little chat. I want to know how you're feeling."

"I'm fine, Mama."

"Are you sure? Maybe you should see the doctor."

"I don't want to see the doctor, Mama. I said I was fine."

"I just want to be sure. I'm upset about you going into Laster with Wiley Hendrix without telling me. I'm afraid it was too much of a strain for you."

"It wasn't. I enjoyed going."

Glenda pursed her mouth and looked around. "Why are you still in my room, Zelda? Are you trying to spy on my son and me or are you afraid we might say something you can hold over Hugh's head?"

"I was simply trying to straighten up your room a little, Glenda. But I'll leave. I'm sure there are deep dark secrets that you and Hugh need to share." She flipped around and left.

Oh, Dear Lord, please help me control my temper. Sometimes I think I'm going to go mad with the way Glenda treats me. I know

I deserve it, but I'm getting so tired of her ways. Please give me patience to cope.

"Hey, Zewie. Be-Be wants us to rock."

"I wish I could sit down and rock with you, sweetheart, but I have to start cooking."

"I help?"

"Yes, sweetie. Come on in the kitchen and you can help."

Seventeen

"That lazy woman drives me crazy. She doesn't do enough work around here to keep her busy, so she enjoys tormenting me."

"She was hanging clothes on the line when I got back. I guess she's tired." Hugh didn't know why he said this. He couldn't believe he was defending Zelda to his mother.

"Tired, nothing. She doesn't have that much to do. Looking after you children isn't a hard job. I just wish I could do it myself."

"I wish you could too, Mama."

"Oh, Hugh. How sweet of you to say that. You're the perfect son."

Hugh glanced away when his mother reached for him. He knew there were some serious things he wanted to talk to her about, but he wasn't sure where to begin. He took a deep breath. "I met a couple of guys in town yesterday, Mama. They invited me to come back and go swimming with them. I'd like to go."

"Oh, no. You can't do that."

"Why not?"

"I'm sure they were only trying to make you think they wanted you to go. Everyone in town knows you're a weak little boy who must be careful about what he does. I can't stand the thoughts of you getting sick again."

He wondered if she was right. Maybe he was weak and maybe they didn't really want him to come back and go with them.

He didn't want to think this, so he changed the conversation. "Mama, when I go anywhere, I have to ride Hector. He's not a very good horse to ride. He's more for plowing and working around here. I want a nice, pretty one to ride on. Maybe a pinto."

"I don't understand, Hugh. Hector is a gentle horse. You're safer on him than you would be on another one. Besides, you don't leave here often enough for me to spend my money on a new horse."

"I ride more than you think."

"Where do you go?"

"Well, you send me to see Mace Palmer. Then I went to town. Besides that, I kind of like riding out on the range with Wiley."

He knew he'd said the wrong thing when his mother's voice grew angry. "That awful man is trying to turn your head. You have no business riding out on the range or anywhere else with him. I knew he was trouble the minute he came into this house. You stay away from him. Do you hear me?"

Hugh couldn't help becoming defensive. "He's not so bad, Mama."

"He most certainly is bad. In fact, he's worse than bad. He's evil. It wouldn't surprise me if he isn't some escaped outlaw or something." She looked into Hugh's eyes and pointed her finger at him. "I forbid you to have anything to do with him."

"Why?"

"For the reasons I just told you. He's a terrible person and the sooner we get him off the ranch the better off we'll all be. When Mace takes over, you'll soon forget Wiley Hendrix ever existed."

"I don't know..."

"Please don't question me, Hugh. Don't you think I know what's best for you?"

He half nodded his head in frustration.

"Then be a good boy and go get your book and relax for a little while. That way you will get the silly notions of having a horse and going out on the range out of your mind. You're my baby and I'm only telling you this because I want to protect you."

It dawned on Hugh that his mother had been calling him a baby all his life. In the last few days he realized he was no longer one. It was time for her to realize it, too.

"Why do you keep calling me your baby? Pansy's your baby, not me."

"Oh, sweetie, don't you realize you're still a baby? Somebody has to protect you, and that somebody is me."

He couldn't control the emotion that seem to boil over in him. He jumped up and pushed his chair back. He swallowed, and despite his determination not to cry, a tear slid down his cheek. In as strong a voice as he could muster, he said, "I ain't no baby, Mama."

"Oh, Hugh, darling. Of course, you are. You're weak and..."

He interrupted. "I'm stronger than you think I am."

"No, sweetie..."

Other tears began to fall. "Quit calling me those baby names."

"But, darling..."

"Dang it, Mama. I've got to start growing up sometime." His voice had become an almost yell as his anger grew.

Glenda's voice rose, too. "This is all the fault of that evil Wiley Hendrix. If I had a gun, I'd shoot that bastard the next time he dared step his feet into my room."

"How can you say you'd kill somebody, Mama?"

"I can kill anybody that messes with my baby."

Hugh didn't say anything else. He couldn't. He couldn't control the tears any longer, so he let them flow.

Glenda reached for him, but again he ignored her outstretched arms and fled from the room without saying anything else to her.

She screamed for him to come back, but he kept going.

~ * ~

Zelda wasn't sure what she should do. Glenda continued to call to her son, but Hugh ran out the back door and to the barn.

"Why Hugh cry?"

"I don't know, Pansy, but I better go see if I can find out what's going on."

"I go."

Zelda took her hand and they stepped out on the back porch, but before they could step into the yard, Hugh came out of the barn riding Hector. Zelda called to him, but he shook his head and rode away.

Since Glenda was still calling him, Zelda turned back into the house. She knew the woman shouldn't get so upset and hoped she could calm her down.

In Glenda's room, she asked, "What happened, Glenda?"

"Don't tell me you weren't listening. You always snoop around when I talk to my children." The woman was still screaming.

"You need to calm down. You know it's not good for you to get so upset."

"How can I help getting upset? You and that rotten Wiley have turned my baby against me."

"What do you mean?"

"Go get him and make him come back in here. We need to clear things between us."

"He gone," Pansy said.

"Where did he go?"

Pansy looked up at Zelda and waited for her to answer. "We don't know where he went, Glenda. He got on Hector and rode out toward the range."

"Why didn't you stop him?"

"I called to him, but he ignored me."

"Likely story. I know you want both my children to hate me. You've been trying to turn them against me ever since John died."

"That's not so. I want your children to have happy memories of you, but the way you're acting lately, they won't have."

"You devil. I hate you, Zelda Jordon. If it weren't for you, I wouldn't be in the shape I'm in and my children wouldn't be facing a future without me."

"I know you believe that, but I'm trying the best I know how to make things better for you around here."

"If you want to make things better, go get my son."

"I can't go out to the range on foot and you know it."

"See. I knew you didn't care a thing about me or my children."

Zelda felt Pansy's hand tighten around hers. She realized the child was frightened by the way her mother kept yelling. As gently as she could, she said, "Glenda, you're frightening Pansy. Please calm down."

"Oh, Pansy, darling. Come here to Mama. Let me hold you in my arms."

Pansy backed away.

Glenda almost screamed when she said, "See what I mean? Now you've made Pansy turn against me."

Pansy threw her arms around Zelda's leg and began to cry.

"She's only scared because you keep yelling, Glenda. If you don't stop it, I'm going to take her outside where she won't have to listen to it."

"Go on. You've already turned her against me anyway." Glenda began to gasp for breath.

Zelda rushed to the bed. "Here, let me get you some of your medicine."

Glenda was gasping so hard that she didn't refuse when Zelda put a spoonful of the liquid the doctor had left in her mouth. In a matter of minutes, her breathing became better and she slipped down from her sitting position in the bed.

"Try to rest. I'm sure Hugh will come and talk with you when he gets back."

"You better let him."

"I will, Glenda." She turned and looked down at Pansy. The child had stopped crying, but her eyes told Zelda that she was still scared. "Come on, honey. Let's let Mama get some sleep."

Pansy didn't answer, but clung to Zelda's hand as they left the room.

~ * ~

Wiley hitched his horse in front of a building with a sign that proclaimed, Avril Crowder and Son, Attorneys at Law. He hoped one of the men were in and that he didn't need an appointment to see him. If so, it would mean another trip into town.

Opening the door, Wiley stepped inside. A sour looking woman, with her head bent over some papers, sat behind the desk in the small reception room. She didn't look up. He removed his hat, walked up to the desk and cleared his throat.

She finished reading whatever it was she was so intent on and glanced up at him. "What do you need?" Her voice was as sour as her look.

"I need to speak with Mr. Crowder, ma'am."

"What about?"

Wiley lifted an eyebrow. "I don't mean to be rude, ma'am, but that's between Mr. Crowder and me."

"Well, do you have an appointment?"

"No. But I won't take much of his time."

"Well, even a little of his time is valuable. He doesn't have enough to waste on you drunken cowboys. Why don't you stay out of trouble in the first place?"

Wiley frowned. "Ma'am, I'm not in trouble."

"That's what they all say."

The door to the right of her desk opened and a middle-aged man stepped outside. "I thought I heard voices in here. What's going on."

"This cowboy wanted to see you, but I told him you didn't have time for him. He's probably just like the rest of them. He got into some kind of trouble, more than likely at the saloon, and now he wants you to defend his evil ways in court."

"Well, Essie Mae, why don't you go back to your work and I'll see what this gentleman wants?"

Essie Mae huffed, but turned back to her reading and ignored them.

"Don't pay no attention to my sister, mister. She doesn't like to come in and sit at that desk and she doesn't do it often. My pretty daughter is usually there. Too bad you didn't get to meet her. She likes to talk to new people."

Essie Mas huffed again, but didn't speak.

Wiley couldn't help being glad that she wasn't always the one to meet the friendly lawyer's customers.

Crowder chuckled. "Come on in my office, young man. What can I do for you?"

"I have a few questions I want to ask you. May I ask if I'm speaking with the senior Mr. Crowder?"

"You sure are. I'm the only one who works here."

"But the sign…"

Crowder laughed. "Yeah. That sign throws people who don't know me. My son was in business with me until a few years ago. He decided there wasn't enough work in a town like Laster to make him rich, so he packed up and moved to Austin. Said he was more needed there and I just haven't bothered to change the sign. Have a seat there and I'll see if I can answer your questions."

Wiley took the seat and decided he liked Avril Crowder, but he couldn't help wondering if the man shouldn't get a new woman to work on the front desk when his daughter couldn't. When seated, he introduced himself. "I've been helping out on the Jordon ranch and I wanted to see if I could clear up some things concerning the place."

"I'm surprised Glenda Jordon has put out the money to hire a hand. Last thing I heard was that she had let the place run down and was about to lose it."

"I'm not working for Glenda Jordon. I'm helping Zelda try to get the place back on its feet."

"That's a good thing. That young woman needs all the help she can get." He took a cigar out of his pocket and offered Wiley one. When Wiley shook his head, Avril lit his and leaned back. "Now start your questions and I'll see if I have the answers."

"You were the lawyer who wrote John Jordon's will, weren't you?"

"I was."

"When I saw how much Zelda loved her father, I was surprised the man cut her out and left everything to his wife. Why did he do that?"

Avril frowned. "He didn't cut Zelda out."

"Well, according to her and Glenda, he did. He left everything to Glenda with the stipulation that Zelda could live on the ranch until she was married."

"Now, that's a downright lie. It was the other way around."

"What do you mean?"

"John left the ranch and all the cattle to Zelda. He did stipulate that Glenda could live there until she married or died. It was written so the children would get a portion of the land when they reached the age of twenty-one. Until then, they could live under the roof with Zelda."

Wiley was not only stunned, but he was confused. "Then why do they tell me Glenda owns the ranch and Zelda has no choice in the matter? Zelda should know what she owns."

"Looks like she would know. I went out there and read the will to them shortly after John's funeral."

Wiley's mind was trying to grasp what the attorney was saying. If Zelda owned the ranch, why was she letting Glenda lord over her the way she was? Why did she say she had no say in the matter if Glenda sold the ranch? What in the world was going on with the Jordon women?

"Wait a minute." Crowder leaned forward and took the cigar out of his mouth. "I remember now. I was reading the will to the women when there was a loud crash in the kitchen. Zelda went running out and it seems the little girl, who had just learned to walk, had tried to climb up and get something out of the cabinet. The stool slipped out from under her and she fell. She screamed and hollered so that Zelda took her outside. She wasn't badly hurt, but she wasn't easy to calm down. After they went out, Glenda then told me to continue reading the will and she would tell Zelda all about it when things calmed down." He shook his head. "Like a fool, I believed her. Because I had to be back in town to attend court, I finished reading it, gave Glenda a copy and hurried away. That was the last time I saw either woman."

After talking for a few more minutes, Wiley thanked the lawyer and stood. "Thank you for seeing me. You've cleared up a lot of questions."

"It was my pleasure, Mr. Hendrix. If there's anything else I can do, don't hesitate to let me know. I'll even come out and explain things to Zelda if you need me to."

Wiley thanked him again and left. On the ride back to the ranch, he tried to decide how he was going to relate this news to Zelda. He wasn't sure if the woman would be relieved to know Glenda didn't own the ranch or would she be upset because her stepmother had let the place get so rundown? He figured she would feel a little of both. He also wondered what she would do when she learned the truth. Would she continue to build the place back up or would she decide it wasn't worth the effort and sell it herself? The one fact he knew for sure was that she would never sell the place to the Palmers.

It then crossed his mind that she might be willing to sell it to him. It would be a good place for him to start over and he sure wouldn't mind if she and the children stayed there as he was building it up. Of course, his conscience wouldn't let him put Glenda out, but he would make sure she treated Zelda with a little more respect. No. A lot more respect.

These thoughts continued to whirl in his head as he and Samson got closer and closer to the ranch.

Eighteen

Wiley frowned when he led his horse into the barn. He hadn't seen Hector in the corral and expected to see him in a stall, but the barn was empty. He removed the saddle and bridle from Samson and reached for the curry brush. "I'll do a better job later, old boy, but I need to get inside and see what's going on. Surely Hugh hasn't gone off to the Palmer ranch again."

He finished brushing the horse and turned him into the corral. He then headed to the house. He wanted to discuss what he learned in town today with Zelda, but first he had to find out what Hugh was up to.

In the parlor, he found Zelda rocking Pansy. At this time of day, this was unusual. He hoped the child wasn't sick and said so.

"She's fine. She just needed a little extra loving. I guess she dozed off."

"Was she upset about something?"

"I'll tell you later. Maybe we can get her to go outside and play with her rocks." She looked down at Pansy and whispered, "Sweetheart, look who just got home."

Pansy looked around and smiled. "It Wiwey."

"I sure am Wiley." He smiled back at her. As he moved closer to them, she held up her arms. He picked her up off Zelda's lap and she flung her arms around his neck.

"Is something wrong with my girl?"

"Hugh cry. Mama yell. Zewie rock me."

"Why don't you let Wiley carry you outside? You can sit under the tree and make designs with all those pretty rocks you have out there."

"I wike rocks."

"I know you do." Wiley chucked her under the chin, then looked at Zelda. "Are you coming with us?"

"I'll be there as soon as I check supper. I want to be sure nothing is burning."

"Then let's go, cutie." He nuzzled Pansy and she giggled.

In a matter of minutes, Zelda joined them. Pansy was already arranging her pile of rocks in the shapes her little mind devised.

"It looks pretty, Pansy."

The little girl looked up and grinned at Zelda, but didn't say anything.

Zelda turned to Wiley. "She's busy now, so I feel I can tell you what happened."

"What did happen?"

"Hugh and his mother had an argument. He was so upset, he ran out of the house to the barn. Shortly, he came out riding Hector. I'm concerned because he hasn't come back."

"Do you want me to go look for him."

"I hate to ask you to go since you just got home, but would you?"

"Of course I will. Which way did he ride out?"

"Across the pasture behind the chicken coop."

Wiley stood. "I won't ask you to tell me what the argument was about, but do you think it had anything to do with the Palmers?"

"I don't know, Wiley. I was in the kitchen until he left. Then I had to go in and try to settle Glenda. All I got from her was the same old things she always says. She tells me it's my fault that she is losing her son because I let you come to the ranch and take over running it. None of it made sense to me." She sighed. "I was afraid she was going to die on me, but soon after I got her medicine in her, she went to sleep. She'll probably stay asleep all evening and maybe all night. I'm sure she'll ask for Hugh as soon as she wakes up."

Wiley wanted to take her in his arms and comfort her. Instead he reached over and touched her cheek. "Keep supper hot for Hugh and me. We'll be back as soon as I can find him."

"Thank you, Wiley."

He smiled, winked at her and headed to the barn.

"Where you go, Wiwey?"

Wiley didn't want Pansy to get the argument she'd overheard on her mind, so he reached won and ruffled her hair. "I'm going to find Hugh so we can eat supper. I bet he's hungry, don't you think?"

"I hungry."

Zelda smiled at her. "Then why don't you finish with your rocks and we'll go inside and finish up supper."

Pansy nodded and muttered, "I hurry." She then began placing other rocks around on the ground.

~ * ~

Before the boy saw him coming, Wiley saw Hugh sitting on a boulder on the side of a small knoll. His horse was ground hitched beside him and he looked alone and scared. Slowing his horse to a walk, he approached the young man. When he was within a hundred feet or so, he got out of the saddle and led Samson to where Hector was grazing. He dropped the reins and let Samson graze too. Without saying a word, he moved beside the boulder and took a seat next to Hugh.

They sat in silence for a few minutes, then Hugh took a deep breath. "I'm mad and I'm confused and I don't know what to do."

"Maybe you need to talk it out."

"I saw the cows you said you had in the canyon."

"Oh? Where did you see them?"

"They were running with the Palmer herd."

Wiley nodded. "I figured that was who took them."

"The mama cow had a scar on her right shoulder just like you said she would. I know it was her because there was a calf with her."

"Now we know for sure who is taking your cows."

He was silent a minute, then went on, "Mama said you probably hurt the cow so I'd think you cared about what happened to us."

Wiley took a deep breath. "I only go after animals for food, and to protect me or someone else. I've never intentionally hurt an animal just to make someone believe something I said, Hugh."

"But Mama said…"

"One day, and that day is coming sooner than you think, you're going to have to decide for yourself who is telling the truth."

"Mama don't like you."

Wiley couldn't help a slight grin. "I know. She's made that perfectly clear to me."

"She wants you to leave the ranch."

"She's made that clear to me, too."

Hugh looked around at Wiley. "Why do you keep staying when you know she don't want you here?"

"I stay because, regardless of what your mama wants, the rest of you need me."

Hugh mumbled something, but Wiley didn't understand it. "What did you say, Hugh?"

"I said, I don't want you to go."

Wiley smiled. "Well, that makes two of you who don't mind my being here."

"I know Zelda don't mind."

"I wasn't talking about Zelda. It's Pansy who likes me."

Hugh kind of grinned, then his face became serious again. "Mama said I couldn't have a horse because I didn't know how to ride. She's afraid I'll get hurt."

"Looks to me like you're a pretty good rider. Old Hector here hasn't thrown you yet, has he?"

"No."

"A good horse is what a guy needs if he intends to work on a ranch and from what I see, you're doing a pretty good job of learning what has to be done."

"I'd like to have a horse."

There was another long pause.

Then, "Zelda's not going to marry Mace Palmer, no matter what Mama says, is she?"

"No, Hugh. She'll never marry him."

"I'm beginning to think Mama doesn't know what's really going on. Maybe it's because she's been in her bed so long."

"You may be right."

Hugh stood. "Then I think we should go get our cows."

"I'm afraid we can't do that, Hugh."

"Why not? They're ours."

"I know that and you know that, but since the cows aren't branded, the Palmers could say we were stealing their cattle. I think we should go into town tomorrow and talk to the sheriff about it."

Hugh looked surprised. "You want me to go with you?"

"Sure I do. You're the one who saw our cows on the Palmers' ranch. You need to be the one to tell the lawman." Wiley stood. "If you don't mind doubling with me into town, we can see about getting you a horse while we're there."

"Really?"

"I don't see why not."

Hugh climbed on Hector's back as Wiley mounted his horse. "I don't care what Mama says, I don't think you're the devil, Wiley."

Wiley laughed. "And I don't think you're that rude young man I first met when I arrived on this ranch."

Hugh laughed too. "I'm glad, because I want to start being a real cowboy just like you."

Wiley didn't say anything as they rode off, but he couldn't help feeling a sense of pride. The boy was coming around faster than he ever dreamed he would. There were still some things he had to learn, but he was going to be just fine. Wiley felt it down to his boots.

~ * ~

Two Feathers whirled around when Elias yelled, "What you doing down in the floor in my room, Injun?"

Keeping a straight face, she jumped up and said, "Looking for your nasty clothes."

"Ain't no nasty clothes under my bed and you know it. You was looking for somethin' to steal."

"I was not." She quickly put the hand behind her that held the coin she'd found under there when she hit it with her toe and it rolled out. She'd only bent down because there was the possibility of another one there. She knew if he found the coin in her hand, he'd accuse her of stealing it.

"What you got in your hand?"

"Nothing."

He walked over to her. "Don't lie to me, you filthy redskin. Show me your hand."

"No." She tried to back closer to the wardrobe so she could drop the coins inside, but she didn't get there.

Elias reached out and slapped her so hard she fell backward. The coin rolled out of her hand and ended up at the toe of his scruffy boot. He picked it up. "I knew it. You're nothing but a damn thief." He reached to hit her again.

She rolled to the side and scrambled to her feet.

"What's going on?" Mace yelled from the hall. "Who you fightin with, Pa?"

"This good-for-nothing thieving Injun. She's trying to steal my money."

Mace came in the door. "Looks to me like you need to give her a licking with your whip. That'll teach her."

Two Feathers tried to dodge them and run out of the room, but Mace grabbed her arm. "You ain't going nowhere. Pa needs to teach you a lesson."

Elias turned toward them. "Take her to the barn, Mace. You're right. I am going to teach her a lesson. A good one. The filthy redskin will never try to steal from me again."

Two Feathers glared at him as he jerked her forward. "How long you been stealing from Pa, old woman?"

"Don't call her a woman. She's nothing but a dirty Injun squaw. She don't deserve the name of woman."

Mace laughed as he practically dragged her down the hall, across the parlor and out the backdoor.

Two Feathers bit her lip. She knew these men had no mercy and there was no way she could get away from them. She'd have to endure whatever punishment they were going to levy on her because she knew Dub was out on the range and couldn't help her. She also knew another thing: she wouldn't give them the pleasure of seeing her cry or beg for mercy. Some way, somehow, she'd repay them in kind for whatever they did to her today and she wouldn't be slow in doing it.

Nineteen

Zelda knew Wiley had wanted to talk to her last night, but things didn't work out to where they could be alone for any length of time. And he'd said it would take time to explain what he wanted her to know. She couldn't help being a little worried. Especially since he'd kept looking at her strangely. She figured he was getting ready to tell her he was leaving. Though she'd expected him to move on, she wasn't ready for him to leave. In fact, she admitted to herself that she didn't want him to go.

It was comfortable with him on the ranch. He knew what he was doing and he'd sparked a hope in her that in some way they'd be able to save the ranch. Not that Glenda would appreciate it, but she certainly would. Zelda loved this ranch. She just wished her father had left it to her instead of his heartless wife. She would have still taken care of Glenda and the children for as long as they needed her to and they sure wouldn't be in the poor financial shape they were in now.

Shrugging her shoulders, she put the last clean breakfast dish on the shelf and lifted Pansy off the stool. "Let's go water our garden, sweetheart."

"Get pumpkin?"

"I'm afraid not. I told you, it will take a while for the pumpkins to grow."

Pansy pursed her lips. "How long while?"

"It will be when the weather turns cold. It's still warm, you know."

They stepped out on the back porch. Wiley and Hugh were carrying lumber from the pile beside the corral fence to the almost dilapidated chicken coop.

"What Wiwey do?"

"Looks like he and Hugh are getting ready to fix a place for the chickens. When it's done, maybe we will be able to get more eggs."

"I wike eggs."

"I know you do." Zelda patted her head. "You sure ate enough at breakfast."

She giggled. "Go see Wiwey?"

"No, sweetie. You can't. He's busy and I don't want you to get hurt."

"Wiwey not hurt me."

"You're right. He wouldn't, but they are going to start nailing and you could step on a nail or get hit in the head or something."

Pansy looked puzzled, but didn't say anything.

Zelda got a bucket of water and went to the garden to douse the hills where they'd planted the pumpkins. She hoped there would be a sprout or two so she could show Pansy that there was something beginning to grow in the ground. They walked down the row and she splashed water where the seeds had been buried.

Pansy's voice was sad. "No pumpkin."

"Just wait. There will be."

They continued in silence until they reached the end of the row. Zelda started to turn back, but Pansy didn't move. "What's the matter, honey?"

"Who dat?" Pansy whispered.

"I don't see anyone, Pansy."

"There." Pansy pointed toward a tree.

"I don't see.... Oh, my goodness. Yes, I do." With her heart pounding, she turned toward the chicken coop. "Wiley, can you come here a minute?"

He put down his hammer and headed in her direction. Hugh followed him.

"What is it, Zelda?"

She pointed. "That looks like a person lying on the ground near that tree."

"Stay here. I'll see who it is." Wiley walked to the tree and in an instant picked up the small woman.

Zelda frowned as he came forward. "Oh, my goodness. What's wrong with her?"

"Looks like somebody has beaten her nearly to death."

"Bring her in the house and I'll see what we can do for her."

Inside, Wiley deposited the woman on the couch. "She's barely conscious. Maybe I should go get the doctor or send Hugh."

"No!" The woman's voice came out in a rushed whisper.

"Ma'am, you're hurt pretty bad. I don't know if we can help you. You need a doctor."

"Don't send ... the ... boy."

Wiley glanced at Zelda and frowned. To the woman, he said, "Why not?"

She didn't answer.

"She's passed out, Wiley." Zelda knelt beside the women. "Pansy, go over there and play with your doll so I can help this lady."

With big eyes showing her fear, Pansy moved to the fireplace and sat near the corner. She hugged her doll close, but didn't say anything.

"She's an Indian," Hugh said in a flat voice.

Wiley nodded. "Looks like it."

"It doesn't matter who she is. She needs help." Zelda looked at Wiley. "Will you get me some warm water and some rags?"

Wiley moved toward the kitchen.

Hugh blurted, "I know her."

They both looked at him. "Who is she, Hugh?" Zelda asked.

"She's the Indian woman who works for the Palmers. I saw her when I was over there."

"I wonder if they did this to her," Zelda muttered.

"I wouldn't put it past them." Wiley continued to the kitchen.

"Whoever did it must be awfully wicked. How could anyone do this to another human?" Zelda placed pillows under the injured woman's head.

Wiley returned with the water and a couple of towels. "What else can I do?"

"Go see if you can comfort Pansy. She's upset. I'll call you if I need you."

"What can I do?"

Zelda looked at Hugh. She couldn't believe he was asking to help. "Just stand by. I might need you to get something for me."

"I could go get the doctor."

"For some reason, she didn't want you to go."

"Wonder why?"

"I have no idea, but for now, let's see what we can do for her."

Zelda washed the woman's face and arms. She wondered if she shouldn't remove her dress and see if there were more cuts and bruises on the woman's body. She made the decision to move her and turned to Wiley. "Would you carry her into one of the bedrooms? I need to undress her."

"Sure." Wiley sat Pansy off his lap. "I'll be back in a minute, honey."

Picking up Two Feathers, he glanced at Zelda. "Which room?"

"I guess you can put her in mine and Pansy's."

Hugh butted in. "Why not use mine?"

Zelda was shocked. "You wouldn't mind?"

"It makes more sense. I can sleep on the couch or in the barn with Wiley. You and Pansy have nowhere else to go unless you clean out the room we use for storage."

Zelda smiled at him. "That makes sense, Hugh. Thank you for thinking of it." She nodded at Wiley. "Follow me."

After getting her cleaned up and bandaged as well as she could, Zelda came back into the parlor. "She's in worse shape than I thought. I'm sure she needs the doctor because I think she has some broken ribs. Her arm is either out of place or broken."

"Then I'll go get him." Wiley stood.

"Can I go with you?"

Wiley shook his head. "I don't think both of us should leave, Hugh. The Palmers might figure out where their housekeeper is and come to get her. I don't want anyone here to get hurt and I'm trusting you to take care of the women while I'm gone. You'll do it, won't you?"

Hugh straightened his shoulders. "Yes, sir. I will."

Wiley nodded. "I know you will."

"Hurry back, Wiley."

"I'll be back as soon as I can, Zelda. In the meantime, you and the kids need to stay inside. I don't know if somebody is watching this place or not, but I don't want any of you to take a chance."

"I'll make sure they stay inside, Wiley."

"Thank you, Hugh." He turned and went out the door.

Pansy went running to Zelda. "I scared."

"Nothing is going to happen to you, sweetheart."

"I won't let nothing hurt you, Pansy. Wiley told me to watch out for you and Zelda and I will."

Zelda couldn't help staring at him. Was she in the wrong family or was Hugh the real Hugh? He'd never acted this way before. So he'd realize she appreciated his protection, she said, "Thank you, Hugh."

"If you have something to do, I'll watch Pansy, Zelda."

"I guess I should check on your mama, unless you want to."

"You can do it." He looked at his little sister. "Want me to read you one of your stories, Pansy?"

She looked confused, but nodded.

Amazed that Hugh would offer to read to his sister, Zelda sat her back on the floor and she toddled over to the table beside the fireplace where she kept her books. She held one out toward Hugh. "Read."

He nodded and moved to the fireplace and had a seat on the hearth. Pansy sat beside him.

Still wondering what had come over the boy, Zelda went down the hall to check on the women. They were both still asleep.

~ * ~

Mace Palmer grinned as he reined his horse into the woods near the Jordon house. He founded a downed pine that gave him an unobstructed view of the ranch house and the surrounding yard. He tied his horse to one of the scrubby little pines and took out a twist of tobacco. He figured he'd have a long wait, so he might as well take advantage of it. Of course, he didn't care how long it was. At least it kept him from having to help their one ranch hand, Dub Veach, brand the cows they'd taken. Mace didn't see the need of that, but Pa said they better do it afore that Hendrix man missed them and came to claim them.

Then Pa suggested they go check on Two Feathers. They had left the crazy Indian in the barn to wallow in her misery until she decided she best get up and come cook supper. But Two Feathers wasn't in the barn. Mace remembered they'd argued a little about what happened to her.

"Recon you beat her too much and she died, Pa?"

"Nah. Old Injuns pretend to be hurt so's you'll quit hittin' them."

"She looked plum passed out to me."

"Probably got up and run away to pout as soon as we was back in the house. Don't worry about her. She'll come back in time to cook supper. She knows she'll get some more licks of my whip if she don't."

Mace wasn't sure his pa was right, but he didn't argue with him anymore. He simply said, "I'm going to see if'en I can grab one of them young'uns on the Jordon ranch like you suggested we do, Pa. I'll be back by supper."

"That's a good idee, Mace. Just be sure you can get one of em before that Hendrix man sees you. As I said afore, try to get the girl."

"I'll make sure Hendrix is nowhere around the house."

Biting off a large chew of the tobacco, Mace settled himself on the log. He figured he'd have a long wait, but he'd only been there a few minutes when that interfering Wiley Hendrix came out of the house in a hurry and went to the barn. In a matter of minutes, he rode out on his horse and headed down the road toward town.

Mace didn't bother to wonder where he was going. He didn't care. Now he felt things were going to work out just fine. He only knew this was the best chance he'd had to grab one of the Jordon children. He decided he'd wait a few more minutes to be sure the man was going to town. If that were the case, he'd have plenty of time to grab a kid. Hendrix would be gone for a while.

Mace knew he had to play it smart. When he'd left home, he'd told his paw he hoped he'd be lucky enough that Zelda would come out and it would be her he could grab, but his pa told him he couldn't get her. It had to be one of the brats. "How're we gonna blackmail them if we done got your woman?" he'd said.

Of course, Mace knew his pa was right, but he didn't like it. He wanted to get Zelda under his roof as soon as he could. He'd already seen the way she looked at that Wiley man. There was no doubt the woman had a hankering for the drifter and Mace was afraid if he didn't get her away from him, she'd never decide she wanted to be Mrs. Mace Palmer. But he wondered if it really mattered. Whenever he got her, there was no way she'd ever think of another man once they were married. He'd see to that. She was like most women. As soon as they were really loved by a man, none of the other males in this world would ever matter to them. And Mace had had dreams of loving on her for years.

But as his pa said, he guessed getting one of the young'uns was the thing to do. He hoped he'd be able to snatch the little girl. Hugh was getting older and he was smart enough to figure out that they were holding him for some reason other than to take care of him, as his mother had drilled in the boy's head they would do.

Laughing and spitting tobacco on the ground, Mace couldn't get over how stupid Glenda Jordon was. The woman actually thought he and his pa would take care of those blasted children. Of course, they'd do it only long enough to get Zelda in front of a preacher. Then he'd laugh in Glenda's face when he sent the little gal to an orphanage and his pa put that lazy Hugh to work on the ranch. He wondered how many times Pa would have to give the boy a lashing with that whip of his. "Shore didn't take me long to do what the old man said. I don't think he used it more than a dozen times on me," he muttered as he stood and walked to his horse.

He decided he'd waited long enough. Since he was sure Hendrix wasn't coming back any time soon, he wasn't going to keep sitting there and waiting for somebody else to come outside. He'd simply go on to the house and talk his way inside and they wouldn't suspect a thing. That way, he knew he'd have his choice of who he was going to kidnap.

Twenty

Zelda heard a horse in the yard and glanced out the window. "Oh, my Lord. It's Mace Palmer."

"What does he want?"

"I have no idea, Hugh, but we don't want him to come in."

"What can we do?"

"We'll try to keep him out, but in case he pushes himself in, how about making sure the Indian's door is shut."

Hugh jumped up, put the book aside and ran down the hall.

"What happen?" Pansy cried and ran to Zelda.

"It'll be all right, sweetheart." Zelda swept her up in her arms and hurried to the front door. She latched it, then hurried back to do the same on the back. She heard Mace's heavy boots hit the porch just as she turned the key in the door leading outside from the kitchen.

Pansy whimpered.

"Please don't cry, Pansy," she whispered and hugged the child to her. "Everything will be fine."

"I shut the Indian's door. Mama's, too."

"Good thinking."

The door knob rattled and Zelda saw he was trying to walk into the house. She knew she had to stop him. Handing Pansy to Hugh, and her voice still in a whisper, she said, "Will you take her and hide?"

"Maybe I should help you."

"I'd rather you and Pansy be safe. When Mace rode up, he looked like he was up to something. He may have seen Wiley leave and knows we're alone here. If he does, I don't want either of you getting hurt. Please, either hide in the bedroom or climb up to the attic. I don't think he could find you at either place."

"Come on, Pansy." Hugh took her hand, but Pansy didn't want to leave Zelda.

"Please go with Hugh, honey."

Hugh added, "If you'll come with me, we'll take your book and read some more."

This must have satisfied the child because she took her brother's hand and they paused to pick up a book, then went down the hall.

Mace pounded on the door. "Open up!" he yelled. "I know you're in there."

Zelda took a deep breath. "Who's out there?"

"It's me. Mace. Why you got this door locked, Zelda?"

"I can't let you in."

"Why not?"

She racked her brain. What could she tell him that would keep him from continuing to harass her to let him in? Then it hit her. "We're afraid you might catch it."

She could almost see the confusion on his face. "Catch what?"

She said the first thing that entered her mind. "The pox."

He was silent for a minute, then he said, "You ain't got no pox."

"You're right. I haven't...yet."

"What do you mean, yet?"

"Hugh got up this morning covered in the blisters. He must have gotten them when he was in town the other day. I heard there was a case or two in Laster."

"I don't believe you and I want to see for myself. Let me talk to Hugh."

"He's in bed with a high fever. I can't let anyone get to him. Pansy went in there earlier and now she's complaining she don't feel good. I think I see a few of those dreadful things popping out on her. I put her to bed and sent Mr. Hendrix to get the doctor."

"I don't think I'd catch them, do you?"

"You're just as likely as anyone to catch them, Mace. They tell me they're a lot harder on a man or a woman than they are a child. Grownups most always die."

She realized Mace must be considering what she said, because there was a long pause. In a minute he asked, "So, how long until I can see Hugh?"

"I'm not sure. It depends on how he handles the disease. Why do you need to see him anyway?"

"Pa and I talked it over and we decided you had too much to do. We thought we'd take one of the young'uns and keep them for a while so you wouldn't have so much work on you."

Zelda shivered. The thoughts of the Palmers getting their hands on either of the children made her feel sick to her stomach. She tried not to let her voice be too sharp when she said, "Well, I can't let you in today. Why don't you check back after the doctor sees the children? He'll surely know when it would be safe for you to come into the house."

There was another pause, then he said, "I'd shore like to get one of them today, but maybe you're right. I guess I better wait and see what the doctor says."

"That's wise of you, Mace. You don't want to catch this disease and maybe take it home to your daddy. It could easily kill an old man like him."

There was a pause, then he yelled, "You might be right, but I'll be back."

She didn't answer, then she heard him turn and his boots go down the steps. Hurrying to the window, she smiled as he mounted his horse and rode out of the yard.

Going down the hall, she opened the door to the room she shared with Pansy. "Are you in here, Hugh? If you are, you can come out now."

There was a scrambling noise and Hugh wiggled out from under the bed. Pansy followed him. She began babbling before she stood. "Hugh say we hide. It be fun."

"Well, was it fun?"

She looked at her brother and nodded. "He make me go first."

"He did."

"I thought if she went first and somebody looked under the bed, they'd see me first and maybe not even see her at all."

Zelda smiled. "I'm proud of you for thinking of your sister's safety."

"Well, Wiley said when there was danger, a man should always try to protect the woman. Pansy's not a woman, but she is a girl. I figured since she was, I should protect her as good as I could." He half grinned at Zelda. "How'd you get rid of Mace?"

"How about I tell you later."

He frowned, but when she nodded toward Pansy, he seemed to understand. "That'll be fine," he muttered.

"Zelda!" Glenda shouted.

Zelda turned around and opened the door to Glenda's bedroom. "Yes."

"Why is my door shut? You know I can't breathe well when it's shut."

"I'll leave it open now."

"I bet you were trying to make my breathing worse. You're so mean to me. I've been calling you for ages and you've been ignoring me again."

"Me and Hugh get under bed," Pansy blurted.

"You what?"

"We get under bed."

"What in the world is she talking about? What have you done to my children, Zelda? It's enough that you're mean to me, but I won't permit you to be mean to them."

"Mama," Hugh butted in. "Let Zelda take Pansy to the kitchen. I want to talk to you."

Glenda's mood changed. "Of course, darling. Go on, Zelda. Just be sure you go all the way to the kitchen. You have no business listening in on mine and Hugh's conversation."

Zelda turned, took Pansy's hand and with a smile for Hugh, she left the room.

~ * ~

"Where you been, Mace?" Elias shouted as his son came into the kitchen.

"You know I went to see if'en I could get one of them Jordon young'uns."

"Well, I don't see nary a one with you."

"Couldn't get to one today." He looked around. "I'm hungry. Where's Two Feathers?"

"That damn Injun ain't come back yet."

Mace frowned. "You don't suppose she went into the woods and died, do you?"

"I told you afore. Injuns don't die from a little whupping. They're too tough for that."

"What are we gonna eat?"

"How the hell should I know? Look in the stove and see what was left from yesterday's breakfast. She usually puts it in there, if she don't sneak and eat it herself."

Mace looked in the oven. "They's some bacon and a couple of biscuits, but they're cold. Ain't been no fire in this stove since morning."

"Then I reckon you better start one if we're going to have any coffee."

"Why can't you start one, Pa?"

"Cause I told you to do it. That's why. Besides, my ankle hurts." Elias took a seat at the table and watched as Mace began piling wood in the iron cook stove. "What happened at the Jordon place? Did that Hendrix man run you off again?"

"No. He weren't there. I saw him headed out toward town. When I was shore he weren't coming back, I went on to the ranch."

"Then why didn't you get the young'un? Looks like it would've been the prefect time."

"That's what I thought. I went to the house, but it was all locked up."

"Why in the world was it locked up?"

"I talked to Zelda through the door. She said the young'uns had the pox and she'd sent Hendrix into town to get the doctor. She wouldn't let me in."

"Why didn't you make her?"

"Pa, if them brats had the pox, we could catch them. I didn't want to take no chance. They say they'll kill a grown man before they do a child."

Elias frowned. "She was probably was lying to you. I bet ain't nobody there got no pox."

"I thought that, too, so I went back to the place where I set to spy on them and waited."

"What'd you do that for?"

"I was waiting to see if the Hendrix man come back with the doctor."

"Well, did he?"

"He shore as hell did. They was riding fast, too."

Elisa frowned again. "Maybe it was a good thing you didn't go in there. I don't want none of them old pox around here."

"That's what I thought." Mace shut the fire box and twiddled with the damper. "There. It should be hot enough to make coffee in a little while."

"Good. We'll eat what's left, then I want you to go out and see if you can find that crazy Injun. I may give her a few more licks with my whip for staying away so long. She shore deserves it."

"Don't do that, Pa."

"Why not?"

"Cause she might run off again and I don't look forward to us having to do the cooking."

"Maybe them pox won't last long and you can get that young'un. Then it won't be long until we swap her for Zelda. I bet that woman

can do some real cooking around here. I'm looking forward to that."
He chuckled. "Be kind of nice to see her pretty little behind twisting
around in here, too."

Mace glared at his father. "Now, Pa. I told you not to get no ideas
about Zelda. She's gonna be mine. Not yours."

"We'll see, Mace. We'll see." Elias stood. "I see Dub headin' into
the barn. He's probably through for the day. I guess I'll go tell him that
we ain't got no supper and he might as well fix his-self something to
eat or head into town and eat at the saloon. Ain't gonna be no cooking
around here today unless that crazy Injun shows up in the next little
bit."

"I figure if she was coming back tonight, she'd be here."

"For once I bet you're right."

Mace shook his head, but said nothing else. He wanted to tell his
Pa that he shouldn't have hit the old woman so hard, but he didn't
dare. He knew Elias well enough that the man wouldn't hesitate to
take the whip to him. It didn't matter that he was his son or that he
was a grown man. Pa had certainly done it many times in the past and
he wouldn't hesitate to do it again.

Twenty-one

Zelda was stirring in a pot when Hugh walked into the kitchen. "Mama went back to sleep."

Zelda nodded. "She's sleeping a lot now."

Hugh glanced at Pansy, who was busy squeezing biscuit dough through her fingers. "Is it because of her illness, Zelda?"

"Yes, Hugh, I believe it is. She's getting weaker."

He bit his lip. "I guess I shouldn't argue with her, but sometimes she upsets me."

Zelda smiled at him. "Sometimes it's hard to control ourselves when we're angry, but we need to try."

"You always seem to be in control of yourself."

Zelda smiled. "Maybe on the outside, but inside I sometimes want to throw up my hands and scream."

"Want make biscuit, Hugh?" Pansy looked at him.

He shook his head. "I'll just watch you."

She nodded and put her hands back in the bowl.

"Can you tell me now, what Mace wanted?"

"I can give you some hints." She turned the slabs of pork she was frying. "He wanted to take one of you children home with him."

"Why in the world would he want to do that?"

"I don't know and what he said didn't make sense. He kept saying I had to work too hard around here and he and his pa wanted to relieve me of some of the work." She shook her head. "I got the feeling there was another reason, though."

"What reason could it be?"

"That's it, Hugh. I have no idea what he had on his mind. He just kept saying he'd take one of you children to his ranch."

"Which one of us did he want?"

"At first, I thought he was talking about you, then he said he wanted one of you. It didn't seem to matter which one." She turned and looked at him. "You know, I'd never allow him to take either of you away from here, don't you?"

"Why wouldn't you want him to take me?"

Zelda smiled at him. "Hugh, I know we've been at odds with each other ever since my papa died, but I still wouldn't want you to be in the hands of a man like Mace Palmer or his father. I've heard the old man has a fierce temper and will use his whip on somebody without giving it a second thought."

"Do you believe he'd really use his whip on somebody?"

"All I have to do is look at that poor Indian woman in your bedroom and I know it's true. She certainly didn't whip herself."

"No. She couldn't have done that."

The sound of horses came through the window. She glanced outside. "That's Wiley and the doctor. Will you unlock the backdoor, Hugh?"

"Yep." He stood and opened the door for the men. "Come on, Doctor Abernathy. I'll take you to the Indian."

"Thank you, Hugh."

The two of them went down the hall and Wiley looked at Zelda with a raised eyebrow.

"I'll tell you about it later."

"Then I guess I'll have to wait." He turned to Pansy. "And how's my pretty girl?"

She plopped the biscuit dough she'd been rolling around in her hand back into the pan and held out her arms. "Take me, Wiwey."

"Let me wash that dough off your hands and I'll be happy to take you." He took the wet cloth Zelda handed him and cleaned, not only Pansy's hands, but her arms and the front of her dress.

Tossing the rag back into the pan of water on the sideboard, he held out his arms and she jumped into them. "Shall we sit here at the table and watch Zelda work?"

She nodded and giggled. "I tell you 'bout bed."

Wiley laughed. "Are you sleepy?"

"No." She giggled. "Hugh make me get under bed."

Wiley frowned and looked at Zelda. "What's she talking about?"

Zelda smiled at him. "Just listen. She'll explain it to you. I'll fill in when I need to."

Looking confused, Wiley said, "All right, Pansy. Tell me about Hugh making you get under the bed."

"Man come. Zewie say hide. Hugh make me get under bed first. He get there, too."

"What man come?"

"Don't know." She yawned.

Zelda interjected. "It was Mace Palmer. I locked the doors and wouldn't let him in, but in case he overpowered me, I had the children hide."

"What in ...uh... the world did he want?"

"Zewie say he want me and Hugh."

"I'll have to give you more details later, but I kept him outside by telling him you'd gone to get the doctor because the children had the pox. I finally convinced him that he might catch them. I guess he believed me because he left."

Hugh came back into the kitchen. "Zelda, the doctor wants you to go in there."

"I need to watch supper."

"No, you don't," Wiley said. "Hugh and I'll take care of things in here. You go see what the doctor wants."

~ * ~

When they were alone, Wiley said, "I'm proud of you, Hugh."

Hugh looked confused. "Why?"

"Zelda told me how you protected Pansy."

Hugh looked a little embarrassed and grinned. "Well, you told me a man should always protect the women. I figured that meant little girls, too."

"You're right about that. It does mean little girls, too."

"Hugh read."

Wiley cocked an eyebrow. "He did?"

"Not under bed. By fireplace."

"I see."

"It dark under bed. He not read."

"I guess it would be too dark to read there." Wiley looked at Hugh. "I knew you had it in you to be a nice guy. Thanks for proving me right."

There was silence for a few minutes, then Hugh asked, "I wonder why Mace Palmer wanted me or Pansy?"

"That's something I'm going to find out."

Before they could talk anymore, Glenda yelled, "Zelda."

When Wiley started to get up, Hugh said, "I'll go. It upsets her too much to see you and I think we need to keep her pacified until the Indian is gone."

"Doesn't she know?"

"No. I didn't think there was any reason to tell her."

"Smart move."

"Zelda!"

Wiley watched Hugh walk from the room. Again, he couldn't help the feeling of pride that he felt. The boy was going to be all right. Oh, he realized there would probably be backsets, but for the time being, Hugh seemed to be taking his rightful place in the family.

~ * ~

"What do you want, Mama?"

"Oh, Hugh, darling. I'm delighted to see you, but where is Zelda?"

"She'll be here in a little while. I wanted to talk to you, so I came when you called her."

"How sweet. You know I'd rather talk to you than anybody. You're the one person in this house who will tell me the truth about what's going on."

"I try to tell you the truth, Mama."

Glenda sighed. "I seem to keep hearing voices. Is there someone here visiting Zelda?"

"I guess you heard Wiley."

"Oh, heaven help us. If we don't get rid of that man, he's going to mess up everything I have planned." When Hugh didn't say anything, she went on. "You have to help me, Hugh, because we can't let that happen."

"What can I do to help?"

"I think he's some kind of outlaw. I'm sure he's only hanging around here to see what he can steal from us. He may even be planning to kill us all."

"I don't believe Wiley would hurt any of us."

"You're wrong, Hugh. He's an evil man."

Hugh didn't know what to say. There were times he also wondered why a man like Wiley was hanging around. He didn't seem to need the job and he didn't really know any of them. People usually had a reason to do the things they did. Was there some way Wiley could have him fooled. Though he didn't think Wiley was a deceitful person, he knew he had to calm his mother down. He sighed and said, "I'll watch him and see what I can find out. If he's an outlaw, he'll slip up somewhere and give himself away."

"That's good thinking, son. I knew you were a smart boy."

"Thank you, Mama." He stood.

"Wait, Hugh. There's one more thing I want to discuss with you."

"He sat. "What is it?"

"I think I need a gun."

Hugh frowned. "Why would you need a gun, Mama?"

She reached for his hand. "Can you keep a secret, Hugh?"

"Sure."

She squeezed his hand. "I'm going to trust you not to tell anyone what I'm about to tell you. Not Mace nor his father. Not Zelda nor that Wiley person. Not even Pansy."

Hugh laughed. "I won't tell a living person, Mama. Not even Pansy. If you want me to promise, I won't even tell a dead one."

"We'll not worry about a dead one. She smiled at him, then changed to a serious look. "I need the gun because I'm afraid."

"What are you afraid of?"

"I haven't told anyone this, more than one time I've seen a man looking in my window at night."

"Who was it, Mama?"

"He looked like ..."

"Don't say Wiley. I know he wouldn't do that."

She bit her lip. "What I was going to say is that the man looked like a wild savage. Besides, the first time it happened before Hendrix showed up."

"Why hadn't you told somebody about that, Mama?"

"I mentioned it to Zelda, but she said I must have been dreaming. I didn't tell her about the other times, but I'd feel so much safer if I had a gun to protect myself if it happens again."

Hugh nodded. "I understand, Mama. Where do I look for a gun?"

"I'm not sure. Check the drawers in the room where Zelda sleeps. Also look in the pantry. I know John had several guns when he was alive and unless Zelda has sold them or got rid of them for any other reason, they still have to be around here somewhere."

"Zelda keeps the rifle in the kitchen behind the pantry door, but the only time I've seen her use it was the day she shot at Mace. I haven't seen any pistols."

"Just keep looking and I'm sure you'll find one."

Hugh heard the rustle of Zelda's skirts and knew she was leaving the room where the Indian was. He stood. "Why don't I go get you something to drink, Mama?"

"That would be wonderful, darling." She frowned. "I hear a man talking again."

"It's just me, Glenda." The doctor stuck his head in the door. "I was out this way and thought I'd stop by. How are you feeling?"

"Oh, Uley. It's good to see you. Come have a seat and talk with me."

"I plan to do just that."

"I was going to get Mama something to drink. Do you want some coffee or something, Doctor?"

"No, thank you, Hugh. I'll just visit with your mama for a bit."

"You can bring me something to drink, later, sweetheart. Right now, I'll just have a talk with the doctor."

Hugh nodded and left the room. As he always was after a visit with Glenda, he felt confused. He didn't believe her when she said Wiley was a bad man, but he did believe somebody had looked in her window and she needed a way to protect herself. He knew he'd try to find his mother a gun without telling anyone because she wouldn't use it unless somebody did try to get in her window. He just wondered where he should start to look for one.

Twenty-two

Wiley lay in his bedroll in the loft of the barn with his hands behind his head. He couldn't help being a little frustrated. He'd wanted to get Zelda alone and explain to her that she didn't have to worry about Glenda selling or giving the ranch to the Palmers, but he hadn't had a chance to talk with her alone. Finding the Indian woman, then having to fetch the doctor and last, the unexpected visit from Mace Palmer, had thrown the whole evening out of kilter.

He thought he'd be able to get her to the side and talk with her after supper, but it didn't happen. The Indian regained consciousness and told them the Palmers planned to kidnap one of the children and hold him or her until Zelda agreed to marry Mace. Of course, this upset Zelda so much that she was in a tizzy the rest of the night. She said they not only had to keep this information away from the children, but nobody was to mention it to Glenda either. Especially after the doctor said Glenda was getting worse and he feared the end was near for her.

Now, he wondered if it wouldn't be better to let Glenda know he knew about the will and that there was nothing she could do with the ranch, even if she did sign a paper to the Palmers. It would easily be disputed in court.

Or would it be better to drop the whole thing for a while and let things settle down? As long as he was there, he knew he wasn't going to let anything happen to any of the Jordon household. He had to smile when he realized that meant Glenda as well as the rest of them. The woman might hate him, but for some reason, though he wanted to shake her until she came to her senses sometimes, he felt a little sorry for her.

He knew it was getting late and he needed to go to sleep, but there were times when there was so much on his mind that sleep didn't come easily. Tonight was turning out to be one of those nights. Not only was he thinking about all that had happened today, but he couldn't forget the way Zelda turned to him and cried against his chest when the Indian woman told them what was going on at the Palmer household.

He'd like to think it didn't affect him, but it did. It affected him a lot. It felt wonderful to have his arms around her and to hold her close to him and smell the faint order of wildflowers. He guessed it came from the soap she'd used to bathe and wash her raven hair. Whatever, it was nice and he didn't want to let her go when she backed away, blushed and mumbled, 'Sorry.'

He'd only smiled and nodded at her because he didn't know what else to say or do.

It had been a while since Wiley had held a good woman in his arms. His wife, Janet, had been dead almost two years and Camilla, the woman who was visiting her uncle on Blake Cantrell's ranch, made it clear to him the only man she was interested in was Blake. Though he'd never really held Camilla, he had tried once to let her know he cared. It was then he realized he didn't have a chance and he'd been right. Camilla and Blake were happily married and from what he'd noticed when he'd left the ranch, they were expecting a baby soon.

He'd stopped at a few saloons on his way to Waco, but he knew the women he'd met there would never be anything except a night to fulfill his loneliness. Tonight, he realized how lonely he really was. Wiley liked being married. He liked having a woman in the house. He liked to come in and see her at the stove when he finished his daily chores. He liked sitting by the fire or on the porch with her and talking about everything and about nothing. He liked holding her close to him in the bed at night and then sharing the love they had for each other. He wanted that again, and though he'd tried not to admit it to himself, he wanted it with Zelda.

This thought pleased him and he closed his eyes. Now that he'd finally settled his feelings for the woman in his mind, he relaxed. Maybe sleep would come now.

But a sudden noise in the yard jerked his eyes opened. He jumped up and ran to the window in the loft. There was a figure of a man sneaking up to the house. He jabbed his feet into his boots and grabbed his gun. Being as quiet as he could, he climbed down the loft ladder and headed across the yard.

The man was standing on tiptoes and trying to look into a window when Wiley jammed the pistol in his back. "What the hell do you think you're doing?"

The man raised his hands. "Didn't mean no harm, mister."

Though Wiley had thought the man was Mace Palmer, he knew by his voice that he wasn't. "Then why are you at this window?"

"Trying to see if Two Feathers is here."

"Who?"

"Two Feathers. The Indian woman from the Palmer ranch."

"Who wants to know about this Indian woman?"

"Me. I'm Dub Veach."

"Turn around than lower your hands." Wiley knew he'd seen this man on the Palmer ranch when he'd been out on the range. "Why are you looking here for Two Feathers?"

"After I realized she'd managed to get out of the barn and leave the place, I started tracking her. She'd left some spots of blood and there were several places where she drug her feet a lot."

Wiley frowned. "How could you track her at night?"

"I didn't. I started out while it was still light, but I stopped back there in the woods and waited until I thought everybody here was settled in for the night. I didn't mean no harm. I just wanted to make sure Two Feathers was all right."

"How do I know you aren't trying to find out about her just so you can report back to the Palmers?"

"I wouldn't tell them damn fools a thing."

Wiley lifted an eyebrow. "But you work for them, don't you?"

"I do, but it ain't because I like them. It's cause it's hard for a man like me to find a job."

"What do you mean, a man like you?"

"Mister, if it was daylight you'd see what I mean. I ain't all white and I ain't all Indian. I looked everywhere for work, but the Palmers were the only ranchers who'd give me a job."

Wiley nodded toward the barn. "We need to get out from under this window before we wake someone up. Let's walk over to the barn and you can explain things so they'll be a little clearer to me."

As they walked away, Dub said, "I don't know if I should."

"Should what?"

"Talk to you."

"You'd better talk to me or you're going to find yourself on the way into town to have a talk with the sheriff."

"Elias told me to stay away from you because you ... well, he said you wouldn't mind shooting me just for target practice. That's why I waited till dark to try to find Two Feathers."

"Regardless of what Elias Palmer says, I don't shoot people for no reason. On the other hand, when I see somebody sneaking around as if he means harm to somebody in the Jordon family, it becomes another matter."

"I swear I don't mean nobody no harm. As I told you, I'm trying to find Two Feathers."

"And why are you so interested in Two Feathers?"

"She tells me some of what's going on in the Palmer house. Like when they're in a bad mood or something and I kind of look out for her cause she's getting older and I feel like I owe her. Shore ain't nobody else on the place gonna do no looking out for her."

"Then why didn't you stop him from beating her nearly to death?"

Dub's voice was angry when he answered. "Cause I didn't know what'd happened till I come in. Mace told me to get my own supper cause there wouldn't be none from Two Feathers. I didn't think nothing about it till I went in the barn and saw the blood on the floor. That told me why Two Feathers weren't cooking."

"So you tracked her to this place?"

"That's right. I wanted to make sure she hadn't crawled off somewhere and died."

Wiley had heard enough to make him think the man was telling the truth. He took a breath. "Set your mind to rest, Dub. It's going to take a while, but Two Feathers is going to be fine. I brought the doctor to see her and he said there were no broken bones, but there were a lot of cuts and bruises. It looked as if she'd been whipped."

"The bastard used his whip on her."

"That's what we figured."

"Didn't she tell you why he whipped her?"

"She was only awake for a few minutes and all she would say was for us to keep the children away from the Palmers. She implied that they planned to kidnap one of them."

"I don't know nothing about that, but I don't doubt it. Those two are as mean as they come."

"I gathered that." Wiley stretched. "It's getting late and as you can see there's no lamp lit in the house. I'm not going to bother them tonight, but why don't you come back tomorrow? I'm sure Miss Jordon will let you see Two Feathers then."

"Then I'll come back." Dub turned and walked across the yard.

Wiley watched him until he entered the woods at the backside of Zelda's garden. He then went back into the barn and climbed the ladder to his loft. He didn't know why, but the conversation with the man had made him tired. He was asleep almost as soon as he was back in his bedroll.

~ * ~

When Dub was deep enough in the woods that he knew he couldn't be seen from the barn or anywhere else on the Jordon ranch, he untied his horse from the small bush in the group of shrubs where he'd tethered him, removed the saddle, gave him some oats from the small sack around his saddle horn, poured some water from his canteen into his hat and let the animal drink. He then hobbled him for the night, spread his bedroll on the ground and settled in to sleep for a while.

He had no intention of leaving the Jordon ranch until he saw for himself that Two Feathers was all right. He half way believed Wiley Hendrix, but he'd learned a long time ago that you couldn't fully trust any white man. Not even your father.

He lay on his bed and remembered the time when he was seven years old. It was the day his father knocked his mother across the teepee and grabbed his arm. "Come on boy, we're gettin out of here. I'm tired of these redskins and I'm going back to the white world and you're going with me. I won't have my son raised by these heathens."

Instead, for almost ten years, his father dragged him from one town to another. From one saloon to another and the only people he was allowed associate with were the dregs of society. There were many times he'd vowed to get away from the man and find his mother and her people. And eventually he did return to their camp.

When he arrived at the place where he'd spent his childhood, he learned that most of the tribe had died from a fever that swept through the camp shortly after he left. The ones who survived had moved to other areas and joined other people. Nobody could tell him what had happened to his mother.

Discouraged and disappointed, he almost gave in and turned to liquor and loose women, just has his father had, but one event stopped him. It happened the day he'd left a bordello, broke and half sick. All he had on his mind was finding a job on one of the surrounding ranches to work long enough to have the money for another bottle and a night with one of the available women. Then he saw a young boy sitting under a tree with a book in his hand. He stopped to talk when he realized the boy had Indian blood in him.

Though he was much younger, Dub and Roddy became instant friends and Roddy insisted that Dub come to his house for supper. There he met the parents. A hardworking white man and a beautiful yellow-headed woman. He learned these good people had taken Roddy in when his mother died in childbirth. They loved the child and treated him as their own. For a few months Dub lived with this family. He helped the man in the fields, around the barn and even helped the woman in her garden. Roddy took the time to begin teaching Dub how to read. He was happy he'd mastered enough words to read simple things and especially proud of the fact that he'd learned to write his name.

Dub thought he'd found a home. He liked these people and they seemed to like him. But it wasn't to be. On a warm Tuesday evening, just as the woman came out on the porch to call them to supper, a group of marauders came riding into the yard, yelling and demanding food and money.

One jumped from his horse and ran up to the porch, grabbed the woman around the waist and yelled, "Look what I found, boys. We're sure gonna have a good time today."

The farmer ran from the barn with his rifle in the air. He didn't get a chance to pull the trigger because one of the gang shot him in the shoulder. Another shot him in the stomach and a third one blew half the man's head off.

Dub ran for the gun the farmer had dropped, but he didn't make it. He fell as a horse bumped him to the ground and a searing pain ripped through him as bullet went into his back. He heard one of them say, "Just make sure he's out. Ain't no need to kill him. When they find them and he's alive, he'll be blamed for it. Nobody'll believe a half-breed, even if he is telling the truth." He then heard nothing and only saw blackness.

When he came to, despite the pain, Dub managed to sit up. The scene around him made him want to throw up, but he managed to keep from it. He stumbled to Roddy. Though he'd hoped there was a chance of life, there wasn't. His friend was dead. So was his father. Moving to the porch, Dub looked at the woman. Her clothes had been torn off her and blood was all around her neck and head and in her yellow hair. Her throat had been sliced.

Dub turned to the edge of the porch and retched until he could retch no more. He then went into the house and found enough bandages to tie up his shoulder. He realized the bullet had gone through and exited his body. He was relieved. He didn't have to worry about infection. Going into the room he shared with Roddy, he got his meager belongings, tied them in a bundle, stuffed them in a pillow case and headed to the kitchen. Here he found a few dollars the robbers had dropped. He felt bad about doing it, but knew it would do the family no good now. He stuffed them in his pocket. He took a few supplies from the pantry and in doing so, he saw a baking powder can tucked behind the basket of potatoes. He'd often heard the man tease his wife about stashing money away in a baking powder can. He opened it and there was more money. Again, he felt bad about taking it, but somehow, he knew the woman would want him to have it. He stuffed the few bills and the change in his pocket and left the house.

After saddling his horse, he mounted and rode to the edge of the yard. Pausing, he turned and looked back at the only place he'd been happy since he'd spent his early childhood in the teepee with his mother. Though he wasn't a religious man, he hoped they were now in a better place. Wishing them farewell in his thoughts, he turned and without looking back again, he headed west. He didn't know where he was going. He didn't care. His heart was breaking and uncontrollable tears rolled down his cheeks, but he kept riding.

Dub turned over and didn't want to remember any more. He willed the thoughts away and soon fell into a light sleep.

Twenty-three

Zelda heard a noise in the room where the Indian woman slept. Easing out of bed, she lit a lamp and carried it into the room. The woman was trying to get out of bed. She sat the lamp on a table and rushed to the bed. She put her hand on the woman's shoulder. "You've been hurt, Two Feathers, and you shouldn't get up. If you need something, I'll get it for you."

The woman's black eyes stared at Zelda for a moment. Then, without speaking, she lay back on the bed.

Zelda smiled. "There. That's better. Now, was there something you wanted?"

After staring for a moment, Two Feathers asked, "How do you know what I'm called?"

"When we brought you into the house, my stepbrother told me your name. He also said you worked for the Palmers."

"What are you called?"

"I'm Zelda Jordon."

"The one Mace Palmer wants to marry?"

"There's no way in the world I'd ever marry Mace Palmer. I've told him this several times, but he continues to harass me about it." Zelda couldn't help wondering if the woman had some reason for asking this question.

"He said you didn't like him."

"He's right about that. I can't stand the man and please don't think I'd ever marry him."

Two Feathers nodded. "I need to get water."

"Is that why you were trying to get out of bed?"

"Yes."

"Stay here and I'll be right back. I'll bring you some water."

Zelda hurried out of the room. She walked softly across the parlor so she wouldn't waken Hugh, who was asleep on the sofa. Thinking Two Feathers might be hungry, she added a slice of the apple pie she'd made for supper on the tray where she'd placed a tall glass of water.

Coming back into the bedroom, she placed the tray on the table beside the bed. "I know you probably haven't eaten in a while. I brought you a slice of pie in case you're hungry."

When Two Feathers nodded, Zelda placed a towel across the woman's knees, then handed her the water and the pie.

Zelda pulled a chair up beside the bed and sat. "We've all been concerned about you and wanted to find out why someone would beat you in such a horrible manner. Do you feel like telling me what happened to you?"

"He used his whip on me."

"The doctor said it looked like you'd been beaten with a whip."

"The doctor?"

"Yes. You were in bad shape when we found you. Wiley Hendrix went for the doctor and he came to treat you. He said he was shocked no bones were broken."

"Then I can go back."

Zelda was shocked at those words. "Surely you wouldn't go back to the Palmer place. That evil man might kill you next time."

"I have to see Dub."

"Who's Dub?"

"He works there. He needs to know what happened to me."

"If you insist he know, we'll get word to him."

After a moment, Two Feathers looked directly into Zelda's eyes. "I have to go back. I have nowhere else to go."

"For the time being, you're going to stay right here. I'm not trying to boss you around, but I don't want you to go anywhere until you're well again."

Again, there was a pause. Then Two Feathers said, "You are a good woman."

Zelda smiled. "I try to be, but there are times I fail miserably."

"I have not trusted a white person in a long time, but I think I can I trust you. I am going to tell you what the Palmers plan to do to you and the other people who live here."

Zelda was stunned at these words, but she nodded and whispered, "Please do."

~ * ~

Zelda turned from the stove when there was a knock on the back door. Moving close to it she asked, "Who is it?"

"It's me, Zelda."

She unlocked it and held it open for him.

He gave her a strange look. "Why in the world do you have the door locked?"

She glanced at the couch to make sure Hugh was still asleep. "I had a long talk with Two Feathers last night. She told me the Palmers plan to kidnap one of the children any way they could. Even if they had to slip in and snatch one of them out of their bed during the night."

"What in the world?"

Hugh stirred and she leaned closer to Wiley. "I hear Hugh waking up. I'll explain in more detail later. Now, come have some coffee. It's ready."

Hugh came into the kitchen. "Boy, that old couch don't sleep too good."

"Maybe you should get your bedroll and sleep in the barn with me tonight."

Hugh's eyes lit up. "I'll do that. I bet the hay will sleep better."

"I don't know…"

"He'd be safe with me, Zelda."

"Sure I would. Can I have some coffee?"

Zelda thought he was too young to drink coffee, but when Wiley gave her a quick nod, she poured Hugh a cup. "Do you want milk in it?"

Hugh looked into Wiley's cup. "No. I'll take it black like Wiley."

"Is Pansy still asleep?" Wiley asked.

"She is. She was a little restless last night, so I hope she sleeps late this morning."

A knock at the door interrupted.

"I'll see who it is." Wiley stood and opened the door.

Dub stood on the other side. "I saw you leave the barn and figured it was all right to come see Two Feathers now."

Zelda walked up behind Wiley. "Two Feathers is still asleep, Dub. But please come in and have a cup of coffee."

"I don't know if I should."

"If Miss Zelda invites you in, there is no reason not to come on in, Dub."

He came through the door with his hat in his hand, but looked as if he might turn and run at any moment.

"Two Feathers told me about you last night, Dub. She said you looked after each other at the Palmer place."

"Yes, ma'am. I just wish I had been at the ranch when that devil started whipping on Two Feathers. I would've stopped him."

"I wish you had been there, too." Zelda handed him a cup of coffee and turned back to the stove. "Have you eaten?"

"No, ma'am."

"I'm sure Dub spent the night in the woods beyond your garden, Zelda." Wiley went on to explain about Dub trying to see if Two Feathers was in the house after everyone had gone to bed.

"Since you've met Wiley, I'm sure he told you the doctor has seen Two Feathers."

"Yes, ma'am." He took a swallow of coffee. "Did she tell you why they beat her?"

"Yes. She found a penny on the floor in his room when she was cleaning. He came in as she picked it up and accused her of plundering in his room to see what she could steal."

"Two Feathers wouldn't steal from him."

"She told me she would occasionally find loose coins on the floor or in the yard and would keep these, but she would never search for money to steal. I believe her."

"You can because she told you the truth."

Wiley stood. "I'm going to go do the milking for you, Zelda. I want you to stay in the house."

Hugh spoke for the first time. "Can I help?"

Wiley shook his head. "No, Hugh. I want you to stay in here with Zelda. She has something to tell you."

Zelda was surprised at his words. "I do?"

"Yes, Zelda. Hugh is old enough to understand what's going on. I think you should tell him everything Two Feathers told you." When she looked as if she might argue, he added, "He'll also be more able to protect Pansy and himself if he knows what's going on."

"If you're sure."

"I am."

Dub stood too. "I might as well help you while I wait for Two Feathers to wake up."

As the two men went out the door, Hugh looked at Zelda. "What are you going to tell me?"

~ * ~

It was hard for Hugh to believe what Zelda told him. It was opposite of what his mama had said. One of them was lying and he decided it had to be Zelda. His mother wouldn't lie to him. Though he listened to Zelda, he didn't argue with her. He waited until she went to take food to Two Feathers, then he slipped into the pantry and searched until he found a gun. He hid it under his shirt and hurried to his mother's room, knowing he'd wake her if he had to. But he found her waking up.

"Here, Mama." He slipped the gun from his shirt and handed it to her. "You better put it under the covers if you don't want anybody to know you have it."

"Oh, Hugh. Thank you." She slid it under the edge of the mattress. "It's the day Zelda will change the sheets, so I better put it here where she won't see it. I put it far enough back that she won't notice when she lifts the mattress to tuck the sheet in."

"I only found one bullet, but I'll look for some more later."

She nodded. "You're such a good boy."

"I need to talk to you about something before Zelda brings your breakfast."

"Sure, son. What is it?"

He told her what Zelda had said, though he knew it would upset her. It did, but when she calmed down, they discussed what they could do about it. Afterward, he knew what he had to do.

When Dub and Wiley were in the room talking to Two Feathers, and Zelda was helping his mother with a bath and Pansy was sitting in the corner beside the fireplace playing with her doll, he knew it was time to act.

"Stay right there until Zelda comes back, Pansy," he said in a soft voice.

Pansy nodded and he smiled at her. He then slipped out the back door, ran to the barn, put the harness on the plow horse and walked her outside. He only mounted when he was behind the barn and out of sight of the house. When he felt safe to do so, he slapped her with the reins and went as fast as he could get her to go in the direction of the Palmer ranch.

When he approached the ranch house, Mace came out onto the front porch and waited.

Hugh stopped at the hitching post and threw the reins around it. Climbing down he started up the steps.

"Hey, Pa!" Mace shouted. "You ain't gonna believe who just come visiting."

"Who?" A deep voice came from inside. Then the door opened and Elias came outside.

A big frown crossed his face. "Have you got them pox, boy?"

"I don't know what you're talking about."

Elis looked at Mace. "I told you that Zelda was lying to you."

Hugh looked up at them. "I got some questions to ask you."

"Well, come on in the house and ask yer questions," Elias said. "We might have a few for you, too."

Mace grinned from ear to ear. "Weren't it neighborly of Hugh to show up like this? Now I won't have to worry about trying to get him."

"Shut up, Mace," Elias bellowed.

Hugh had the sudden feeling that maybe he'd done the wrong thing by slipping out here because his mama told him to. She said he needed to see that Mace and his father were not as evil as Zelda said they were. At this moment, he had the urge to turn around, climb on his horse and hurry back home. But it was too late to think of such a thing.

Elias grabbed him by the shoulder, shoved him through the door and into the house.

~ * ~

After finishing Glenda's bath, Zelda rolled her on one side and changed the bed in that area. She then rolled her onto the side with the clean sheet and pulled the sheet to cover the rest of the bed. "Now that we have you all cleaned up, would you like some coffee or tea before you relax and take your nap?"

"I need something to relax. You couldn't have been rougher with me if you'd tried."

Zelda bit her lip and headed out of the room. She knew it didn't matter what she did for her stepmother, it would never be enough to please the woman.

In the parlor, she looked around and frowned. She'd told Hugh to stay in here and watch Pansy until she finished his mother's bath, then he could visit with her if he wanted to.

Trying not show the panic she felt, Zelda looked at Pansy. "Where's Hugh, honey?"

"Go outside."

"Oh, no." Zelda ran to the back door and opened it. "Hugh! Where are you?"

There was no answer.

She started to run outside to search for the boy, but thought better of it. If she went out, Pansy would follow her. She turned and ran down the hall. Without knocking, she opened the door to the room where Dub and Wiley were talking with Two Feathers. She couldn't keep the panic out of her voice when she said, "Wiley, Hugh has slipped outside and I have no idea where he is."

Wiley jumped up and came out of the room. "I'll go check."

Dub followed and the two men went out the back door on the run.

"What's going on out there?" Glenda yelled. "And who is that strange man with Wiley? Have you brought another outlaw to my ranch, Zelda?"

Pansy came running down the hall. "I scared, Zewie."

"Come here, honey." She swooped the child up in her arms. "Everything will be fine."

"Zelda, get in here!"

Zelda started to Glenda's room, but Wiley came back into the house and met her in the hall. "Hugh took the old horse. I'm not afraid to bet he's headed to the Palmer place."

"Why in the world would he go there?"

Glenda yelled again, "I said get in here, Zelda."

Wiley followed Zelda to her door. "Do you know where Hugh would have gone, Glenda?"

She gave him a snide look. "Maybe I do and maybe I don't."

Wiley turned to Zelda. "I don't have time to fool with her. I don't think God Himself could convince her that she's probably killed her boy."

"Oh, no." Fear flooded Zelda's face.

"I've got to go. Dub should be through saddling my horse by now." On an impulse, he leaned down and kissed her cheek. "Don't worry. I'll bring Hugh back."

"What is that fool man going to do? I'm sure Hugh is fine. He's gone to take a message to Mace for me. Nothing could happen to him there."

Zelda stared at her for a few seconds and then before she could stop herself, she said, "Glenda, you're the biggest fool I've ever seen. You've let your hate for me control everything you do even to the point of sacrificing the son you profess to love." When she saw Glenda start to interrupt, she went on, "Don't say another word to me. I'm too worried about Hugh to listen to your crazy rants. Instead of spewing your venom, you need to say a prayer that Wiley gets to Hugh in time. It's no telling what those evil Palmers will do to him."

"How dare you talk to me..."

Zelda interrupted her sentence by walking out of the room and slamming the door behind her.

Twenty-four

Elias's eyes grew dark. "So, you say Two Feathers is at your ranch?"

"Yes, sir. She came up all bloody and hurting and Zelda had Wiley put her in my bed."

"Well, at least we know where she is now. I was going to send Dub to look for her whenever he shows up this morning."

Mace said, "He probably spent his night getting drunk at the saloon. I figure he's like all half-breeds. He likes the bottle."

Hugh started to tell them that Dub was at their ranch, but Mace spoke before he could say anything.

"What you going to do about Two Feathers when she shows back up, Pa?"

"As soon as I get my hands on her, I'm going to kill her, that's what. Ain't no bloody redskin squaw gonna get away with trying to rob me then running away because I give her a few licks for it."

Hugh's eyes got big. "Would you really kill her?"

"Shore I would. She ain't nothing but an old Injun squaw. Nobody'd miss her."

Mace looked at Hugh and kind of smiled. "Forget about the old Indian. Maybe you can help us out around here."

Though he wasn't sure what was going on, Hugh managed to ask, "What do you want me to do?"

"Can you cook?"

"No."

Elias laughed. "If I give him a lick or two with my whip he might be willing to fry us up somethin' that's fit to eat."

Hugh had felt uneasy since he'd arrived at the ranch. Now he was beginning to feel scared. He stood. "I think I should go home. Mama will be worried about me."

"Set down and shut up, Hugh. You ain't going nowhere." Mace pointed a finger at him.

"But I want to leave."

Mace got up, knocking his chair over. He grabbed Hugh's arm and slung the boy backward toward the chair he'd been sitting in earlier. Hugh missed the chair and landed on the floor. "I said, set down and shut up."

Hugh couldn't help it. A tear slid down his cheek and soon he was openly crying. He didn't try to get up because he was afraid Mace would hit him again.

Mace laughed. "Look at that, Pa. The baby is going to cry. Does he think that'll make us let him go home?"

"Please. I want to go home," Hugh said through his tears.

Without warning, Mace backhanded him across the face. "If you don't stop that blubbering, I'm going to take you to the barn and let Pa give you a few licks with his whip. He knows how to make a crying boy shut up. He done it to me plenty of times."

"No. Please don't whip me."

"We ain't got time to take you to the barn now, boy. That will have to be put off till later. Right now, we gotta get a letter wrote to your mama afore that Wiley man comes over here with his gun." Elias looked away from Hugh and toward Mace. "Get some paper."

"What'll you do if he gets here before we get the letter wrote, Pa?"

"I'll be watching with my shotgun. Blow him right out of his saddle, that's what."

Quivering, but holding back the tears, Hugh swallowed. He couldn't believe his mother could have been so wrong about two men as she had been about Mace and his father. Why did he listen to her? Wiley and Zelda had been right all along. These men didn't mind killing people. They were really mean. Now what was he going to do? He felt he had to get away from them somehow. But how? If he tried to get out now, they might decide they did have time to use the whip on him.

"Here's the paper, Pa. What should I say?"

"First write it to that stupid Glenda." The old man chuckled. "Of course, don't put stupid in there. Then tell her that we've got the boy and if Zelda don't come over to our ranch with the preacher by dark today, we're going to kill him."

Hugh grew terrified. "Are you going to really kill me?"

Elias looked at him and grinned. "We might and we might not. I've been thinking I want to get rid of that half-breed that works here. Once I get you trained, I may just let him go and you can do his work."

Hugh swallowed and didn't say anything else. He was just glad he hadn't told them Dub was at their ranch. It might make things worse if they knew. They'd probably plan to kill him, just like they planned to kill Two Feathers and everybody else they'd mentioned.

Mace licked the end of a stubby pencil and bent over the table to write. Nobody said anything until he raised up and said, "How does this sound, Pa?"

"Let me have it. I'll read it myself." He grabbed the paper from Mace's hand and began to read aloud. "*Glenda, we got Hugh at our ranch. If you want to see him alive again you make sure Zelda shows up at our ranch with the preacer by supper time. When me and her is maried, we will let the boy come home.*" Elias nodded. "Sounds good to me. I don't think no words is spelt wrong nor nothing. Now fold it up and put it in..."

"I hear a horse coming, Pa." Mace jumped up and looked out the window. His face grew relaxed. "It's just Dub."

"Good. Go out and tell him to come in here."

Mace did and in a minute Dub came into the kitchen. "What's up, Elias?"

"It's about time you showed up. I want you to take that there note Mace has writ over to the Jordon place. Make shore that they know it has to be given to Glenda Jordon."

Dub glanced at Hugh, who still sat on the floor. He lifted an eyebrow, but said nothing.

Hugh started to say something, then thought he better be quiet. Maybe Dub would see that he was here against his will and help him in some way.

"What's that boy doing here and why's he sitting in the floor?"

"Never mind about him. Just take this note like I said."

"And don't read it," Mace added.

"You know I can't read," Dub said.

"Good."

Dub took the note. "Anything else you want me to do while I'm there, boss?"

"Keep an eye out for that Hendrix character. I hear he's a mean one. He may try to keep you from giving the note to them."

"I ain't never met the man, but from what I've seen of him, he don't look too tough."

"Good. Just don't let him get in your way."

"I won't, boss." He turned to go out. When his head was looking at Hugh and he was sure the Palmers couldn't see his face, he winked at the boy.

"Tell Zelda I'm all right," Hugh said.

"Shut up, Hugh," Mace barked. He looked back at Dub. "Don't you tell Zelda nothing."

Dub nodded and went out the door.

Hugh put his head on his knees and tried not to cry again. His only hope was that Wiley would rescue him before Zelda had to come and marry Mace. For the first time since it was mentioned, he didn't want his stepsister anywhere near this mean man.

~ * ~

Dub reined his horse up on the small knoll where Wiley waited. They were out of sight of the Palmers' ranch house. Dismounting, he handed the paper to Wiley. "Read this!"

"Have you read it?"

"As soon as I got outside the house. I'm not the best reader in the world, but the fools don't think I can read at all."

"Even with all the grammar and spelling mistakes, it doesn't take a good reader to understand what this note means."

"Right. I don't think the boy is in danger yet. He did have a smear of blood on his cheek, where somebody had slapped him, but otherwise, he seemed fine."

"One of them probably hit him for backtalking or something."

"What's our next move, Wiley?"

"Maybe you should suggest something. It was your idea that I wait here while you went to the house to see what was happening. It was a good idea, by the way. I probably would have rushed in there and got Hugh or myself killed."

"You'll be all right. Those two are kind of easy to outsmart. Two Feathers and I have been doing it for months."

"I understand." Wiley looked at the note again. "When Glenda sees this, it might finally convince her the Palmers are not her saviors."

"Why don't you take it home and show it to her? In the meantime, I'll stay here and keep an eye on things. After enough time has passed for me to have gone to your place and back, I'll go back in and let them know I've delivered the note. I can then make sure the boy is all right."

Wiley hesitated. "I don't know. I think it might be better to let her see the note after we rescue Hugh. She's a dying woman and I sure don't want to be the one to push her over the edge, even if she hates me."

Dub nodded. "Then I tell you what. Whenever enough time has passed, I'll go back to the house, like I said. Maybe I can get them to let me take the boy to the barn to do some work or something. In the meantime, you can work your way around to the back of the barn where you won't be seen. If luck is with us, we all might be able to slip away without them even knowing we're gone."

"Dub, if this thing works out like you said, will you be needing a job?"

He gave Wiley a funny look. "I thought the Jordon ranch belonged to the widow."

"Everybody thinks so, but it actually belongs to Zelda."

"Then you don't have the right to offer me a job, do you?"

"Not yet, but I will have."

Dub frowned. "How's that going to come about?"

Wiley chuckled. "I decided this morning that I'm going to convince her to sell me the ranch, then I'm going to marry that woman."

Dub lifted an eyebrow. "This morning?"

"Yep. When you were saddling my horse and I went in to tell them I was going to get Hugh, I had an impulse hit me and I acted on it. I leaned down and kissed Zelda on the cheek. In that instant I knew kissing her on the cheek wasn't enough. But I had sense enough to know that marrying her was the only way I was going to get more."

"Just like that?"

"Yes, just like that. In that instant I knew I was going to marry her and we would build her ranch into a profitable one and we'd raise the two Jordon kids. Hopefully, we'll eventually have children of our own to raise along with them. I also knew we'd take care of Glenda as long as she lives, even though she hates both of us."

"And you want to hire me to work on this ranch you plan to build?"

"Yes, I do. I see the way you are with Two Feathers and I know I can trust you to do the right thing by me."

Dub nodded. "What about Two Feathers?"

"Don't worry about Two Feathers. There'll always be a place for her on our ranch."

"Then, Mr. Hendrix, I accept the job."

"None of that Mr. Hendrix stuff. I'm Wiley and you're Dub. It started that way and it will always be that way. Deal?"

"Deal."

The two men shook hands.

~ * ~

Zelda wasn't sure she was doing the right thing, but when Two Feathers heard Glenda's tirade, she insisted on going to talk with her. "I want to tell her what the Palmers are really like, Miss Zelda."

After she saw Two Feathers wasn't going to give up, Zelda helped her walk into Glenda's room. Pansy walked on the other side of the Indian. "This lady wants to talk to you, Glenda."

"Who the hell is she?"

"I'm Two Feathers. I work for the Palmers."

"Well, what are you doing here. I don't like strangers in my house."

"Do you mean because I'm an Indian?"

Glenda swallowed, but didn't say anything.

Zelda helped Two Feathers to a chair. "Pansy and I will leave you two alone."

"Don't you dare!" Glenda blurted.

Zelda took another chair and pulled Pansy into her lap. "Then we'll sit here and listen."

Glenda seemed to find her tongue. "Well, say whatever it is you have to say to me, then get out. I'm upset about my little boy."

"You should be. I heard them plan the whole thing and you helped them pull it off."

"You're crazy."

"Did your son go to the Palmer ranch?"

"Yes, he did. I told him to go get Mace because I needed his help." Glenda looked pleased with herself.

"You sent your son straight into their trap."

"What do you mean?"

"They planned to take one of your children and hold it for ransom."

"That's ridiculous. I don't have any money. All I have is this ranch and they know they're going to get that for agreeing to take care of me and my children."

"Old man Palmer wants the ranch and will do or say anything to get it. Mace wants Miss Zelda. Neither of them wants you or your children and they don't plan to look after any of you when you sign the ranch over to them."

"You're lying."

"No, ma'am. I don't lie. I heard Elias Palmer say he was going to put the little girl in an orphanage, but he might keep the boy and whip him into shape as a cowhand."

"You're crazy. He wouldn't do that."

"Look at me, Miz. Jordon. Where do you think I got all these whip marks? Elias Palmer loves to whip people. He don't care if it's a man, a woman or a child. Your son will be no exception. He'll beat him until the boy does what he wants him to do."

"I don't believe you."

"What he plans for you is even worse."

"What lie are you going to tell me now?"

"He said after they got rid of the children, and Zelda was married to Mace, they were going to let you lie here in your bed until you starved to death."

"No!" Glenda turned horrified eyes toward Zelda. "Get her out of here. I'm not going to listen to any more of her vicious lies."

Zelda stood. "Come on, Two Feathers. I can tell you're in pain. I'm going to give you some of the medicine the doctor left for you. It will help you rest."

"But, I should try to make Miz Jordon understand how evil the Palmers are."

"You told her what they are. Now it's up to her whether she believes it or not."

Twenty-five

After he felt enough time had passed, Dub headed back to the ranch house as Wiley began working his way around to end up behind the barn. He'd only come into the yard when Mace appeared on the porch. "Did you give 'em the note?"

Dub nodded.

"What'd you tell 'em?"

"I give it to the woman and told her it was for Miz Jordon."

"What'd she say?"

"Said she'd give it to her."

"Was that all she said?"

"She didn't have time to say no more. She slammed the door in my face."

Elias came out on the porch and asked practically the same questions as Mace did. He got the same answers. "Well, hell," Elias frowned. "I thought at least they'd send a message back."

"I waited for a few minutes to see if they were going to, but like I said, nobody came back outside. I turned around and came back here."

"Did you see Two Feathers?"

Dub tried to look surprised. "Why would I see her? I figure she's in the kitchen cooking."

"Well, she ain't. The boy said she was at their ranch."

"What's he doing here anyway?"

Elias gave him a sharp look. "Don't be so damn nosey, Dub. It ain't none of your business why he's here."

"I'm sorry, Mr. Palmer. I just thought maybe you'd hired him to help me out in the barn since your foot is messed up."

Mace jumped into the conversation. "That ain't a bad idee, Pa. Dub could start teaching him what has to be done in the barn. That way he'll be that far ahead on his training and he wouldn't be setting around in the kitchen whimpering to go home."

"For once, you've got a good idee. I'll get the boy."

Mace turned to Dub. "Teach him how to take care of the horses and how to muck out the stalls and how to get the food together for the animals."

Dub nodded. "I'll do it. Just call us when supper is ready."

Elias came back shoving Hugh through the door in front of him. "I heard that, Dub. It's like last night. There ain't no supper in the house. You'll have to take care of yourself."

Dub started to ask why, but decided he wasn't going to push it. "I guess I can handle another night at the saloon."

Elias turned to Hugh. "Go with this man. He's going to teach you some things a boy your age ought to already know. If you learn them right, I'll spare the whip tonight. If you don't, then I might have to give you a lick or two."

"Come on, boy. I want to get this work done so I can head for town." Dub took Hugh's arm to keep Silas from shoving him forward. He headed to the barn, leading his horse with one hand and keeping the other one on Hugh.

When they were several yards away, Dub continued to look straight ahead, but he said, "Don't look at me and don't look back. They're watching so we're going to do something to make them think I'm not going to treat you very nice."

"What?" Hugh's voice came out in a shaking sound.

"Jerk your arm away from me and act like you're going to run. I'm going to jerk you back and yell at you so they'll think I'm mad."

"Why should I?"

"You want to get away from here, don't you?"

"Yes."

"Then do it."

Hugh jerked his arm away, but Dub was fast. He grabbed the boy and almost threw him down.

There was laughter on the porch, then Mace yelled, "That's the way, Dub. Don't let the little rat get the better of you,"

"No danger of that," Dub yelled back.

Before they reached the barn, Dub heard the door slam. "Looks like they've gone back inside, but don't relax yet. They could be watching out the window."

Once they were inside the safety of the barn, Dub let go of Hugh's arm. "You can relax now. They can't see us here."

Hugh turned and stared at him. "Did you give that note to my mother?"

"No, Hugh. Wiley has the note. He said your mother was too sick to get something like that."

"But you told them you gave it to Zelda."

"I lied."

"Why?"

"It's all in the plan that Wiley and I came up with to rescue you. We want to get you out of here and home before your mother has a chance to worry."

Hugh became excited. "Is Wiley in here? Where is he?"

"Calm down, boy. Wiley will be here shortly. He'll be sneaking in the back." He put his hand on Hugh's shoulder. "In the meantime, how about saddling your horse and getting ready to go."

"I don't have a saddle, but I'll put the harness on him."

It wasn't long until the back door eased open and Wiley came into the barn.

Hugh saw him, went running to him and threw his arms around Wiley's waist. "Wiley, I'm glad to see you. I thought they were going to kill me."

"You know I wouldn't let that happen." Wiley hugged him then pulled back. "I'm glad to see you too, Hugh, but what happened to your face?"

"Mace hit me a couple of times, but I'm all right. I just want to go home."

"I ought to kill that man."

Hugh reached up and took Wiley's arm. "Don't kill him."

"Why not? He deserves it."

"If you kill him you might have to go to jail or get hanged. I don't want you to go to jail and I sure don't want to see you hanged."

Wiley chuckled as he remembered the first time Mace rode up to the Jordon ranch. Hugh announced that Mace was Zelda's boyfriend. Then he said, 'Shoot him, Mace. He's just a stranger and nobody will ever know you done it.' Now he was begging Wiley not to shoot Mace because of what might happen. He wondered if Hugh remembered the day, but didn't remind him. Instead, he said, "If you won't let me shoot him, how about you let me take you out of here. We need to let your Mama and Zelda know you're all right."

"I'll be glad to go home. I never thought I'd get away from here alive."

"You and Hugh go on ahead, Wiley. I have a couple of things I need to do here."

Hugh looked at Dub. "Don't do anything foolish. I don't want to lose my only hand."

"I won't. I'm just going to make them think I will."

"You'll be taking a chance."

"I know that, but they have to pay for what they did to Two Feathers."

"I understand. I want to make them pay for what they've done to the Jordons, but we can take care of all that later."

"I'm not going to kill them, if that's what you think. I'm just going to get started on their punishment."

Wiley nodded. "In that case, we'll meet you at the house around supper. You should know from breakfast that Zelda is a good cook."

"I do know and I'll be there by supper time."

Wiley told Hugh to mount. They then slipped out the back door of the barn with Wiley leading Hugh's horse.

~ * ~

As soon as Wiley and Hugh left, Dub gave his horse some special oats and let her rest in the stall, still saddled. When he thought they had enough time to get away, he turned and walked toward the house.

He walked in the back door to find Mace at the stove stirring something that smelled awful. He was glad he wasn't going to have to eat it.

Mace turned. "What the hell are you doing here? Don't you know that boy will run away when nobody's there watching him?"

"Mace is right." Elias's voice thundered as he came down the hall. "Get back out there and watch him."

In a quiet voice, Dub said, "Nobody can run anywhere when they're tied up tight." He knew this was a fact and hoped they wouldn't ask if Hugh was tied.

Mace grinned. "Good thinking, Dub."

"I have to hand it to you. You've got more sense than I thought you had." Elias dropped to a chair at the kitchen table. "What did you come to the house for anyway?"

"A couple of things. First one is to let you know I saw some unbranded cattle on the way in. Thought it might be a good idea to run them into a pasture before it got too late. The kid would be no help doing that."

"He's right, Pa."

Elisa nodded. "I guess it won't hurt to let him stay tied up in the barn till you get back. It'll keep him out of here and we won't have to listen to his moaning and crying and begging to go home."

"Did he do any work in the barn?" Mace asked.

"He did everything I told him to do."

"Good. I figured since you was a Injun he'd be a little afraid not to. Thought you might scalp him or somethin'." Elias laughed. "Tell him that you'll take his hair if he gives you any trouble when you get back."

"I'm cooking up some stew and it should be done in a couple of hours. You won't have to go to town tonight. You can eat with us."

Dub nodded.

"What was the second thing you wanted to say?" Elias asked.

"Wanted to find out if you ever learned what happened to Two Feathers."

Elias shook his head. "Don't know what happened to her. She must have run off."

"Why would she do that?"

"What business is it of yours, Dub? Just cause she's Injun, too, don't mean you have to be concerned about her."

"You should know that as an Indian, I can sense when something isn't right with another one of my race."

Elias glanced at Mace. "I didn't know that? Did you?"

"No."

"Well, it's true. Ever since the white man came west and took our land, it's become important that we communicate with one another. I'm sure since she's older, Two Feathers knows how to use the spirits to send a message."

Elias glanced at the floor. "She may have decided she don't want to work here no more."

"I don't think it's that. I sense that she's in pain. You didn't happen to use your whip on her for some reason, did you?"

"Of course not."

"Good."

"Why do you say that?"

"Because if Two Feathers comes to harm, I pity the man who lays a hand on her."

Mace frowned. "Why?"

"You may not know this, but Two Feathers has strong powers. She hasn't used them in a long time, but I'm sure she can still conjure them up."

"What kind of powers?" Elias was beginning to look uncomfortable.

"If someone has hurt her, and I'm sure they have, and if she doesn't die from the attack, she will bring ruin down of the person who caused her pain."

Elias shook his head. "That's a lot of nonsense. That old Injun squaw couldn't do nothing to hurt nobody."

"I just wanted to be sure it wasn't something you had done, Mr. Palmer."

"Why?"

"Because I don't want to be around when the trouble starts if you're the one who hurt her."

"Pa told you he didn't do it, Dub. He also said it weren't none of your business. Now, accept that and get back to work or he might decide to use his whip on you."

Dub's eyes narrowed. "Just so you know, if he ever tries to use his whip on me, you'll be an instant orphan."

Mace's mouth quivered, but he didn't say anything else.

Dub turned back to Elias. "As for you, if you decided you're going to try whipping me, think twice. I haven't done it in a long time, but I haven't forgotten how to scalp a man."

Elias couldn't hide the slight fear that crept into his eyes. "I ain't gonna use the whip on you, Dub. I've never thought of such a thing. Mace there is just running his mouth like he usually does."

Dub nodded. "In that case, I will go get those cows now."

He went out the door, happy that things went the way he wanted then to. He hadn't lied as much as he thought he'd have to. He just hadn't told the truth the way the Palmers thought he had. He was sure Two Feathers didn't have any magic powers, but it was fine if they began to think she had. As for him, he had never scalped anybody, but he had seen it done. He was a little boy when it happened. It made him sick and as soon as he could get away from the scene, he went behind a tree and threw up. As for the cattle, he was going to get around forty head. Cattle that he'd been hiding in a canyon on the back side of the Palmer property. Though they thought he'd branded all the cows they'd run on the land without brands, he hadn't. He'd kept them in case he needed to take a herd with him when he left this place. He'd thought they might give him a new start somewhere away from Mace and his father. A place where he could take Two Feathers with him the way they had planned.

He smiled to himself when he thought of the reaction of the Palmers when he didn't show back up tonight and when they went to the barn and didn't find Hugh there. They would be furious and probably act irrationally. They might even go to the Jordon ranch. He couldn't help hoping they would. At least if he shot them there, it wouldn't be called murder. Shaking those thoughts away, he turned his mind to the task at hand.

Now, he was going to round up the cows in the canyon and run them back to where they probably belonged in the first place, the Jordon ranch. He didn't need them now because, thanks to Wiley Hendrix, he'd not be leaving here any time soon. Neither would Two Feathers.

Twenty-six

Zelda heard the horses come into the yard and set Pansy from her lap where they were sitting in the rocking chair by the fireplace. "I need to see who that is, sweetheart."

Pansy followed her to the kitchen, where Zelda looked out the window. "Oh, thank the Good Lord. It's Wiley and Hugh."

She rushed to the door, opened it and stepped outside. She watched as they turned their horses into the corral and dismounted. Wiley took the saddle off his horse and threw it on the top rail of the corral fence.

Hugh turned and ran toward the house as fast as he could. He started waving when he saw Zelda and Pansy. Leaping onto the porch, he startled Zelda when he threw his arms around her neck. "I didn't think I'd ever see you again." He let her go and picked up Pansy. "I didn't think I'd ever see you again either, Pansy."

Wiley walked up and Zelda asked, "What happened?"

Hugh started to speak, but Wiley put his hand on his shoulder. "Have you told Glenda any more about Hugh's disappearance?"

"Two Feathers insisted on telling her what the Palmers planned to do to him, but I'm not sure she believed her. She's been moaning and crying ever since the Indian talked to her, but I couldn't take her accusing me of making everything up any longer. Pansy and I have stayed away from her."

"Mama was all wrong, Zelda. Those Palmer men are mean."

"Yes, they are, Hugh. What happened to your face? Did they hit you or something?"

"Mace did."

Wiley butted in. "Let's not stand here on the porch and discuss it." Wiley nodded toward the door. "Let's go inside and let your mama see that you're all right."

They went inside and to Glenda's room. As soon as Hugh stepped over the threshold, she held out her arms and screamed, "My baby!"

Hugh let him hug her, then he pulled back. "I'm fine, Mama. Wiley saved me."

"Oh, my heavens, look at your face. What have you done to my little boy, Wiley Hendrix?"

"Mama, didn't you hear what I said? Wiley saved me. He didn't hit me in the face. Mace Palmer did."

She stared at him. "Don't lie to me, Hugh. That evil Wiley Hendrix probably made you say that."

"No, Mama." Hugh pulled a chair up beside his mother's bed. "We need to talk."

"My baby wants to talk to me. The rest of you get out of here."

"No, Mama," Hugh said again. "I want them to stay."

She stared at him. "Why?"

"Because they need to know what happened."

"I don't see why...."

"Be quiet and listen, Mama."

Zelda took a chair near the bedroom window and lifted Pansy to her lap. Wiley stood beside them.

When Glenda finally quit trying to talk, Hugh went on, "I did what you told me to do. I slipped out of the house and went to the Palmer ranch to tell them that you wanted them to send a paper back so you could sign it, but I didn't get to tell them."

"Why not?"

"They were glad to see me…"

"Of course they were."

"Mama, if you interrupt me one more time, I'm going to walk out of here and you'll never know what happened."

Glenda bit her lip.

"As I was saying, they acted glad to see me and I felt I'd done the right thing by going over there. They took me in the house and asked what was going on at the ranch. I told them Two Feathers was here, because I didn't think I was doing anything wrong." Glenda started to speak, but stopped herself and he went on. "Then they started talking about how they were going to kill her. I was a little scared, but I got more afraid when they said that since I'd showed up they wouldn't have to kidnap me or Pansy. I got really scared then and told them I wanted to go home. They told me to shut up. They kept talking about how they were going to make Zelda marry Mace and they were going to write you a letter and tell you they would kill me if Zelda didn't do like you said. I told them again I wanted to go home and I got up to go. That's when Mace hit me in the face and knocked me down on the floor."

"I can't believe this."

"It's true, Mama. Mace and his papa have no intention of taking care of us. They're going to make me do all the work and get rid of Dub. Then they're going to send Pansy to an orphanage and Zelda will have to do all of Two Feathers' work when they kill her. Wiley and Zelda are right about them. They're mean and I never want to see them again."

Glenda swallowed. "They didn't send me a letter."

"They gave it to Dub to bring to you, but him and Wiley decided it might kill you if you got it before they rescued me." He turned toward Wiley. "Dub said you had it, Wiley."

"I do."

"I want to see it." Glenda glared at him.

Wiley took the letter out of his pocket and handed it to her.

She read it, then bit her lip. "I bet you wrote this and tried to blame it on Mace."

"Read it to me, Mama." She did and Hugh said, "Mace wrote that because that's the same letter they read out loud while I was in their kitchen."

Glenda began to cry. "What in the world are we going to do?"

"I think I can answer that." Wiley looked at her. "The first thing you're going to do is be honest with Zelda, Glenda."

"What do you mean?"

"You're going to show her a copy of her father's will."

"She knows what the will says."

"No, she doesn't. She only knows what you've told her, and you and I both know that you've told her nothing but lies."

"You can't accuse me of something like that."

"If you refuse to tell the truth, I'll have the lawyer come out here and explain it all to Zelda, just like he explained it to you."

There was a moment of silence, then Glenda shouted, "Everybody except Hugh, get out of my room. I need to think."

"No, Mama. I'm not going to stay here and listen to you tell me how everything is Zelda's fault because she let Wiley come to stay on our ranch. If it wasn't for the way she's looked after all of us, I don't know where we'd be. And Wiley has done nothing but make this a better place to live. With his help, we might just have a good ranch again someday. The kind of ranch it was before John Jordon died."

"Hugh, you're just a little boy. You don't understand."

"I'm not grown up yet, but I'm not a little boy either. I'm learning how to do things and I hope I'll be able to help Wiley run this ranch one day. He's teaching me a lot of stuff."

"But your illness..."

"Mama, I'm not sick. You're the only one who keeps saying that. I believed you for a long time, but I don't believe you any longer. I'm able to do a lot of things and I intend to learn to do a lot more."

Wiley put his hand on Hugh's shoulder. "Son, why don't you have a heart to heart with your mother. I'll go tend to our horses and I'm sure Zelda won't mind stepping out. We can have the discussion about the will when I come back."

"I don't want to talk to her alone. She'll try to make me do something else wrong. If you have to leave, can't Zelda stay?"

"If she wants to."

"If Hugh wants me to stay, I will."

"I do want you to stay, Zelda." He turned back to his mother. "Now, what did you want to tell me."

"I can't talk with her in here."

"Then I guess we don't have anything else to say."

Glenda cried again. "How can you turn your back on me, Hugh?"

"I'm not turning my back on you, Mama. I'm only letting you know that I'm growing up and I have to make some of my own decisions. I'll make mistakes, like I did today when I went to the Palmers, but I'll get better at doing things right."

"You may think you're grown, honey, but you're still my baby boy."

"I'm your son, but I'm not a baby boy. I love you, Mama. I always will, but you have to let me grow up. You keep trying to make me as little as Pansy, but I'm not. I never will be again."

"But ..."

"That's it." Hugh stood. "Zelda, I haven't had anything to eat. Do you happen to have anything in the kitchen I can have?"

"Why haven't you fed my son, Zelda? You know better than to let my boy go hungry. Get in there and fix him something to eat."

"Don't order Zelda around like that, Mama. I haven't eaten because the Palmers were holding me prisoner. Zelda had nothing to do with it."

"She should have fed you when you got home."

"She's always fed me when I was here at mealtime. I just never appreciated what she did for us until recently."

"Hugh, you can't mean..."

"Don't say anything else, Mama, 'cause I'm upset and I'm hungry and I'm not going to talk to you until you will listen to what I'm trying to tell you." He looked around at his stepsister. "Let's go to the kitchen, Zelda."

Zelda stood and with Pansy in her arms she followed him out of Glenda's room, but she didn't say anything. She was still trying to comprehend the change in Hugh.

~ * ~

Wiley came through the door and frowned. "I can't believe Two Feathers can sleep with all the moaning and carrying on Glenda is doing."

"She probably wouldn't be able to sleep if I hadn't given her a dose of laudanum. It knocked her out."

Hugh looked up at him from his seat at the table. "Zelda gave me something to eat, but I'm almost finished. I'll go back and see if I can calm Mama down when I get done."

"I'll go with you. I need to talk to Glenda about the will. We were interrupted before, but it's important that the truth of it come out. I think you should come too, Zelda."

"Do I really have to? I know how much Glenda hates me and it will just make her harder to talk to if I'm there."

"I'm sorry, but I think you should come."

Hugh stood. "Then let's go before she screams any longer."

Pansy, who was saying very little, reached up her arms and said, "Carry, Wiwey."

"Come on, sweetheart." Wiley picked her up and she smiled.

Hugh went into Glenda's room first and she smiled when she saw him. It turned to a frown when he was followed by Zelda and Wiley with Pansy. "I thought you were coming to talk to me alone, son."

"Wiley said you needed to finish the conversation you were having about the will."

"I've said all I'm going to say about that."

"I think not, Glenda. Where is the copy the lawyer gave you?"

"It's none of your business, Wiley Hendrix. I'll not show it to you or anybody else. It's mine and it's in a safe place."

"Then do you want me to tell Zelda and Hugh what it actually says?"

"I've told them."

"No, you haven't, Glenda. You've told them what you wished it said, but what you've said is a lie. You and I both know that. So, now you're going to tell everyone the truth."

"Lies! Lies!"

"No, Glenda. You're not going to intimidate me the way you have done Zelda, but if you don't want to tell her the truth, I will."

Glenda reached out and grabbed Hugh's hand. "Don't listen to him. He's making all this up. Listen to me. I'm your mother."

Hugh looked at her and his mouth quivered. "Have you been telling lies, Mama?"

"I would never lie to you, baby."

"I'm sorry I have to expose your mother's deceit right here in front of you, Hugh, but I don't have a choice. The truth has to come out." When nobody said anything, Wiley went on, "Your mother doesn't own this ranch, Zelda does."

"What?" Zelda stammered.

"Is he telling the truth, Mama?" Before she could answer, he added, "And for once, please tell me the truth."

Glenda dropped her head and began to sob. "I didn't lie. John wanted me to have this place."

Wiley shook his head. "No, he didn't, Glenda. He made this will the day you were in town. The day that he was killed on the way home. The lawyer told me that, and if you won't show us the copy of the will you have, as soon as I can get to town again, I'll get a copy of John Jordon's will and prove this to everyone."

Hugh's voice sounded serious and grown up when he said, "Where is the will, Mama? I want to see it."

"Hugh, you're too young to be bothered..."

He interrupted her. "I want to see it, Mama."

"But..."

"Now, Mama! Where is it?"

"I'm not going to show it to you, Hugh."

"Why don't you check under her mattress, Hugh? That's where people hide things. And since your mother can't walk, that's probably where it is."

"Shut up, Wiley Hendrix. I'll not have my son corrupted by your lies."

Hugh reached under the mattress.

"Reach as far as you can under the mattress, Hugh," Wiley said. "I bet it's way under there because if it wasn't, Zelda would have seen it when she changed the bed."

In a minute Hugh brought his hand out. In it was an envelope. "I bet it's in here."

"Give me that." Glenda grabbed toward the envelope.

Hugh held it back. "No, Mama. As Wiley said, it's time for the truth to come out."

Twenty-seven

"Wonder where that Injun is. He should've been back here with them cows a long time ago." Mace looked out the kitchen window at the setting sun.

"No telling when he'll come back." Elias shook his head. "Can't trust none of them redskins."

"Reckon he'll kill us when he finds out Two Feathers is at the Jordon ranch?"

"We ain't going to let that happen."

"How can we stop him, Pa? I know Injuns sneak around at night and they're so quiet nobody knows they're there until they have a knife on you."

"Like I said, we ain't going to let him kill us."

"And like I said, how are we going to stop him?"

"We're going to kill him first, you fool."

"Oh."

"I swear, Mace. I don't think I could've had a stupider young'un than you even if I'd tried hard to do it."

"Maybe if'en I'd had a smarter pa, I wouldn't be so stupid, as you say."

Before Mace could duck, his father slapped him hard across the face. "Don't you talk to me like that."

Mace looked as if he was going to hit Elias back, but must have changed his mind. Instead, he said, "Think I ought to go get that Jordon young'un and bring him to the house?"

"I reckon so. I guess if we're going to work him, we have to feed him and it shore don't look like Dub's going to get back in time for him to do any work in the barn tonight. Is there enough of that stew left to fill him up?"

Mace looked in the pot. "Looks like there's at least a half bowl full."

"That'll be enough. Go get 'em."

"I'll be right back."

Mace was only gone a minute when Elias heard him yelling. "He ain't here, Pa."

Elias went out to the back porch. "What do you mean, he ain't here?"

"He ain't in the barn and his horse is gone."

"Damn! That stupid redskin probably didn't tie him tight enough and he got away."

"I don't know, Pa. I didn't see no ropes laying around and there ain't no work been done in the barn. The animals ain't even been fed."

Elias lumbered off the porch. "I'll kill that bastard redskin if he's let that boy go on purpose."

Mace waited until his pa reached the barn. "Why would Dub let him go, Pa?"

"How the hell should I know? Injuns think different to us. He could of done it just to be mean. Them people do things like that." Elias looked around the barn. "Look over there. The back door is open part way. I bet that's the way he went out."

"Looks like Dub would of come back to the house and told us the boy was gone before he took off to get them cows."

"I don't know about that. I told you, Injuns don't think like white people. They just ain't smart as we are."

"What are we gonna do now that we ain't got the kid to bargain with, Pa?"

"I'll think of somethin', Mace. Give me time. I can always get a good idee when I think on it for a while."

Mace didn't say anything, but he did wonder if his pa could really come up with a plan. So far anything they'd tried hadn't worked. He still wondered if he shouldn't just ride over to the Jordon ranch and kidnap Zelda. Glenda would probably sign the papers if he told her he was taking Zelda and wasn't going to do anything to help the rest of the Jordons unless she signed the ranch over to them. This sounded like the most logical plan to him, but he didn't voice it to his pa. The mood the old man was in would probably push him into grabbing his whip. Since there was nobody else to use it on, it'd probably end up strapping his back. For this reason, he didn't mention the plan he'd thought up to his father. He might just wait until his old man was asleep and slip off and pull off his plan by himself.

~ * ~

Zelda sat at the kitchen table and re-read the will for the fourth time. She still had tears in her eyes. Not because she was mad that Glenda had lied to her. Not because of Zelda had sold off their stock at a loss and expected the ranch to run the way it always had. Not even because she'd not had access to what was lawfully hers.

It was because she was so touched that the father she'd loved so dearly hadn't turned his back on her. He'd made it clear she was his daughter and she deserved to have what she'd helped him and her mother build over the years. "Oh, Papa. I'm so sorry I thought you'd abandoned me. I should have known you loved me too much to do such a thing."

"Did you say something, Zelda?" Wiley asked from his seat in the rocking chair near the fireplace.

"I didn't mean to speak out loud." She looked around at him and smiled. He looked so natural sitting there with a sleeping Pansy in his lap. She folded the paper and stood. "I need to get supper finished. I know you must be hungry since we didn't have a mid-day meal."

"I'm fine. I felt there were other things we needed to clear up."

"You were right." She moved to the stove and stirred the beans she had put in the pot earlier. "At least things seem quiet in Glenda's room. Hugh must have convinced her to calm down and face reality."

"I think he'll be able to do that." He stood. "If you don't mind, I'm going to put Pansy on the couch and move over there so we won't have to whisper."

She nodded and he carefully lay the little girl down and covered her with the small quilt Zelda had placed on the back. She wiggled a little, but didn't wake up.

Moving to the kitchen area, Wiley walked up behind Zelda. "Have you finally accepted the fact that you are the sole owner of this ranch?"

She turned to him. "Thanks to you. I'd never know if you hadn't found out about it."

"No problem, ma'am." He smiled down at her. "Now that you know, what do you plan to do with the ranch?"

"I don't know. I'm still trying to cope with the fact that it's mine." She sighed. "I don't have the money to get it back on its feet. I'm sure Glenda has managed to run through what little cash Papa left." She sighed again. "I guess I'll have to sell the place... but not to the Palmers. I don't want them to have one foot of this property. They've already cheated us out of enough."

"Maybe there's more money than you think."

She shook her head. "I kept the books for Papa. There wasn't a lot of cash. Most of what he had went back into the running of the ranch. I don't know exactly how much Glenda got for selling the livestock, but I know it was not nearly as much as it should have been."

"Things will work out, Zelda." He reached out and hugged her. "You deserve for things to go right with you for a change."

"Oh, Wiley." She threw her arms around his waist and looked up at him. "I'm so thankful for the day you came into our life. Things have been so much better since you've been here."

He held her a little tighter. "The pleasure has been all mine."

Zelda pulled away. "I'm sorry. I didn't mean to throw myself at you. I'm just grateful and I want you to know it."

"I do know it, Zelda." He chuckled. "As for throwing yourself at me, you can do that any time you wish."

She blushed. "No I can't, Wiley. I know you've been here for a few weeks, and all I really know about you is you're a nice man who was on his way to Waco."

"What do you want to know about me, Zelda? I'll answer any of your questions"

"Mainly, I want to know if you have a family waiting for you in Waco. A wife and children, maybe."

He laughed and led her to the table. Sitting down, he nodded for her to take a chair.

"I need to finish supper."

"Humor me. This won't take long." She sat and he took her hand in his. "I'm going to give you an abbreviated version of my life's story."

"I'd appreciate that."

"I was born and raised in Texas. Ranching is in my blood and it's what I want to do for the rest of my life. I worked on a large ranch as a foreman for a while then I met this sweet lady named Janet, from Chicago. We were married and she was content to live in a cabin on that ranch with me until I saved enough money to buy a little place of our own. We were on our ranch for almost a year then she became sick. When the doctors there couldn't help her, I sold the ranch and took her back to Chicago. I felt the doctors would be better there. It didn't matter. She died a little over two years ago. We never had any children, though we both wanted some. After her death, I came back to Texas and worked on my friend's ranch for a year. When he married, it hurt too much to see him and his happy family. Something I'd always wanted for myself. He understood when I told him I'd heard there were some large ranchers near Waco that needed cowhands. I was on my way when I was waylaid by a beautiful young girl with berry juice all over her face, hands and clothes. She stole my heart when she called me *Wiwey*." He smiled at Zelda and squeezed her hand. "And that, my dear, is about all there is to me and my life before I met you."

"Thank you for telling me, Wiley. And I must admit, I'm glad little Miss Pansy brought you home from her berry picking expedition."

He winked at her. "Then whatever happens in the future, we can always be thankful to Pansy for it."

Zelda blushed.

"Hey, folks," Hugh came into the kitchen, keeping his tone low. "I see Pansy is asleep. So is Mama. I thought I'd come out here and check on supper."

Zelda let go of Wiley's hand and stood. "It won't be much longer. Why don't you have a seat and talk to Wiley while I finish it up, then we'll all eat."

~ * ~

Zelda looked into Glenda's room and was surprised to see the woman awake. "You should have called me when you woke up, Glenda. I need to bring you your supper."

Glenda bit her lip. "I was afraid I'd bother you."

"No bother." Zelda went into the kitchen, made a plate and returned to the room. She placed a towel across Glenda's knees and then handed her the tray. She would have sworn Glenda mumbled a thank you, but she said, "Is there anything else you need?"

"I need to talk to you."

"Of course." Zelda took a seat by the bed and waited for her stepmother to continue.

It took her a minute, but she finally said, "I'm not going to pretend that things have changed so much that I'm now going to love you like I do my children, Zelda."

"I don't expect you to do that, Glenda."

She nodded. "You know that I'm practically helpless. I'm going to have to have someone to look after me as long as I live, which the doctor says isn't going to be much longer." When Zelda nodded, Glenda went on, "I need to know what you intend to do. Are you going to send me to some home or am I supposed to try to find a place for the children and me to go where I can get somebody to help me?"

"I am not sending you anywhere, Glenda. As you know, my father's will states you have the right to live on this ranch for the rest of your life. So do your children. In fact, when they are grown and responsible, they'll get part of this land and they can either sell it or settle on it if that is their wish. Things will remain just as they have been, with one exception."

"What's that?" Glenda's voice was sharp, though Zelda could tell she was trying to control her irritation.

"There will be no visits to or from Mace and Elias Palmer. After what those men did to Hugh, I might shoot either of them if they show up here making demands."

"It's still hard for me to believe they did that to my boy. They've always been so nice and have talked to me with respect."

"I know you thought so, Glenda, but you saw only one side of them. I've lived beside their place all my life and they have always been sneaky and mean. Papa wouldn't have nothing to do with them after the day he caught them trying to steal a calf and its mother from our place."

"Maybe that's why they bought the herd from me. They needed more cattle."

Zelda decided she wasn't going to say anything else. "Well, at least you have that money. I know you don't like for me to advise you what to do, but I think you should put that money back for Hugh and Pansy. When they're older, it will give them a good start in life."

"I will when they pay me."

Zelda was startled. "Pay you?"

"They said they'd pay me later and no matter what you say, I believe them."

Glenda shook her head and stood. She refused to argue with Glenda. "That's between you and them. Now, you can put your mind to rest about where you'll be going. You and the children will stay here as long as I own this ranch. I know you hate me, and to be honest, you're not my favorite person either, but no matter how you and I feel about the situation, we're still family. We have been since the day my father married you and nothing we do will change that. He loved you and because of that, you and I have to learn to tolerate each other."

When Glenda only looked at her and didn't speak, Zelda got up and left the room.

Twenty-eight

Zelda couldn't go to sleep. She knew everyone in the household had drifted off a long time ago, but she didn't think sleep would ever come to her. Not that it mattered. If she was awake she could build a dream around what Wiley had said to her. Or at least implied, if not voiced. She only hoped she had correctly interpreted his words.

They had finished supper and she had put Pansy to bed. Hugh had gone to talk with his mother and Two Feathers had been in pain. Zelda had given her more laudanum and she was sound asleep. Wiley and Zelda sat at the kitchen table having a cup of coffee and talking about the ranch.

"I've tried to think of a way that I might be able to keep the ranch, Wiley, but as bad as I want to stay here, it seems impossible."

"I've always believed that anything is possible if you believe it is and you work hard to achieve it."

"I've worked hard for almost a year, but I'm not making any progress."

"But you are not working alone now. I'm here and Hugh is taking an interest in things. He'll be here to help us because he wants the ranch to prosper, too."

"I'm so glad he's beginning to grow up, but he and I can't do it alone."

He smiled at her. "Didn't you hear me say I'm here? And if you think you have to sell the place, I'll buy it, but only on the condition that all of you Jordons will live here with me."

Hugh came into the room. "Mama went to sleep. I'm ready to go sleep in the barn with you, Wiley."

"Then maybe we better go. I'm sure we're going to have to put up with a visit from the Palmers tomorrow and we need our rest." He stood and patted Zelda on the shoulder. "Remember what I said."

She did remember. Every word. But what did he mean? Did he really mean he'd buy the place and let them live here with him? If he didn't buy it, was he going to be here to see that Hugh learned how to help her run the ranch? If she didn't sell it to him, would he go on to find a job in Waco? Or was he going to be here as long as she wanted him to be? If that was so, he would be here forever.

When she was no closer to an answer than when she began thinking, she yawned. Maybe sleep would come to her soon. She hoped so, because she, too, wanted to be rested to face the Palmers in the morning.

~ * ~

Dub heard Wiley and Hugh climb the ladder to the barn loft, but he didn't let them know he was hidden on the straw in the corner. When he'd put the stray cows in the Jordon's north pasture, he'd circled back by the Palmer ranch and watched until he saw a light come on in the barn. He figured Mace and his pa were planning to sneak onto the Jordon place to see if they could capture one of the children, kill Two Feathers or kidnap Zelda. He wasn't about to let that happen. He had too much to lose.

An hour passed and nothing happened, but he was still sure it would. He heard Wiley's light snoring in the loft and occasionally Hugh would turn over or mutter something. He was going to let them sleep as late as they could because he might need their help if the Palmers had planned to split up. He knew he wouldn't be able to go in all directions.

Then he heard them. Whispers.

He didn't move. He barely breathed. He listened and could understand what they said.

"Are you shore they're all asleep, Pa?"

"Of course. The lights in the house have been out for over a hour and we saw that Hendrix man and Hugh come to the barn. Must be sleeping in the loft."

"Reckon we can get in the house now?"

"I'm gonna make shore we can. We're going to wake Hendrix up and when he comes down..."

His voice dropped and Dub couldn't hear the rest of his statement.

Then he heard a rock hit the side of the barn. He started to get up and stop the man, but in the same instant, he heard Wiley jump up and start down the ladder. Hugh was right behind him.

Dub waited. If they met Wiley with a gun, he'd stand a better chance of freeing the man when they moved away from the barn door.

But it didn't happen that way. As soon as Wiley stepped out the door, one of them hit him on the head and the other grabbed Hugh.

"You've killed Wiley!" Hugh screamed.

"He ain't dead, boy, but if you don't shut your mouth, I'll shoot him right here and now."

Hugh got quiet.

Dub slipped toward the door. Wiley was on the ground just outside and the Palmers were at the back porch ready to go into the house. Dub checked Wiley as quickly as he could. The man was alive, but out cold.

He started for the house and saw the back door open. He wondered why Zelda hadn't locked it before she went to bed. *Probably thought with Wiley in the barn they were all safe.*

A light came on and he realized that one of the Palmers must have had a lantern. He hung back a little to see what they planned to do because by this time, Hugh was shouting, "Zelda, get a gun! The Palmers are here and they've killed Wiley."

Dub eased up to the back door and pushed it open. There was nobody in the kitchen and he saw the light going down the hall.

"Shut up, Hugh," Mace's voice shouted at him. "We've come to get your mama to sign the ranch over to us, and I'm going to get my woman tonight."

"What's going on?" Glenda shouted.

"You turn Hugh loose!" Zelda shouted. Dub knew she must have come into the hall.

Still, he held back. He didn't want to get anyone killed, unless it was a Palmer, so he knew he had to wait until they were all in one room.

They went into Glenda's room and set the lantern on the chair. "Miz Jordon, we've come to get what's rightfully ours." Elias's voice showed no mercy. "If you don't sign this paper right now, we're going to shoot your little boye here right in the head."

Mace took out his gun and pointed it at Hugh's head.

"Don't you dare hurt him!" Zelda yelled and started toward Mace.

But he saw her coming and backed handed her across the face. She fell backward against the table.

"Let my boy go." Glenda began to gasp for breath. "You know I want to give you this ranch so you will look after me and my children."

Dub wondered, even after all the evidence, if she still believed the Palmers would take care of them as they had promised. If so, she certainly was a stupid woman.

"I can't sign anything over to you...."

"Yes, you can, Glenda," Zelda said as she got up off the floor. "Go ahead and sign the paper."

"But..."

"Please. Just sign it. You can't let them hurt Hugh."

"All right. I have a pen right here. I've been figuring out some things today." She began feeling around under her covers. "I must have dropped it when I went to sleep.

Mace let Hugh go and he ran to Zelda. "Go ahead and let the boy hug you, honey. It'll probably be the last time you ever get a hug from another man except me."

Dub thought it was time to intervene. He pulled his gun, but hesitated when he heard the back door open. He whirled around to see

Wiley, with blood running down the side of his head, enter the room. He motioned for the man to be quiet. Wiley must have understood, because he nodded and eased toward the hall.

"Can't you find the damn pen?" Elias demanded.

"Yes, I've got it."

"Good." He handed her the paper.

Glenda shook her head. "No, that's not it. I must have put it on the table."

"See if it's there, Mace." Elias demanded.

He glanced at the table and handed the pen to Glenda. "Now, sign Pa's paper so we can get out of here." He grinned. "I'm anxious to get my woman to my house."

"Shut up, Mace." Elias give him an evil glare.

Glenda quickly wrote her name on the paper. "Here you go. You do remember your promise to me, don't you?"

"Don't worry about no promise. Your little girl will make friends in an orphanage and that boy there will whip into a fine cowhand."

"And what do you plan to do with me?"

"Don't worry about it. You ain't got that much longer to live. We'll just help you reach the end sooner."

"Would you really use a whip on my son?"

He gave her an evil grin. "I shore will and I'll enjoy ever minute of it."

"That's what you think, Elias Palmer."

Before anyone knew what was happening, Glenda pulled a gun from under the covers and fired. Elias Palmer fell across the foot of her bed and blood was pouring from his chest.

Mace screamed and ran to his father. "You shot Pa."

Dub and Wiley entered the room at the same time.

Mace turned toward them and screamed, "I'll kill every one of you. I'll do it this very minute. He grabbed the gun from his pa's holster and turned to fire, but didn't have a chance. Two guns went off and two bullets sailed into the man. One in his shoulder. The other in his chest. He crumpled to the floor.

Chaos reigned for a few minutes, but it turned into a good chaos after the Palmers' bodies were dragged out of the room.

Zelda insisted that before she clean up Glenda's room, she bandage Wiley's head.

"My head will be fine."

"Don't argue with me."

"Might as well listen to her, Wiley," Dub said. "Hugh and I will get some water and begin to clean up the mess. You and Zelda can help after you're taken care of."

Glenda told Hugh to stop working and come to her so she could hold her baby in her arms. "I'll hug you when I get some of this blood up, Mama. I'm proud of you for shooting that awful man."

Pansy stumbled into the room. "Where Zewie?"

"I'm here, sweetheart. Did I wake you?"

"Huh, huh."

"Why don't you sit on the bed with Mama and let us bandage Wiley's head."

"All right." By the time she crawled up on the bed, she was again asleep.

"Come along, Wiley. I have some bandages in the pantry. We'll doctor your head in the kitchen."

"I think I'll be fine."

Zelda put her hands on her hip. "You're wasting time arguing with me. I'm going to fix your head before I let you start bending down and cleaning up the floor. You might pass out on me."

Dub laughed. "As I said before, listen to her, Wiley. You're going to end up getting your head doctored whether you want it done or not."

~ * ~

Wiley shrugged and let Zelda lead him out of the room. She sat him at the kitchen table, pointed her finger at him and said, "Don't move. I'll be right back with the bandages."

"Yes, ma'am." He winked at her and gave her a big smile.

She returned and began cleaning and doctoring the wound. "You're probably going to have a knot on your head for a few days."

"He hit me pretty hard."

"I'm sorry you were hurt."

"Makes it all worth it just to get you to baby me like this."

She smiled down at him. "So, you like to be petted?"

"Of course. Doesn't every man?" When she said nothing, he added, "I especially like being petted by you."

She stopped applying the cream to his wound and gave him a serious look. "Why me, Wiley?"

He reached up and took her hands in his. "Let's stop acting like we don't know there's something special happening between us, Zelda Jordon. I'm going to come right out and say it. I'm falling in love with you."

"Oh, Wiley. I've been hoping that would happen."

He stood. "Really?"

"Yes."

He didn't hesitate. He took her in his arms and kissed her passionately.

Hugh walked into the room. "What are you doing holding Zelda like that? Don't you dare hurt her."

Wiley laughed and looked at the boy. "I'll try never to hurt her, Hugh. She's special, you know."

"Yeah, I've just learned she is and I'm not going to let some drifter come in here and take advantage of her. She's my sister, you know."

"What if I told that I'll not be drifting any farther than this ranch for the rest of my life?"

"What do you mean?"

"I mean if Zelda will say 'yes' she'll marry me, I'll be living here on this ranch for the rest of my life." He looked down at Zelda.

She could hardly believe his words. Did he mean what he was saying? Could she really depend on him to marry her and make her a happy woman?

"Well, Zelda. Are you going to marry him or not?"

"Yes, Hugh. I'll marry him." She looked back at Wiley. "I said yes because I'm not falling in love with you, Wiley. I've been in love with you for some time."

"In that case, you can kiss her again, Wiley, but hurry up. We need help to get Mama's bedroom clean. It's an awful mess and she's complaining about it."

Wiley looked down at Zelda. "I guess we'd better go help them get it all cleaned up, then we can make them go to bed."

"Aren't we going to bed, too?"

He lifted an eyebrow and chuckled. "Do you mean before we're married?"

Zelda blushed and playfully hit him on the arm. "You know good and well what I mean. You'll be going to the barn and I'll stay with Pansy as I usually do."

He shook his head. "In that case, we'll go help them, but before we do, I wish I could get one more kiss from my future wife."

She put her arms around his neck and whispered, "Your wish is granted, my love."

~ * ~

When everything was cleaned up in Glenda's room, they all stood back and looked at their handiwork. "You would never guess what happened here tonight," Zelda declared.

"What happened?"

They all turned to see Two Feathers holding the doorframe to help her stand. She had a puzzled look on her face as she looked from one to the other.

Dub couldn't help it. He laughed as he walked over and put his arm around her. "A lot has happened here tonight. The Palmers raided this room a short time ago. They were trying to come in here and kidnap Zelda. Elias was holding Hugh with a gun at his head, but Glenda didn't want him to hurt her son, so she shot him. When Mace tried to help his pa, Wiley and I shot him at the same time and I don't which bullet killed him, but it doesn't matter. They're both dead."

Two Feathers looked confused. "All that happened?"

"Yep, but on a happier note, while Zelda was doctoring Wiley's head wound, he asked her to marry him and she said yes." He looked down at Two Feathers. "I can't believe you slept through the whole incident."

"Zelda gave me some of that sleeping medicine. It knocked me plumb out."

"That's no excuse. Indians don't let things like them dull their senses and I can't believe you slept through all this, medicine or no medicine."

"I must have."

Dub hugged her closer to his side and kissed the top of her head. "Yes, you did. I just want to know one thing. After missing all this, how can you call yourself a full-blooded Indian, Mama?"

Epilogue

Though spring approached, it was still cold when Zelda and Pansy went outside to call the men to supper.

"Give us a time to find a good stopping place, honey," Wiley called down to her from the roof of the bunkhouse.

"Don't wait too long."

"We won't." He turned back around and said something to Dub and Hugh.

Zelda moved to the bench under the tree and took a seat. Looking down at Pansy she said, "If they don't take too long, we'll wait for them to come down off that roof." She pulled her shawl tighter around her shoulders.

"I play with rocks." Pansy squatted at her knees.

"You do that, sweetheart." She smiled down at the child. "But first, let me button your coat. I don't want you to get cold."

As Pansy played, Zelda watched the threesome on the bunkhouse roof. Her heart swelled with happiness and pride when her eye settled on her husband. Though they'd been married for almost four months, she still couldn't believe how fortunate she was to be Wiley Hendrix's wife. Every day was a new adventure with him. And every night she knew she would never get closer to heaven on this earth than she did when she lay in his strong arms. She doubted if any woman could love her husband more. Marrying him had been the greatest blessing of her life.

She remembered the days following the deaths of the Palmer men. It seemed chaos wanted to take over. Glenda was sure she'd be arrested and hanged for shooting Elias. Hugh was almost hysterical because he'd been the one to give his mother the gun. Zelda was again riddled with guilt because she was sure she was somehow at fault. Only Pansy was her sweet normal self and...

Then Wiley took over. He arranged for the Palmers to be transported to town for burial in Potters Field. He went to the sheriff and explained everything. He convinced everyone that things would work out fine. He even told Zelda how Glenda had insisted her husband bring her home the day of the accident, though he had wanted to spend the night in town with her. Though she never let Glenda know she knew the truth, the guilt seemed to slip from her shoulders and she accepted that the event of that terrible day really was an accident.

The day after the burial, the sheriff showed up and informed them that he'd investigated the Palmers' death and found papers in their house that indicated they'd not only got the stock from Glenda Jordon and never paid her, but found a record of the cows they'd stolen from the Jordon range. He insisted that all the cattle that could be found was to be returned to the Jordon place. Since there was nobody to care for the other livestock on the ranch, he said they should take the chickens, pigs, horses, the one milk cow and any other animals on the ranch. To Pansy's delight, that included the big fuzzy black and white dog. Hugh tried to be nonchalant about it, but he was thrilled with the dog, too. Almost, but not quite as thrilled as he was with the pinto Wiley let him trade one of the Palmer horses for when they found it for sale at the livery. Because Wiley's horse was named Samson, Hugh named his filly Delilah.

Once she found out she wasn't going to be hanged, Glenda slipped back into her old habits of trying to baby Hugh and ordering Zelda around. Especially when she was told Zelda and Wiley were getting married.

"He's just marrying you to get this ranch, Zelda. Don't you know that?"

"As far as I'm concerned, he deserves the ranch."

"He'll probably throw us all off the place once you marry him."

As became the custom, nobody argued with the woman because she seemed to grow weaker every day. They simply ignored her."

Three weeks after the shooting, Zelda and Wiley said their vows at the little church in Laster with Pansy and Hugh standing with them.

Hugh helped Wiley clean out the large bedroom that had been used for storage. In her heart Zelda felt her parents would have been happy to know she was married to a wonderful man and sleeping in the room they had once shared. The one Glenda would never consent to sleep in after her marriage to John.

Though Glenda never came to like Zelda, she did tolerate her and would occasionally mumble a thank you when she was fed or cared for. It was hard for Zelda to know the woman died in early January still hating her. The only good thing was the fact that Glenda finally admitted they both loved Hugh and Pansy. The woman did die knowing her children would be well taken care of by their sister. Because she felt she should, Zelda had her buried on the other side of her father in the family graveyard. Hugh seemed to be pleased by this and Zelda knew it was the thing to do because, with all her faults, her father had loved the woman.

After getting over the shock that Dub was Two Feathers' son, they were all delighted that the two of them were now living on the ranch. Wiley and Hugh had helped him build a snug two-bedroom cabin in the edge of the woods where Dub had camped the night he'd traced his mother to their place.

Nobody could have been more excited than Pansy when the pumpkin vines sprouted and little pumpkins appeared on them. Now that winter was ending and spring was on the way she was excited about the things she and Zellie were going to plant this spring and she could watch grow into different vegetables.

The ranch grew and became self-sustaining faster than any of them thought it would. It was a happy place and they were now a happy family.

Zelda smiled as she watched the men working on the bunkhouse. They had said this was a necessity because they were going to have to hire a couple of hands to help with the spring roundup. Two Feathers insisted they put a kitchen in one end of the place because she intended to be the bunkhouse cook.

Zelda insisted on sharing the farm animals and their products with Two Feathers. The woman was always there to help with chores and Zelda knew she'd be there for the spring planting and later for the harvesting and preserving vegetables. The two women had become friends and knew they could count on one another.

Another thing Zelda insisted on was giving her husband the ranch so he'd have a free hand in running it as he felt it should be run. He didn't want to take it at first, but finally relented when she said they'd run it together.

As she sat here watching them work on the bunkhouse, she realized he hadn't made one decision about the running of the place without talking it over with her. She appreciated him doing this, but she also knew she'd never buck him on anything he wanted to do or any changes he wanted to make. So far, he hadn't make one mistake.

"Zewie." Pansy's voice brought her back to the moment.

"Yes, Pansy."

"Why you smiling?"

"Just because I'm happy." She touched Pansy's head. "Don't you smile when you're happy?"

Pansy gave her a little frown. "I can't smile now."

"Why not, honey?"

"I hungry. I cold, too."

"So am I." Zelda continued to smile, but she stood and held her hand out to the little girl. "Let's go see how much longer they'll be before we can go eat supper."

They didn't get far because the men headed toward them. Wiley gave them a big smile. "Well, ladies. We're at a good stopping place. Now we can come in for supper."

"It's about time." Hugh laughed. "My stomach told me it needed food a long time ago, and I'm glad we finally stopped."

Wiley placed his hand on Hugh's shoulder. "You know, son. My stomach was saying the same thing. I think Dub's was, too because he's already half way to their cottage."

"Then, please come in. Pansy and I have supper ready and waiting."

Pansy held up her hands. "Take me, Wiwey."

He scooped her up in his arms. Then he and Hugh followed Zelda into the house.

Wiley and Hugh washed up as Zelda put supper on the table. The children took their chairs, but Wiley waited until she put the last bowl on the table. He then escorted her to her place and pulled out the chair.

"Thank you, Wiley," she whispered.

He leaned down and kissed her. "It's my pleasure, sweetheart."

"Pansy," Hugh said in a loud whisper. "I wonder if they'll ever get tired of kissing each other."

Pansy giggled and shook her head.

Wiley shook his head, too. "Pansy's right, Hugh. We'll never get tired of it. So, you and little Pansy are going to have to accept that and put up it with for many years to come."

Hugh smiled then shook his head. Pansy giggled again. Zelda blushed and smiled at her husband. He laughed out loud, then leaned down and kissed her again.

Meet Agnes Alexander

Since childhood, Agnes Alexander has been intrigued with all things western. On her first vacation in the west, she knew this was a part of the country and a history she wanted to write about.

Her first Western book was published in 2012. She now has fifteen in print. *Zelda's Guilt* is the sixteenth. When not writing she loves to spend time with her two grandchildren, both of whom have an interest in writing. Of course, she encourages this interest. Agnes loves to hear from her readers and can be contacted at www.agnesalexander.com

Other Works From The Pen Of

Agnes Alexander

Valissa's Home – Penniless, after her brother gambles away everything they own, Valissa has to cope with the big cowboy who now owns her home.

Opal's Faith – In the West, Opal's family not only has to adjust to the strangeness of the land, but cope with a neighbor who is making slaves of young boys.

Ulla's Courage – Knowing her aunt and uncle are trying to cheat her out of everything she owns, Ulla agrees to become the bride of a stranger and accompany him and his children to Oregon.

Letter to Our Readers

Enjoy this book?

You can make a difference

As an independent publisher, Wings ePress, Inc. does not have the financial clout of the large New York Publishers. We can't afford large magazine spreads or subway posters to tell people about our quality books.

But, we do have something much more effective and powerful than ads. We have a large base of loyal readers.

Honest Reviews help bring the attention of new readers to our books.

If you enjoyed this book, we would appreciate it if you would spend a few minutes posting a review on the site where you purchased this book or on the Wings ePress, Inc. webpages at: https://wingsepress.com/

Visit Our Website

For The Full Inventory
Of Quality Books:

Wings ePress.Inc
https://wingsepress.com/

Quality trade paperbacks and downloads
in multiple formats,
in genres ranging from light romantic comedy
to general fiction and horror.
Wings has something for every reader's taste.
Visit the website, then bookmark it.
We add new titles each month!

Wings ePress Inc.
3000 N. Rock Road
Newton, KS 67114

www.ingramcontent.com/pod-product-compliance
Lightning Source LLC
Chambersburg PA
CBHW061031120726
47910CB00006B/2193